THE MAID'S SECRET

A Penny Green Mystery Book 3

EMILY ORGAN

THE MAID'S SECRET

❧

Emily Organ

❧

First published in 2017 by Emily Organ

emilyorgan.co.uk

Edited by Joy Tibbs

ISBN 978-0-9929093-9-0

CHAPTER 1

LONDON, 1884

"**M**r John Morrison?" I asked.

The tall, dark-skinned man beside me nodded, and I wrote his name down in my notebook. John looked to be about twenty. His brow was crumpled and he kept loosening his necktie, as though it would help him breathe.

"I'm supposed to be at work," he said.

"I'm sure your employer will understand on a day like today," I replied.

"I don't know about that." He pulled at his tie again.

"Elizabeth Wiggins was your sister?" I asked.

"Yes." His voice cracked with emotion.

"I'm so sorry," I said. "Thank you for agreeing to talk to me. I know this must be extremely difficult for you."

We were standing on Gonsalva Road in Battersea: a drab street lined on both sides by cramped, brown-brick houses. Number sixteen looked just like all the others, aside from the police officer trying to keep onlookers away from the front door. A light drizzle fell, leaving small sparkling raindrops on my woollen jacket. Trains rumbled along the viaduct behind the houses, and the damp pages of my notebook tore beneath my pencil.

A small crowd had filled the street. Men stood with hands in their pockets and dirty-faced children chased each other around, while women holding babies shouted at them.

"What can you tell me about your sister?" I asked. "What sort of person was she?"

John wiped his brow with his hand. "I can't get used to that word *was*. I can't believe she's not here no more. I only saw her yesterday! She's kind-hearted, like. She'd do anything for anyone. She worked north of the river 'til she lost her job. She's a hard worker, she is. I'll miss her. My wife and son'll miss her too."

He quickly rubbed the tears from his eyes to prevent me from seeing them.

"And what of your brother-in-law?" I asked. "Had he ever harmed Elizabeth before?"

"No. I don't think he did, anyway. She never told me so. The policeman told me he was drunk. He didn't usually drink much. Mrs O'Donnell says she heard shouting. They must have argued, I suppose. Elizabeth would've been angry on account of him being drunk. She didn't like drinkers, our Elizabeth. Because of our father, that is. Me and her saw what drink does to a family. He must have lost his temper with her. He wouldn't normally have done it, but it was the drink. And now..." John wiped his hand over his face. "He's ruined everything!"

I wrote down what he had told me in shorthand. "The police are holding him now. He'll face trial," I said.

"And so he should! I hope he hangs!"

"John Morrison!" a voice called out from behind me. I turned to see Tom Clifford from *The Holborn Gazette* approaching with his pencil and notebook. His jaw moved up and down as he chewed on a piece of tobacco.

"How old was your sister?"

"I'm not speaking to no more reporters now," said John tremulously. "I have to get back to me wife. She's in a delicate state, she is."

"Of course," I said. "Thank you for your time, Mr Morrison."

"Only speakin' to Miss Green, are yer?" Tom Clifford taunted as John walked away.

"Leave him be," I said. "His sister has just been murdered."

"What did 'e tell you?"

"That's none of your business!"

Tom Clifford spat out a globule of tobacco. "You won't of got much from the likes of 'im. What can you say about a battered wife? Husband comes home in a foul temper, husband beats wife, wife dies, and husband gets hanged for it. Happens every week. What we need is another killer like we had in St Giles. How's about that, Miss Green? It's a bit more exciting, ain't it? Sells newspapers, that kinda thing."

"It's not about excitement, Mr Clifford. We're reporting on real people's lives. I don't wish to report on murders in order to sensationalise them. I do it to pay my respects to the victims. Mrs Wiggins should be remembered."

Tom Clifford cackled. "You 'ave a nobler cause than the rest of us, don't yer, Miss Green?"

I ignored him and noted down the date and time at the top of my page: Tuesday, 4th March, 1884. Ten o'clock.

I folded my notebook closed, put it into my carpet bag and took out my umbrella, while Tom Clifford walked over to the police officer and began questioning him.

Reporting on domestic tragedies such as these was upsetting. The death of a woman at the hands of her partner should have been avoidable, and sadly it happened far too often.

I wiped the raindrops from my spectacles, opened my umbrella and walked down to Wandsworth Road, where I could take the horse tram up to Westminster Bridge.

CHAPTER 2

The typewriter was situated in the corner of the newsroom in the offices of the *Morning Express* newspaper. I sat myself in front of the machine beside a narrow dirty window which looked out onto Fleet Street. If I had cared to peer through the grime, I would have been able to see the upper section of a letter 'N', which formed part of the large iron signage across the facade of our building.

"You're not about to start making an infernal racket on that contraption, are you, Miss Green?" asked my colleague, Edgar Fish. He was a young man with small, glinting eyes and a thin, mousey-brown moustache. "Can't it wait 'til later? My head hurts."

"As a result of the beer in Ye Olde Cheshire Cheese yesterday evening, or of Mrs Fish scolding you when you returned home?" laughed another reporter, Frederick Potter, who was portly and curly-haired.

"Neither, thank you, Potter. And I don't appreciate the slur. I have a headache because I've been working too hard."

Frederick was still roaring with laughter when the editor,

Mr Sherman, strode into the room. Edgar swiftly removed the pencil from behind his ear and began scribbling on a piece of paper in front of him.

Mr Sherman removed the pipe from beneath his thick black moustache. "What's so funny, Potter?" His shirt sleeves were rolled up and he wore a grey serge waistcoat. His slickly oiled hair was parted to one side.

"Nothing, sir."

"Good. Well it seems Downing Street has finally realised that Sir Hercules Robinson is a man worth listening to," said Mr Sherman. "Now he can resume his duties as high commissioner in South Africa with the government's full support. Fish, you'll need to be at the Empire Club this evening to hear his address."

"Yes, sir."

"It will be interesting to hear the details surrounding Sir Robinson's uniform system of frontier policy."

"It will, sir, yes," replied Edgar, sounding unsure of himself.

"You haven't any idea what I'm referring to, have you, Fish?"

"Well, I do sir, I—"

"It will put an end to the clashes between the Europeans and the natives. May I suggest that you take yourself off to the reading room sharpish and read up on the topic? You don't want to end up looking a fool this evening."

"Too late for that!" laughed Frederick.

"What was that, Potter?"

"Nothing, sir."

"I need to speak to Purves, the parliamentary reporter, but he's not here again. Ah, Miss Green!"

I jumped at the sound of my name. Until that moment I had hoped Mr Sherman wouldn't spot me in the corner of the room.

"Stop typewriting. You're required in my office. Mr Conway wishes to see you."

The mention of the proprietor's name provoked a sharp intake of breath from Edgar. My heart began to pound wildly in my chest.

"May I ask why?" I replied, tentatively rising from my seat and smoothing out my skirts.

"All will be explained. Come along, now. Mr Conway is a busy man."

I followed the editor to his office and tried to recall which of my recent articles was most likely to have upset the owner of the *Morning Express*.

Perhaps someone had made a complaint about me.

My mouth felt dry as we walked into Mr Sherman's office. The room smelled of pipe smoke and had greasy, yellowing walls. A gas lamp hung down from a long chain over the desk, where the piles of books and papers were stacked high. Mr Sherman had worked in this room, at the helm of the *Morning Express*, for almost ten years.

Mr Conway sat in a low chair with his legs spread apart to allow room for his large stomach. His trousers, jacket and waistcoat were of a baggy brown tweed, and he had a fine head of wavy grey hair accompanied by long, bushy side-whiskers.

"Miss Green." He slowly moved his great bulk out of the chair and stood up. He nodded at me and looked me up and down before gesturing toward the two empty chairs next to him. "Please do sit."

He slumped back down again, the chair creaking under his weight. I sat down cautiously and wondered for whom the third chair had been reserved. Mr Sherman took a seat behind his desk.

"Have you told Miss Green what we want her to do yet, William?" wheezed Mr Conway.

"Not yet, sir."

"Well, don't you think you'd better?"

"Certainly, sir."

The proprietor breathed noisily through his nose as the editor began his explanation.

"Have you heard of an Alexander Glenville, Miss Green?" asked Mr Sherman.

"I'm afraid I haven't."

"He owns the Blundell's vinegar factory in Vauxhall, and has just bought a second factory in Bermondsey."

"I have heard of Blundell's."

"There's been heavy criticism of his manufacturing methods for some time. Workers are required to work long hours in his factories, and there has been a high volume of accidents there. It's rumoured that Glenville has children under the age of ten working at Blundell & Co."

"Which is a contravention of the factory code," Mr Conway interjected.

"Last year he lowered wages at the factory, and the workers who protested about the move lost their employment," continued Mr Sherman. "The social reformer Dorothea Heale has published some articles about Blundell's. Last year she attempted to help the workers form a committee that could stand up to Glenville, but her efforts came to nothing. Rumour has it she was warned off."

"Threatened?" I asked.

"Something of that nature."

"I don't like the sound of Alexander Glenville," I said.

"He's a loathsome chap," said Mr Conway. "And he's a cripple, to boot."

"He has one arm missing," said Mr Sherman. "Does that render him a cripple? The chap can still walk."

Mr Conway dismissed this last remark with a wave of his hand. "Glenville has friends in high places," he wheezed. "The factory in Bermondsey belonged to a good friend of mine, Mr Albert Archdale. Archdale's Vinegar was established one hundred years ago in Shoreditch, and Albert took over the factory from his father. Somehow, this Glenville chap has bought the place from him, and not for a fair sum either. It has ended poor Albert's fortunes for good. When I saw him last at the Garrick Club, he could barely put a sentence together. A family business lies in ruins."

"There are many more rumours," added Mr Sherman. "There are numerous alleged frauds and conspiracies."

"He keeps a tight circle of friends," said Mr Conway. "He's a secretive chap, so you won't see him at any of the London clubs. It's said he has plans for a cartel. Albert wouldn't play ball, and that's why Archdale's was seized from him."

"Can I ask what it is you wish me to do?" I enquired.

"Mr Conway has hired a detective from Scotland Yard to investigate Glenville's unscrupulous business activities," said Mr Sherman. "Once we have understood what the man is up to, we can publish our findings, embarrass the people who are helping him, and ultimately put him out of business."

"And who *is* helping him?"

"That's what we want the detective to find out for us," replied Mr Sherman, blowing a puff of pipe smoke out from the side of his mouth. "We know of one associate by the name of Mr Ralph Lombard, who is the owner of the Lombard gin distillery in Vauxhall. His business is located close to Blundell's, and Lombard's son, Dudley, is engaged to be married to Glenville's daughter. The plan appears to be for the son and daughter to inherit their fathers' businesses and combine them into some sort of gin and vinegar conglomerate.

"Glenville's other associates are a mystery at present. We know he had a connection with Viscount Wyndham some time ago, but they appear to have had a falling out. He met

Wyndham through his wife's family. She's from the ancient line of Noel-Johnstones, but the family's wealth has been gambled away by her father."

"I wish I'd brought my notebook with me, sir. There is a good deal to remember."

"You'll be acquainted with the detail of it all soon enough, Miss Green," my editor replied. "As Mr Conway mentioned, Glenville isn't a member of any of the clubs. He's not part of the establishment. He joined Blundell & Co as a lowly factory lad, and within eighteen years he owned the place. He lives with his wife in Kensington, close to Hyde Park. It's said that she married him for money, and that he married her for respectability. Their eldest child is a son, but as he's a lunatic the family business cannot pass to him. The next child is the daughter who is to be married into the Lombard family."

"I'm still not quite sure what you would have me do," I said. "Do you want me to work with the detective? Who is he?"

"I asked for Chief Inspector Cullen," said Mr Conway. "He's worked on similar cases in the past. But he's a busy man, so we've acquired a more junior detective. I do hope he will be up to the task."

We were interrupted by a knock at the door.

"Enter!" Mr Sherman called out.

I turned to look at the door, and in walked Inspector James Blakely.

CHAPTER 3

A few weeks had passed since James and I had last seen each other down in St Giles' Rookery. He smiled at me as he hung his overcoat and bowler hat on the cloak stand. There was a sparkle in his blue eyes, and I felt a warmth in my face. I adjusted a few pins in my hair and rubbed at a spot of ink on the sleeve of my jacket.

Mr Conway heaved himself out of his chair again and onto his feet. The two men shook hands.

"Have you met our reporter, Miss Green, before?" the proprietor asked James.

"I have indeed. Good morning, Miss Green."

I tried to temper the wide grin which had spread across my face. "Good morning, Inspector Blakely," I replied calmly as I lowered my eyes from his gaze.

He sat in the chair next to me, and I tried to pretend that I didn't find him handsome. He wore a dark blue suit and waistcoat, with a blue and green patterned tie. His dark hair was neatly parted, and he was clean-shaven.

"Inspector Blakely and Miss Green have worked together in the past," said Mr Sherman to Mr Conway.

"Have they indeed?" puffed the proprietor as he lowered himself heavily back into his chair. "Well that is of some reassurance, I suppose."

"We both worked on the Lizzie Dixie case. And the St Giles murders," said James.

"You look rather young, Inspector," said Mr Conway. "You are an experienced fellow, though, I presume?"

James told him about the recent cases he had worked on, and mentioned that both his father and grandfather had been in the police force. I listened intently to his voice and felt privileged that I already knew the information he was imparting. However, I felt it wise to feign indifference by examining the ink stains on my fingers.

"Jolly good," said the proprietor when James had finished. "I'm looking forward to seeing what you're made of, young man."

"We've just explained the nature of your investigation to Miss Green," said Mr Sherman. "Are you all prepared?"

"Yes, I think so," replied James. "Glenville is a rather intriguing character. I can't say I like the man, but I'm impressed by his rise from factory boy to owner of Blundell's."

Mr Conway snorted. "I don't see what there is to be impressed about. The man's a criminal."

"That's what we need to prove, isn't it, Mr Conway?" said James.

"He *is* a criminal. Everyone knows it, but the evidence required to convict him in a court of law continues to evade us."

"If his working practices are in contravention of the Factory Code, surely it should be easy to prosecute him?" I said.

"Exactly, woman," replied Mr Conway. "But it doesn't seem to happen. This is precisely why we need to find out who's helping him. Someone with influence is looking out for the man."

"May I ask again what I shall be required to do?" I said. "Will Inspector Blakely keep me informed about his work in order for me to write about it?"

"More than that," said Mr Sherman. "Much more than that. We plan to attempt something we have never tried before. Do you recall your colleague, Edgar Fish, working undercover for us down in St Giles earlier this year? That was a great success."

"But he returned covered in lice!" I replied.

"A hazard of the occupation, I'm afraid. He entertained our readers with a great number of tales from the slums, and that's what matters."

"You wish me to work undercover?"

"Exactly, Miss Green. And don't worry, there won't be any lice. The Glenvilles are advertising for a governess, and you are well placed to fill the role." He gave me a rare smile. "What do you make of that, Miss Green?"

I stared at him and wondered whether I had heard him correctly.

"A governess?"

All three men looked at me.

"A governess looking after children?" I asked.

"Yes, that's what governesses do," replied Mr Sherman. "You have something of a governess about you, Miss Green. You're well educated and I've no doubt you possess a nurturing streak. Most women do."

"No, not a governess. It's impossible, I could never do such a thing. I have no idea how to do the job."

"It's just teaching children letters and numbers. And a bit of French. You know French, don't you, Miss Green?"

"I'm sorry, Mr Sherman, but I refuse to work in the Glenville household as a governess. I understand why you wish to carry out this investigation, but I would be too busy with the children to pay any attention to what was going on in the household."

Mr Sherman suddenly appeared less cheerful. "It wouldn't be for long, Miss Green. A matter of weeks."

I turned to James. "I'm sorry. I can't do it."

"Not even for a few weeks?" he asked.

"That's the problem!" I replied. "Those poor children would grow accustomed to me, and then I would have to leave them. It's not fair on them. They require a proper governess, not a news reporter pretending to be one. I don't object to working undercover, but I simply couldn't deceive the children. It wouldn't be fair. They shouldn't be caught up in this investigation."

The room fell silent.

"Miss Green has a point," said James eventually. "I don't intend to argue with her any further on this matter. I know that when her mind is made up about something there is little use in trying to change it."

Mr Sherman sighed. "Miss Green, it's not sporting to disobey an order."

"I understand, sir. I take pride in my work and am happy to do what is required of me. But involving the Glenville children in my undercover work is too much to ask of me, I'm afraid."

"Never mind, Blakely," said Mr Conway. "You'll just have to do what you can. I will still pay you what we agreed."

My mind whirled as I searched for an alternative answer. Mr Glenville was clearly an unpleasant man, and we had been presented with an opportunity to uncover his misdeeds. Without my help on the inside, James would likely find the task much more difficult.

"What about a maid's position?" I asked.

Mr Sherman's bushy eyebrows met above his nose as he

frowned. "You're no maid, Miss Green. You're of a different class."

"I should be willing to try."

"You'd be completely unconvincing. You don't even speak like a maid."

"I'm sure that I could act the part."

"You have no experience of service."

"Mr Sherman, a moment ago you thought I would be a suitable governess despite my having no experience whatsoever. A maid would be easier, surely? I could come up with a story to explain my background. Perhaps my family was middle class but fell on hard times. Service was the only work I could find at the time, and then I realised that I enjoyed it."

"It's vaguely plausible, I suppose," wheezed Mr Conway. "Are the Glenvilles currently looking for a maid?"

"Perhaps, Miss Green, you could call at the house and enquire," said Mr Sherman. "It would be the first test to discover whether you'd be convincing in the role or not."

"I'm happy to try. What would I do about a reference?"

"My aunt, Mrs Fothergill, said she was happy to declare that you were in service to her as a governess. I can ask her to stipulate that you worked for her as a maid for some years."

"Thank you." I paused to think over what I was agreeing to. "It all seems rather deceitful, doesn't it?"

"It's what we call undercover journalism, Miss Green! This line of work is particularly popular in America. Americans tend to know what they're doing, I keep my ears pricked at all times for interesting developments from across the Atlantic."

"Quite right, too," added Mr Conway. "Inspector Blakely, do you think this woman could pass for a maid?"

James smiled at me. "I think she has a good chance, sir. Miss Green is a very determined lady."

"Jolly good," said Mr Conway. "In that case, let's get on with it."

He began to rise out of his chair and we all rose to our feet.

"In the meantime, Miss Green, it might be an idea to ask your own maid for some advice on how to do chores," said Mr Sherman.

"I don't have one, sir."

"You don't? Then how on earth are you to understand the duties of a maid?"

"To be honest, sir, I have no idea."

CHAPTER 4

"**A**re you playing a prank on me, Miss Green?"

"I wish I were, Mrs Garnett."

My landlady's eyes were wide with disbelief, the whites contrasting starkly with her dark skin. One of her hands held a feather duster, which was poised over the table in the hallway. "So you're telling me you're going to get a job as a maid?"

"It's an undercover job."

"I don't even understand what that means. I was talking to my niece about you last week."

"Really?"

"Yes. I used you as an example of what happens to a woman when she isn't married. Once a spinster reaches a certain age, she has a tendency to undertake all manner of escapades. It's what happens when there's no husband about."

"It's my profession, Mrs Garnett. I'm a news reporter. The matter of whether I have a husband or not is irrelevant."

"But now you're going to be a housemaid! What do you know about being in service?" She sucked her lip disapprovingly.

"That's why I'm asking for your help. You were in service once, weren't you?"

"That was a long time ago."

I estimated that Mrs Garnett was around the age of fifty. She had come to London from British West Africa and had been widowed following the death of her husband, a circus performer called Hercules Garnett.

"I wouldn't go back to those days," she continued. "The hours were long and the work was hard. A lady such as your-self wouldn't understand what it's like to have a job."

"But I have a job."

"I mean a *proper* job. Servants work sixteen hours a day. When I worked for Lord Brinsley, I was the first to rise and the last into bed. I got up at six o'clock and cleaned the grates, prepared the fires and emptied the slops. Then I swept the carpets and dusted the whole house."

"You must have been extremely busy, Mrs Garnett."

"That was before I even ate my breakfast! I had to wake the household, and while they breakfasted I made the beds and filled the coal boxes. And there was the carrying of water up and down the stairs. There was always somebody asking for water. And I washed the front steps and blackened the grates. Have you ever blackened a grate? Or cleaned silver?"

I shook my head.

"Have you ever waited at table before?"

"It's probably quite straightforward, isn't it?"

"That's what *you* think." She pointed her feather duster at me. "And mind that if there's no butler or footman, you'll be the one answering the door. I also used to take all the deliv-eries at the back door because the kitchen maid was lazy. Lady Brinsley had me running errands to the post office, and taking messages to her friends. And she and her daughters were always ringing their bells! Five storeys that house was, and I can't tell you how many times I climbed up and down those stairs each day answering bells. I wore the soles out on three pairs of shoes. I don't think you have a clue what you're letting yourself in for."

"I think I'm getting some idea now."

Although I didn't doubt that service was hard work, I also knew that Mrs Garnett had a tendency to exaggerate.

"And you want me to teach you everything you need to know about becoming a maid? Everything I learnt from ten years in service?"

"Yes please, Mrs Garnett."

She sucked her lip again. "I always said you were one button short, Miss Green, and once again you've proved me right."

I climbed the stairs up to my attic room, where Tiger was waiting at the window. I pulled up the sash and she jumped onto my writing desk with a miaow. As I stroked her, I felt a pang of sadness that I would be away from her for several weeks while I worked undercover.

"I'll ask Mrs Garnett to look after you," I said.

Tiger stopped purring and jumped off my desk, as if offended by the suggestion. It was true that my landlady barely tolerated the roof cat who had turned up at my window six years previously, begging to be let in from the cold.

I lit the paraffin lamp and sat at my desk, looking out over the city as dusk fell. Lights twinkled in windows, and plumes of smoke and steam rose up from Moorgate station.

Could I really fool a household into thinking that I was a maid? What if I happened to be found out?

Although I enjoyed adventure, the thought of this undercover assignment made me rather nervous.

A pile of my father's letters and diaries sat on my desk,

waiting to be transcribed into my book about his life. He had been a renowned plant-hunter, but had gone missing during an expedition in Colombia nine years previously. My progress on the book had stalled while I deliberated over the extent to which I should edit his adventures. Although he had done a lot of good work in bringing new plant specimens to England, I had been particularly perturbed to read about a massacre of natives, which he had carried out in self-defence. I kept reminding myself that he had only done it because he had been attacked and had no other way of saving his life and the lives of his companions, but I still couldn't reconcile such action with the memories I had of my father as a gentle and docile man.

His last known location had been the Tequendama Falls near Bogota in Colombia. Mr Edwards, a clerk at the British Library, had helpfully provided me with some more information about the falls, and had also drawn a detailed map of the area. But all the books and maps in the library could shed no light on my father's fate.

Could my book about his life ever be complete without a proper ending?

It seemed a shame to spend so much time compiling the records of his travels without ever knowing what had actually happened to him.

My sister, Eliza, and I assumed that our father had died, but I felt the chapter could never be properly closed without discovering his final resting place.

An expedition had been sent to locate my father in the March of 1876. Among my father's papers I had saved a cutting from *The Times*, which read:

Explorer Mr. Isaac Fox-Stirling sails from Liverpool tomorrow on the steamer Bolivar to the United States of Colombia. The purpose of

his mission is to establish the whereabouts of the plant-hunter, Mr.
Frederick Brinsley Green, who has not been seen since the March of
1875. Mr. Fox-Stirling is a seasoned explorer, and he told our reporter
that he was confident Mr Green could be found.

He said: "The jungle is a large place and it is relatively easy to
lose contact with the outside world. I remain hopeful that we will
find our esteemed friend, Mr. F. B. Green, safe and well."

Mr. Green has made a good number of trips to South America
and has transported many exotic plants back to the shores of Britan-
nia. At the time of his disappearance, Mr. Green had been collecting
orchid specimens on behalf of Kew Gardens.

Mr. G. W. Brice of Kew Gardens spoke to our reporter: "Although
it is not unknown for illness or misfortune to befall one of our brave
plant-hunters, it is unusual for one of our men to disappear without
trace. With the generous patronage of private individuals, we hope
that our mission will offer a successful outcome."

Mr. Fox-Stirling plans to proceed up the River Magdalena in a
steam launch to Honda. From there, he will strike out in a south-east-
erly direction to Bogota, and from thence along the River Funza to
the Falls of Tequendama, where Mr. Green was last seen. The cost of
the expedition has been generously borne by the famed actress, Mrs
Lizzie Dixie, a friend of Mr. Green's daughter, Miss Penelope Green.

Mr. Fox-Stirling is to speak at a dinner held in his honour at The
Athenaeum this evening. He is at the present time employed by Wilde
Nurseries, on whose behalf he has made many journeys to the South
American continent.

Isaac Fox-Stirling had returned later that year with various
sketches he had found in a deserted hut. There was no doubt
that the sketches had been drawn by my father, but sadly
there had been no trace of the man himself. Now that I was
working on the book, I wished to meet with Mr Fox-Stirling.
I hoped that he was still working for Wilde Nurseries, which

I knew was located close to the Botanical Gardens in Chelsea.

I loosened my stays and pulled on an old overcoat for warmth. Then I boiled some coffee and wrote a short letter to Mr Fox-Stirling to request a meeting.

CHAPTER 5

The following afternoon I sat beneath the great dome of the reading room and read an article written by the social reformer, Dorothea Heale, about the Blundell & Co vinegar factory.

"Good afternoon, Miss Green. Busy researching a new topic, I see," a man's voice whispered close to my shoulder.

I turned to see olive-green eyes staring at me through spectacle lenses. They belonged to the reading room clerk.

"Hello, Mr Edwards." I felt a prickle of irritation at being disturbed. "Yes, I have a new story to work on."

"Dorothea Heale, eh?" He peered at the article on my desk. "She's an interesting woman, I believe. She has a lot to say."

"Indeed."

"And how's the book coming along?"

"Slowly, Mr Edwards. Slowly."

"I trust that the map I drew for you is useful?"

"It is, thank you."

His eyes remained on mine and I felt my toes curl in my

boots as I realised that he was about to mention the note which he had sent me a few weeks previously.

Mr Edwards pushed his hair away from his spectacles and cleared his throat. His uneasiness made me distinctly uncomfortable.

"There is something which I have yet to receive an acknowledgement from you about," he ventured. "Perhaps you have forgotten it. In fact, it's extremely likely that you have, as you're so busy." He gestured toward the papers on my desk. "Yes, you have probably forgotten about it altogether, I imagine."

His note was still sitting in the biscuit tin on my writing desk back at my lodgings. I had been at a loss as to what to say in reply.

"I haven't forgotten about it, Mr Edwards. I must apologise for the delay in responding to you."

"No matter, there is no need to apologise. Can I ask if you would be amenable to the arrangement which I have suggested in it?"

His voice was so quiet that I could barely hear it, and his face was flushed red. He was clearly finding the situation so unbearable that I began to wonder why he had instigated it in the first place.

"Do not worry about offending me with a *no*," he continued. "I would rather hear a *no* than not know anything at all. If that makes sense, which I'm not sure it does."

His green eyes were wide and earnest, and he seemed to be putting himself through so much discomfort that I felt I should give him the answer he desired.

How could I turn him away now?

I cursed myself for not having replied sooner and allowing the situation to escalate to this.

"Yes, I would be amenable, Mr Edwards."

He gave a great sigh of relief and grinned. "Thank you,

Miss Green," he whispered breathlessly. "I am most honoured."

"You suggested a walk in Hyde Park, didn't you?"

"Yes, with a chaperone if you wish."

"Of course. I will ask my sister to accompany us."

"Well, that's wonderful, Miss Green, simply wonderful. Would this Saturday afternoon be agreeable?"

I tried to think of a reason to arrange our meeting for a day several weeks hence but felt unable to come up with a suitable excuse while he stood there, eagerly awaiting my reply.

"I will have to check with my sister."

I felt cruel for hoping that Eliza would be unavailable.

"Absolutely. I am certainly looking forward to becoming acquainted with her. Shall we meet at Marble Arch at half past two? If your sister is unable to make that time, you could simply leave a note for me at the desk here."

He grinned again.

"I will do."

I was distracted by the sight of someone walking toward my desk, and my heart leapt when I saw that it was James.

If only he had arrived five minutes sooner.

James waved when he saw that I had noticed him. I got to my feet and quietly introduced the two men.

"A detective," whispered Mr Edwards. "How fascinating! Do you enjoy your work?"

"Most of the time," replied James. "Although there are some days when being surrounded by books seems more appealing." He glanced around the circular room and his gaze lingered on the impressive tiers of bookshelves.

"Yes, I can't complain about it. I had always wanted to work in a library," said Mr Edwards.

I gathered up my papers and put them into my carpet bag.

"Have you finished with Dorothea Heale already, Miss Green?" There was a note of disappointment in Mr Edwards' voice.

"Yes, do please excuse us, Mr Edwards," I said. "James and I need to go and discuss some developments relating to a news story I'm working on."

I knew that James would want to talk further about the Glenville case in the nearby Museum Tavern.

"Very well," said Mr Edwards. "I shall see you this Saturday, Miss Green. I am very much looking forward to it!"

CHAPTER 6

"This Saturday?" asked James as we walked down the steps of the British Museum. A damp breeze blew drops of rain onto my spectacles. "You're seeing that chap this Saturday? Remind me who he is again."

From the corner of my eye, I could see that James' face was turned towards me, but I stared resolutely ahead at the terracotta-brick building across the road.

"Mr Edwards. He works as a clerk in the reading room."

"And you're seeing him this Saturday?"

"Yes. He asked me."

"And you immediately agreed?"

"He asked me a few weeks ago, and I neglected to reply because we were so busy with all that business down in St Giles. I felt I should agree to it as he'd been waiting so long for me to respond.

"I see."

We stepped through the gate of the British Museum and out onto the busy street.

"He's been assisting me with my research on Father's travels." I had to raise my voice over the sound of hooves and carriage wheels.

"That's noble of him."

"He's been very helpful."

"I expect he has."

We crossed the street and reached the swing door of the Museum Tavern.

"Does it bother you?" I asked.

James paused with his hand against the door. He fixed me with his blue eyes, his brow furrowed.

"No." He gave the door a hard shove. "I don't suppose it does."

Clouds of tobacco smoke and a loud hum of voices greeted us inside the tavern. Flickering gaslight danced in the carved glass mirrors, and my spectacles instantly steamed up.

We sat at a table which was partitioned either side by a wooden screen. James had removed his overcoat and jacket, so that he wore only a checked grey waistcoat over a white shirt. His sleeves were rolled up.

"How is your family faring since your grandfather passed away?" I asked. "And how is your grandmother?"

It had been a while since James and I had found the chance to have an informal conversation.

"She could be better." He sighed. "She's staying with my parents at the moment. She's struggling to live in her house in Battersea without him. It must be lonely. I can only imagine what it's like for her now, having spent so much of her life with him there."

"I don't think I would ever want to return. Surely everything in the house reminds her of what she has lost."

"It probably does. I don't even like to think how it must feel. The garden will need tending soon, as the spring weather arrives. I've helped them with the garden there for the past several years."

"You gave me some leeks and potatoes from their garden, do you remember?"

"So I did! Didn't I bring them into the reading room?"

"Yes."

We both laughed.

"Where do your parents live?" I asked. There was still so much that I didn't know about James.

"In Wembley."

"That's some distance from Battersea."

"Yes. I think my grandmother is enjoying the change."

"Did you grow up in Wembley?"

"I did."

"I didn't realise that."

"I assumed I had told you."

"I don't even know where you live now."

"Don't you?"

"There's no need for me to know," I added quickly. "After all, you wouldn't want me paying you a surprise visit, would you?"

James looked bemused and laughed. "Why would you do so? It's not that I shouldn't want you to, of course, but it would be a surprise indeed."

"But there would be no need."

"No."

We held each other's gaze for a moment, and then I busied myself with my sherry.

"I live in St John's Wood. Henstridge Place, to be precise," continued James. "It's pleasant enough. Primrose Hill and Regent's Park are both close by."

"And the zoo?"

"And the zoo. So if you were to pay me a surprise visit, perhaps we could go to Regent's Park Zoo."

"I would like that. Although I feel sure the future Mrs Blakely would disapprove."

"Do you think so? There would be no reason for her to. Perhaps Mr Edwards would disapprove."

"Of course he wouldn't! There is no attachment whatsoever between myself and Mr Edwards. You, on the other hand, are engaged to be married. That's rather different."

There was an uncomfortable pause, and I took a large sip of my sherry.

"I think we should discuss that crook, Mr Glenville, now," said James, opening his notebook, which lay on the table. "That's the reason I came to find you."

He assumed a formal air as he read from his notes.

"Mr Alexander Glenville is forty-eight and manages Blundell & Co, a vinegar-brewing business which comprises of a factory in Vauxhall and another in Bermondsey. The Bermondsey factory is the old Archdale's factory, which previously belonged to a good friend of Mr Conway's. Glenville began working for Blundell & Co when he was just ten years old. I understand that he comes from a poor family background. He lost his right arm in an accident at the factory at the age of twelve."

"Goodness, what happened?"

"I don't have any further details. But it seems the accident did nothing to put a stop to his ambitions, because by the time he was eighteen he'd been promoted to supervisor. And he was clearly a favourite there, because following Mr Thomas Blundell's death the factory passed to Glenville rather than to Mr Blundell's eldest son. I understand that two of Blundell's younger sons remain on the board, but Glenville is in charge."

"And what of the eldest Blundell son? Surely he bears great animosity toward Glenville."

"I've heard that's the case. In fact, I'm sure most of the

family bears some resentment toward Glenville, because old Thomas Blundell considered him to be more proficient at running the business than any of them."

"But there has been much criticism of conditions in the factories, hasn't there? I've just been reading the accounts written by Dorothea Heale. I copied some of them out."

I rummaged in my bag for my notes and found one of the articles I had transcribed in the reading room. I read it out to James.

"Work commences at half past six each morning and concludes at six in the evening. Half an hour is allowed for breakfast and dinner. A typical worker earns between three and four shillings a week, and this salary is subject to fines if they are untidy, arrive late or cause any breakages or spillages. In some departments, there is a fine of three pence for talking.

"Many of the factory workers live in single rooms, often shared with family members or acquaintances because the weekly rent of two shillings accounts for at least half of the workers' salary. They live only on bread, butter and tea, with meat on a Sunday should they be able to afford it.

"Earlier this year, Blundell & Co paid a dividend of thirty percent to its shareholders. This large sum of money was achieved by paying such a paltry sum to the company's workers."

"That's interesting research, Penny. Glenville seems to be an unpleasant man, doesn't he?"

"I also read that the factory workers attempted to attend a meeting about the conditions, but were threatened with instant dismissal. I'm concerned that Mrs Heale is no longer as vocal about the conditions at Blundell's. It's as if she, too, is afraid to speak up. Do you think Glenville might have threatened her?"

"It's possible. The man has a ruthless reputation.

However, it's said that he is devoted to his family. He has six children, and the eldest daughter, Sophia, is engaged to the son of his friend, a local gin distillery owner."

"Mr Conway and Mr Sherman explained that to me. Apparently, Glenville's eldest son is a lunatic."

"That would be Maurice. I've heard reports that he's an idiot or an imbecile of some description, but I don't know the details. He lives in the family home, though. He's not kept in an institution."

"And you want me to find out whom Glenville is associating with?"

"Yes, that's what Mr Conway has asked me to investigate. As you've no doubt realised by now, he bears a grudge toward Glenville because Glenville bought his friend's factory. It's Conway's view that Glenville is getting away with a great deal. He has managed to inherit a successful family business whilst being an outsider. He has acquired himself a new factory, treats his workers like animals and has survived a number of financial fraud allegations. He is rumoured to have friends in high places. Members of parliament, successful industrialists, that sort of thing. But the question is, who are they?"

"Do you not think this investigation might stem from sour grapes on Mr Conway's part?" I asked. "Glenville may not be any more corrupt than the average industrialist, but perhaps Mr Conway begrudges his success for personal reasons?"

"It's possible, isn't it? Especially when you consider that Glenville is from a poor background and has been working since the age of ten. Mr Conway was educated at Eton and Oxford, and it's possible that he may object to seeing a working-class boy achieve the level of success Glenville has. However, there's no doubt that there's a whiff of unpleasantness about Glenville. I've met the man once myself, and he's a slippery fellow. Untrustworthy. Shifty."

"I'm looking forward to meeting him," I laughed. "If I get the job as a maid, that is. I intend to call at the house tomorrow."

"Good luck, Penny. You have a tricky job to do."

"I hope I manage to uncover the answers you're looking for. But what will happen if they discover who I really am?"

"Hopefully you won't be there long enough for them to find out. I don't see why you should want to stay longer than a few weeks unless you discover that you enjoy the life of a maid!"

"I consider that highly unlikely."

James checked his pocket watch. "Goodness, I need to be back at the Yard to meet Cullen." He leapt up from his seat and put on his jacket. "As I've already said, good luck with it all, Penny. I hope you manage to secure the position."

I smiled. "Thank you, James."

"If all goes well, I shall see you in a few weeks' time," he continued. "Don't forget to send anything you discover to me at Scotland Yard."

He retrieved his coat and hat from the cloak stand, then regarded me for a moment. "You'll be careful, won't you, Penny?"

"Yes. I always am."

"Is that so?"

He grinned and placed his hat firmly on his head. He paused for a moment, as if considering something, then reached into his waistcoat pocket.

"Here, have this," he said.

I held out my hand and he dropped a gold ring onto my palm.

"James! I can't!"

"No, please do. It was my grandfather's and I've been walking around with it in my pocket since he died, unsure of what to do with it. It won't fit on any of my fingers. He had peculiarly small hands, my grandfather. I don't mean for you to wear it. It may be too big, of course. Or perhaps it will fit. I'll let you try it and decide. But keep it with you for luck. My grandfather always had a lot of luck in his life, and I like to think that whoever carries the ring will also have the same."

"James, this ring is precious to you. There must be someone more important than me to have it!"

I tried to hand the ring back to him, but he pushed my hand away.

"There isn't, Penny. Please keep it."

He quickly walked away.

"James!"

But he was gone.

CHAPTER 7

The following day, I called at the Glenville household in Hyde Park Gate. It was an imposing, cream, stuccoed house, five storeys high with large sash windows and two stone columns supporting a classically styled porch. Two gas lamps hung from either side of a wrought-iron arch at the foot of the steps.

Although my clothes were rarely fancy, I had decided to wear the drab overcoat I usually reserved to keep me warm within my lodgings. Beneath it I wore a simple linen dress, which I imagined a maid of little means might wear on her day off. Pulled around my ears was an old-fashioned bonnet with faded cotton flowers sewn onto it, and I slumped my shoulders in imitation of a put-upon maid I recalled from my childhood home.

My heart thumped heavily as the door was answered by a short, plain woman in a grey ticking-dress that was buttoned up to her neck. Her greying hair was neatly pinned at the back of her head, and a bunch of keys hung down from her waist. I assumed that she was the housekeeper. Her mouth was turned down in a stern pout, and she looked me up and down with her suspicious grey eyes.

"The governess position is filled. I'm assuming that's what you've come about."

"I haven't. I came to enquire about something else." I felt disappointed that I didn't give the instant appearance of a maid. "My name is Florence Parker, and when I saw the advertisement for the governess position I wondered if you might also be looking for a maid. I have a good reference."

The housekeeper surveyed me a while longer, as if making up her mind about me.

"You'd better come in," she eventually replied.

She stepped aside and I joined her in the tiled hallway, where the tick of a grandfather clock echoed and light flickered from a large and ornate gasolier above our heads. The wide staircase had a carved mahogany banister and was carpeted with a dark flock motif, which matched the gloomy pattern of the wallpaper.

Paintings of people I assumed to be family members hung from the walls in heavy gilt frames. I felt their eyes on me as I followed the housekeeper along a corridor that ran parallel to the staircase. The house had a sombre, oppressive feel to it. The furnishings were tasteful and orderly, but everything seemed rather dark and quiet. It was a house which seemed well-suited to its dour housekeeper.

"I have a small room along here," she said.

The austere woman turned the handle of a wooden door beneath the staircase and showed me into a dim little office with a sloped ceiling. Rows of keys hung from little hooks on the wall. Above them, several shelves stored oil lamps, candles, cloths and little glass bottles. Pieces of paper arranged neatly on the desk bore shopping lists and menus.

"I'm Mrs Craughton," she said.

She didn't bid me to sit, so I remained standing.

"May I read your character reference?"

"Yes." I took a folded piece of paper from the inside of my overcoat and gave it to her.

"Mrs Fothergill in Berkeley Square." The scowl from the housekeeper's face lifted slightly as she read. "She thinks highly of you."

"I have worked for her the last seven years."

"So I see."

"She's a widow. Although I was her maid, I was also a companion to her."

"Were there other staff there?"

"There was a cook and a general housemaid."

"Hmm." She folded up the reference and returned it to me. I could feel her scrutinising my looks, and my face began to redden.

"You don't seem to be the usual sort of maid. Who are your family?"

"My mother lives in Derbyshire and my sister is in Kent." I didn't wish to admit that my sister was married to a wealthy banker and lived in Bayswater.

"Kent. I know it well. Whereabouts?"

I felt a prickle of cold perspiration beneath my arms as I tried to think up something in reply. Although I had prepared a story about myself, I hadn't anticipated enquiries about my sister's whereabouts.

"Chatham."

"Your sister is also in service?"

"Yes, she's a governess. We both received an education; our parents were insistent on that. But we've always been a poor family."

"It's interesting that you're not also a governess."

"I tried it once, but I wasn't very good at it. I prefer working as a maid."

I could hear my heart thudding in my ears, and I felt sure

the housekeeper would see through my deception at any moment.

"You prefer maid's work? Well that is unusual, but I can't fault your excellent reference from Mrs Fothergill, and I think the Glenvilles will like you. You have impeccable manners. When can you start?"

"Next week."

I wasn't sure whether to feel relieved or concerned that she appeared to be offering me the position.

"Very good. Please arrive here on Sunday evening with enough time for me to show you to your room. You will start at six o'clock on Monday morning."

"Thank you, Mrs Craughton."

"Have you any questions?"

"Who are the other staff here?"

"There's myself and Mr Perrin, the butler. There's also Cook and a general maid called Maisie Brown. The new governess started this week, and there's an errand boy who also does scullery work. Everyone will be extremely pleased to have you with us."

"Thank you. I'm looking forward to starting work here." I forced a smile.

"Don't you wish to know what your wages will be? It's usually the first question I'm asked."

"Oh yes. What are the wages?"

"Fifteen pounds a year. It's not much, I know. A woman of your age would find a better-paid position in another household. But you seem to be keen to work here. You'd be Betsy's replacement, and that's how much she was paid. I'll show you to the door."

Back in the hallway, I was startled by peals of laughter and a flash of colour, which revealed itself to be a young woman sliding down the banister towards us. Her red hair was coming loose from its pins. Two younger girls followed her, and I couldn't help but smile as they made a well-practised leap off the end of the handrail and tumbled onto the tiled floor, laughing.

"Miss Sophia!" scolded the housekeeper. "You know better than to encourage your sisters in such bad habits! This is no way for a lady to behave!"

The two girls, aged about eight and six, ran back up the stairs. Sophia smoothed out her skirts and fixed the house-keeper with a defiant eye.

"You leave me with no choice but to speak to your father again!"

"You do that, Mrs Craughton," replied Sophia dryly. She gave me a lofty glance, then walked past us and into a room on our right.

"You'll need to watch that one," said the housekeeper quietly. "Fortunately, she'll be off our hands soon, as she's about to be married. I pity her poor husband!"

CHAPTER 8

"**D**o you know how many years it is since I was last your chaperone?" asked Eliza as we made our way through the rain in Hyde Park.

Having hoped that Eliza would be unable to accompany me on my walk with Mr Edwards, I had been disappointed to discover that she was overjoyed to have received my invitation.

"I can't remember." I recalled the prior occasion, but had no wish to discuss it.

"Eight years ago. Can you believe it was that long? It was that Mills fellow. What was his name? It began with an R, I'm sure of it. Roger? Robert? Richard?"

"Benjamin."

"That was it! Benjamin Mills! So you *do* remember? Do you know what he does these days?"

"No."

Eliza was riding her bicycle. It had a large wheel on one side and two smaller wheels on the other. At the centre was a small seat and two pedals. The bicycle was steered by two handles either side of the seat. Eliza held on to one of these, brandishing her umbrella in the other hand. My sister was two years my junior and we were similar in appearance: both of us blonde-haired and brown-eyed. She had always been the larger, louder one.

"Oh, Penelope, you look terribly miserable on what is supposed to be a happy occasion. You're finally meeting with a gentleman! I have waited so long for this to happen. I've written to Mother about it."

"You told *Mother*?" I stopped and glared at her.

Eliza bicycled on ahead, pulling an apologetic expression. "I felt it was my duty. She worries about you, you know that. The knowledge that her spinster daughter is meeting with a suitor is of great comfort to her in her dotage!" she called back over her shoulder. "Just think how happy she will be at the present time in her cottage in Derbyshire! She will be thinking of you every minute of this afternoon, I feel sure of it!"

I sighed and jogged to catch up with her. "I don't want her to be happy and expectant about this, Ellie. I only agreed to this meeting to please Mr Edwards."

"But you wouldn't have agreed to it if you despised the man, would you? There only needs to be a glimmer of interest in the beginning. That's how it began with me and George. In fact, I quite disliked George when I first met him, but true love takes time. You need to nurture it, and allow it to grow. It doesn't happen in the way it's described in poems. That's probably why you've reached the age of thirty-five without being married. You've been waiting for love to come from nowhere and seize you where you stand. It doesn't happen that way."

"I'm still thirty-four!"

"Only for a month longer," she replied. "Remember to look cheerful, Penelope! The last thing an admirer wants to see is the object of his desire looking miserable. This meeting is important. It may finally distract you from that inspector chap."

"I don't need to be distracted from him," I snapped.

"No, I suppose that his own impending marriage should be enough to dissuade you from harbouring any intentions towards him."

"It certainly does."

I thought of James and his wife-to-be, and wondered if their relationship had begun as Eliza described love: a glimmer of interest which had steadily grown into affection.

Or had their hearts been consumed by a sudden fiery passion for one another, which left them with a constant yearning to be together? Did James think about her so much that his mind span, and his stomach felt knotted? Was she the first person he thought of when he laid down to sleep at night and when he awoke in the morning? Perhaps passionate thoughts of her even kept him awake at night.

I felt a bitter taste in my mouth as these unwelcome ideas ran through my mind.

"Is that him?" asked Eliza.

We had almost reached Marble Arch, and a man in a brown overcoat was standing under a large black umbrella by the white stone archway. I wiped away the specks of rain which had blown onto my spectacle lenses.

"Yes, that's Mr Edwards."

"He looks simply charming."

Mr Edwards' eyebrows rose as he watched my sister bicycling towards him.

"Good afternoon!" I called out. "This is my sister, Mrs Eliza Billington-Grieg."

"Delighted to meet you," replied Mr Edwards with a smile. He removed his hat and gave Eliza a slight bow. "I thought you were in an invalid carriage as you approached, but it's a bicycle! How marvellous!"

He walked around the contraption, surveying it as Eliza delightedly described its features.

"Would you like to have a ride on it, Mr Edwards?" she asked.

"Oh no. No, no. I would make rather a fool of myself, I'm afraid. I'll leave the bicycling to you. I'm very much looking forward to our walk, Miss Green. It's a rather damp afternoon, courtesy of Jupiter Pluvius, but I'm sure we shall enjoy it all the same. Shall we wend our way to the tea rooms by the Serpentine?"

"Yes please," replied Eliza. "They serve delicious egg sandwiches there."

"You know the tea rooms well?"

"Yes, I go there with my ladies." Eliza gave a polite laugh. "I apologise, you must be wondering who *my ladies* are. I should elaborate. I'm chair of the West London Women's Society."

"How fascinating." Mr Edwards' eyes were wide with interest. We commenced our walk toward the tea rooms with Eliza on her bicycle between us.

"We campaign for women's rights; more specifically to do with suffrage, employment rights and rational dress," continued Eliza.

"Rational dress?"

"Yes, you have no doubt noticed the divided skirt in which I'm riding this bicycle. Can you imagine the immodesty a woman would suffer should she try to ride a bicycle in her usual skirts?"

"I think so." A flush of red appeared on Mr Edwards' cheeks.

"For that reason, I wear a divided skirt. It appears to be a skirt, but is actually an extremely loose-fitting pair of trousers. It's high time that women were allowed to wear clothing, which suits the physical demands of their lifestyles. I've not worn a corset for a year now."

"Oh." There was a strangulated tone to Mr Edwards' voice.

"I don't believe that women should be forced to wear clothing that constricts their movement. And it's about time, don't you think, that women were able to choose clothing better suited to their lifestyles? I can't imagine that you would like to be laced into a corset every day, would you, Mr Edwards?"

"No, I certainly would not."

"Or to wear a multitude of petticoats and skirts so heavy that your natural locomotion is hindered?"

"Indeed, no."

"Do you support women's suffrage, Mr Edwards?"

"Indeed, I do. With half of the population being female, it makes sense to me that educated women should have as much say in the running of this land as educated men."

"Thank you, Mr Edwards. I approve of him already, Penelope! Perhaps you would like to join our meeting with the London Society of Women's Suffrage, Mr Edwards? There will be plenty of men there, of course. Our cause is now supported by most of the liberal members of parliament."

"That is progress, indeed. I should be delighted to come. You are pursuing a range of worthy causes, Mrs Billington-Grieg. Will you be attending the meeting, Miss Green?"

"I shall encourage her to," said Eliza. "Although she is so busy with her work that it is often rather tricky for her to find the time for causes."

"I'm very supportive, Ellie, as you well know," I said.

"Yes, you are, Penelope, but these days you need to stand up to be counted. By turning up in person you are physically adding to the numbers. There is a march planned in support of women's suffrage in this very park next week. I shall expect you both to attend."

"If my work permits, I shall attend and write about it for the *Morning Express*."

"Thank you, Penelope. Mr Edwards, has Penelope told you about the latest adventure she is to embark upon?"

"No, I believe not."

He gave me an expectant glance, but my sister explained before I had a chance to do so.

"She is to work undercover as a maid! Can you believe that, Mr Edwards? A consummately educated lady working as a maid!"

"A maid, Miss Green?" he asked. "But you're a news reporter!"

"I'm to be a news reporter pretending to be a maid. It's called working undercover."

"I don't understand. Why would you do such a thing?"

"The plan is secret. You mustn't tell anyone about it."

"Certainly not. You have my word."

We paused our walk and the rain pattered on our umbrellas while I explained further.

"I intend to work in the household of Mr Alexander Glenville. He's the owner of the Blundell & Co vinegar factory, where there has been criticism of the working conditions."

"Ah, that explains why you were reading about Dorothea Heale earlier this week," said Mr Edwards.

"Dorothea Heale?" said Eliza.

"Yes," I replied. "She has attempted to help the workers at Blundell's campaign for better conditions."

"I know that," said Eliza. "Why didn't you tell me sooner? She's a very good friend of mine. You don't need to spend time reading about her. I can arrange for you to meet her!"

"Can you really, Ellie?"

"Yes, we cross paths on a regular basis. She'll be at the march. I shall arrange for you to meet her when I see her next."

"But I still don't understand why you must work as a maid, Miss Green," said Mr Edwards with a puzzled look.

"My advice is to give up trying to understand it," replied my sister. "Has she told you about the time she was shot yet?"

"Shot?" A flash of horror passed across his face. "Are you all right, Miss Green?"

"Yes, I am fully recovered now, thank you, Mr Edwards."

He stared at me as if disappointed to discover that I wasn't the person he had thought me to be. His expression confirmed to me why I had remained a spinster.

I knew that I would never find a husband who could accept my chosen profession.

CHAPTER 9

My attic room in the Glenville household was small
and draughty. The only other room on this floor
of the house belonged to the maid, Maisie, and
we shared a narrow wooden corridor.

The mattress on my iron bedstead was thin, and an
inspection of the sheets and blankets revealed numerous
patched holes. A threadbare rug lay on the floor, and the
remaining furniture consisted of a washstand, a narrow
wardrobe and a small dressing table, which had seen better
days. The little window overlooked the street.

I unpacked my trunk in this comfortless room and reassured myself that my stay here would not be for long. Mrs
Craughton had instructed me to change into my uniform and
meet her outside the drawing room, where I was to be introduced to Mr and Mrs Glenville. My mouth felt dry and the
palms of my hands were clammy.

*Would the Glenvilles notice that I wasn't the person I claimed
to be?*

I imagined James at my side and thought of the reassurances he would give me. The ring which had belonged to his

grandfather hung from an old locket chain around my neck. When I rested my hand against my chest I could feel the ring beneath my blouse.

Keep it with you for luck.

I intended to do as James had instructed.

I changed into my uniform: a high-collared cotton black dress with a white apron. I pinned my long hair tightly to my head, so that it would fit beneath the white cotton cap. Whenever I dressed at home, Tiger would curl herself around my legs or watch me from my writing desk. I missed her already.

I hung the rest of my clothes in the wardrobe and decided to keep my remaining belongings locked in my trunk. These included the notes for my book and some of Father's papers. I hoped that I would have time in the evenings to continue with my writing and research, and had brought plenty of ink and writing paper with me to that end. James and Mr Sherman expected me to write to them as soon as I discovered anything which would help in the investigation.

I locked my trunk and pushed it underneath the bed. Then I placed the dressing table chair by the wardrobe, climbed onto it and placed the key on top of the wardrobe. It was unlikely that anyone would be interested in finding the key to my trunk, but I didn't want to take any chances.

I felt nervous.

Would my fellow servants be suspicious of me?

There was a small, tarnished mirror on the dressing table. I looked into it and felt I was looking at a different person. For the forthcoming weeks, I would have to be an actress and play the part of Florence Parker. I needed to forget about Penny Green for the time being.

Household noises rose up from the floors below me. I could hear footsteps and voices on the stairs. Somewhere from deep within the house a young child was crying. The large grandfather clock chimed the hour, its tone reverberating throughout the Glenville residence from the hallway.

I knew I couldn't afford to delay a moment longer. My legs felt unsteady as I left the room and made my way to the servants' staircase. The heels of my boots echoed on the steps, and the steepness of the stairs made me feel quite dizzy. Lit by a small window on each storey, the staircase wound down through the five storeys. I briefly made the mistake of peering over the banisters down to the basement. My head whirled, and I gripped the thin stair rail to steady myself.

Mrs Craughton was waiting for me outside the servants' entrance to the drawing room.

"Are you ready?" she asked with a smile.

Her demeanour was warmer than it had been during the interview in her cupboard office. I deduced that she was most likely a pleasant lady who assumed the stern, authoritative air of her position when it suited her.

"Yes." I wiped my hands on my apron. "I think so."

"Don't be nervous. Mr and Mrs Glenville will put you at ease in no time, just you see."

I held my breath as we walked through the door and emerged into the corner of a grand, high-ceilinged room, which was beautifully decorated in deep green and gold. A strong scent of lilies hung in the air. Large windows at one end of the room were covered by green velvet curtains, which draped from an elaborate pelmet. A display of china plates was laid out on the black marble mantelpiece, and more china pieces were displayed in a glass-fronted cabinet next to it. A small piano stood at one side of the room, and in front of the fireplace lay a thick, deep-coloured rug with an oriental design.

Seated in two chairs either side of the fireplace were Mr and Mrs Glenville. I was immediately struck by the darkness of Mr Glenville's eyes and the fiery red of Mrs Glenville's hair.

Mr Glenville rose and gave me a wide grin. The informality of his expression surprised me. His large, dark eyes were slightly hooded beneath a prominent brow, his dark hair streaked with grey. His face was handsome, with a well-set jaw. He had a thin black moustache, but was otherwise clean-shaven. Had he grown whiskers, he would have been able to hide the angry jagged scar that ran down his left cheek to his neck. I wondered why he felt happy to remain clean-shaven. Perhaps he was proud of his scar and felt there was no need to hide it.

He wore a dark suit with a burgundy cravat, which was held in place with a tie pin that sparkled with a diamond. The right arm of his jacket was neatly folded and pinned to his upper arm. I glanced at his half-arm and quickly looked away, as if I shouldn't have taken note of it. A smile played on his lips, and I wondered if he had noticed my awkward glance.

"Florence, isn't it?" His voice had a pleasant tone. It was deep, yet soft.

"Yes, sir." I performed a small curtsy.

"Welcome, Florence!" he said. "What do we call you? Florence? Florrie? Flo?"

He wasn't what I had imagined him to be. After everything I had heard about him, I had expected his manner to be either rude or dismissive.

"I think Flo sounds appropriate," said Mrs Glenville, who spoke with a well-bred, clipped accent. She remained seated as she worked on a piece of embroidery. She had sharp blue eyes with faint lines at the corners, and pale skin. Her forehead was wide and her face tapered to a receding chin. Despite this, her features were pretty, and I could see the likeness between her and the young woman who had slid down the banisters during my previous visit. She wore a beautiful satin dress of deep blue that had a tight bodice fastened with countless shiny buttons.

"I shall be happy to be called Flo," I replied, curtsying once again.

I could feel Mr Glenville's eyes resting on me, and I couldn't help but meet his gaze. There was something oddly magnetic about it.

"Mrs Craughton tells me you have come from Mrs Fothergill in Berkeley Square," continued Mrs Glenville.

"Yes, that's right," I replied.

She raised a well-shaped eyebrow before I quickly added, "My lady."

"And how did you find your time there?"

"I enjoyed it very much, my lady. I was a companion to her as well as a maid."

She smiled. "Good. Well, we look forward to seeing how you get on in our household. Mrs Craughton will explain everything, but do please ask me directly if you have any questions."

As Mrs Craughton accompanied me from the room, I felt relieved that my new employers seemed so pleasant. There was some frostiness in Mrs Glenville's manner, but perhaps I only detected it because I had taken up the position of a servant. Had she known me as Penny Green, she would no doubt have addressed me differently.

"They seem to like you," said Mrs Craughton as we paused on the servants' staircase. "Make sure you get a good night's sleep. Maisie will wake you at six."

The keys on her belt jangled as she descended the stairs. As I climbed the staircase to my room, the recollection of Mr Glenville's dark eyes created a tingling sensation in my stomach.

CHAPTER 10

I woke long before Maisie knocked on my door. As the dawn crept into my room, I lay in bed worrying about the chores I would have to do that day. I felt sure that my lack of experience would be obvious to everyone around me. Perhaps I'd even be dismissed before the day was through. Mrs Garnett had given me some instruction, but I had finally realised how ill-prepared I was.

Maisie was a small, thin, cheery-faced girl, and she put me at ease as soon as I opened my door.

"You must be Flo," she said. "Come wiv me, I'll show yer what to do."

She looked about fourteen, and had a generous dusting of freckles across her nose and cheeks. Some of her teeth were missing and she had a fidgety manner about her. I instantly liked her, and she seemed keen to help me settle in.

I followed Maisie around the house as we crept into silent bedchambers with a candle and lit the fires. Then we lit the fires in the drawing room, morning room and library. I helped with carrying the coal, loading it into scuttles from the coal bunker in the yard. Once the fires were lit, we opened the curtains in the main reception rooms, then dusted and plumped up the cushions, making sure everything was clean and tidy for the family's use.

There was just enough time for a quick breakfast of toast and a boiled egg at the large oak table in the basement kitchen. I met Cook, a red-faced woman with heavy jowls and a wide vocabulary of curse words. Mr Perrin, the butler, leafed through the *Morning Express* as he ate, and I tried not to peer over at the paper to read my colleagues' words.

Mr Perrin had acknowledged me with a perfunctory nod when we were first introduced. He looked about fifty and wore a smart dark suit over his solid, broad-shouldered frame. His expression was one of refined passivity, which could only have been brought about by many years of service. I struggled to imagine him displaying any emotion.

Much as I was wary about giving away any clues to my identity, I realised that I needed to talk if I wanted to find out the information James' investigation required.

"Mr Glenville has a vinegar factory, is that right?" I asked.

"Yes, Blundell's," Mrs Craughton replied. "You must have heard of it."

"I have. It's not the same factory there have been complaints about, is it?"

"It might be. Although it's much the same as any other factory in London. The workers are always complaining. I suppose they're the ones whose manners are too unrefined for service. I know that sounds rather harsh, but I'm afraid there's some truth in it."

We were disturbed by the ringing of the bell for Mr and Mrs Glenville's room.

"Come on, everyone. Back to work," said the housekeeper, rising from her seat.

Mr Perrin folded his newspaper and placed it on the table. He and the housekeeper left the kitchen.

"I couldn't work in a fact'ry," said Maisie, chewing on a piece of toast. "Too loud and dangerous fer me. And I don't agree wiv Mrs Craughton. I didn' 'ave no manners afore I come 'ere, but you learns 'em, don't yer? Anyways, some rich people don't 'ave no manners neither."

"Do the Glenvilles receive many visitors?" I ventured, hopeful that Maisie might be able to give me a few clues as to Mr Glenville's acquaintances.

"Yeah, they gets a fair few of 'em."

"Some of them must be important, with Mr Glenville being a factory owner."

"Some of 'em is, but I wouldn't know it," said Maisie. "I can't never remember their names."

I smiled, trying to hide my disappointment. *Perhaps Mrs Craughton or Mr Perrin would be more helpful.*

Maisie showed me how the water pump in the yard worked, then we carried water up and down the servants' staircase to each bedchamber and to the nursery. It wasn't long before my arms and legs began to ache and my corset felt extremely restrictive. Mrs Garnett had warned me about the physical demands of a maid's work, but I had been rather dismissive on this front.

Mrs Craughton told me to clear the plates after breakfast, but when I reached the dining room I noticed that the family hadn't quite finished eating. I waited in the room by the servants' door, grateful for a brief rest. The walls were wood-panelled, and heavy, red velvet curtains hung at the windows. There was a large, glass-fronted dresser at one end of the room, and a shaft of morning sunlight glinted on the treasures within it.

Mr and Mrs Glenville sat at the long, mahogany dining

table with the young woman I recognised as the banister-sliding Sophia, alongside two other adolescent children. One was a young man with red hair, like his mother and sister. He had an odd, twisted way of sitting, and as I watched I noticed that his arms suffered from some form of involuntary movement. Despite this, he was able to eat his breakfast quite proficiently. It dawned on me that this young man must be Maurice, the Glenvilles' eldest son. I had heard him described as an idiot, but I saw no sign of mental incapacity as I looked on.

A pretty, dark-haired girl also sat at the table, and I guessed she was the younger sister of Sophia and Maurice. I couldn't remember if James had told me her name. She looked about fifteen.

Mrs Glenville discussed the plans for the day with her children, and I avidly watched their progress with each cup and plate, waiting for the moment when it would be appropriate to begin clearing the table. The Glenvilles didn't appear to be in a hurry.

Mr Glenville said little, occupying himself with reading some newly delivered letters. He had noticed my presence, and on two occasions had looked up from his correspondence and smiled at me. Those two glances were enough to spark the strange, ticklish sensation in my stomach again. I tried to keep my eyes averted, but it was difficult not to look at him every now and then.

A sharp tone in Mrs Glenville's voice drew my attention back to the conversation.

"You're not getting involved with any sort of demonstration." She glared at her daughter, who sat across the table from her. "Such events are dangerous. They attract all manner of troublemakers."

"No, this is a different sort. There is no need to worry, Mother. Many of the people there will be women."

"One of those women's suffrage events? You are not to go, Sophia!"

I felt my heart flip. It struck me that Sophia was talking about the march Eliza had mentioned to me.

"You could come with me, Mother." The corners of Sophia's mouth rose into a mischievous smile.

"Such impertinence!" Mrs Glenville snapped.

"I didn't intend to be impertinent, Mother. It was a genuine invitation."

"Mother has no interest in women's suffrage. You know that," said the younger sister.

"But perhaps she should. Perhaps you both should. Don't you wish to have the vote, Jane?"

"I don't know."

"There is no need for it," said Mrs Glenville. "And the breakfast table is no place to discuss politics. In fact, I have no wish to discuss politics at all. It's not a womanly pursuit."

"But why not?"

"Sophia..." Mr Glenville warned. He had put down his correspondence and was listening intently.

"Women have enough to attend to, Sophia," said Mrs Glenville. "Their homes and families provide more than enough to occupy their thoughts and time. I don't wish to hear another word on the matter."

"But what of the future, Mother?"

"Sophia, we don't need to hear any more," said Mr Glenville.

"More girls are receiving proper schooling now," continued Sophia, disregarding her father's warning. "Do you think well-educated women will find satisfaction in being confined to their homes?"

"Of course they will!" her mother retorted. "It's their duty! And while I agree with improved education for girls, I don't believe it should entitle them to live the life of a man.

What a preposterous idea! Men and women have different roles, and that's the way it always has been."

"But what if a woman doesn't wish it to be that way?"

"Then she must learn to accept it. It's what my generation has done and the many generations which have gone before us also did. Imagine what my own mother would think if she heard you talking this way. Imagine how disappointed she would be. You have been educated to be a lady, and that's the role you must pursue, just as I did. Marching about in parks complaining about one's lot in life is not only ungrateful; it shows a lack of respect for society and order. You have been brought up to be a better young lady than that."

"Dorothea Heale will be there."

"Sophia, that is enough!" Mr Glenville brought his fist down on the table, startling everyone, including myself.

There was a loud clatter of crockery, and several pieces of cutlery fell to the floor.

"You know better than to argue with your mother!" he warned.

Sophia stared back at her father, her eyes unblinking. Jane looked down at her hands, and Mrs Glenville mopped her brow with her serviette.

Mr Glenville held his daughter's gaze for some time before looking away. Once he had returned to his correspondence, Sophia stood and dropped her serviette onto her plate before walking away from the table.

"You sh-should excuse yourself b-before leaving," said Maurice.

It was the first time I had heard him speak.

"I'm too angry!" she snarled in reply.

The door of the dining room closed behind her with a slam.

"That child!" said Mrs Glenville to her husband. "I can't bear it any more, Alexander. I really can't!"

"It won't be much longer now," he replied calmly.

"I can't wait until she's married," added Jane. "I'm counting down the hours to her wedding day. Then she'll be Mrs Dudley Lombard and won't be under our roof any longer!"

Mrs Glenville got up from her seat and the others followed suit. My heart pounded in my chest as I stepped forward to clear away the plates. I felt like an intruder, and was sure that I wasn't supposed to be privy to the family's most private moments. I sympathised with Sophia's sentiments, but I felt sorry for her family that she had been so rude to them.

"Thank you, Flo. I apologise that you had to witness that on your first day here," said Mr Glenville.

"She could have witnessed far worse!" laughed his wife.

CHAPTER 11

After helping with the breakfast plates, I scrubbed the front steps and mopped the tiled floor of the hallway. Having done what I had thought was a good job, Mrs Craughton informed me that my work had been less than thorough.

"I'm sorry," I said. "I was fortunate not to have to do too much cleaning for Mrs Fothergill. I became more of a companion to her after a while."

"So you have already mentioned," said Mrs Craughton, scrutinising my work.

I tried to wield the mop as expertly as I knew how.

"I witnessed an argument between Miss Sophia and her parents at breakfast," I ventured. "Is that a common occurrence?"

"Sadly, it is. She's a headstrong girl."

"How old is she?"

"Almost eighteen. Her birthday is this Saturday, and there will be a small celebration in her honour."

"A happy event!"

I pushed the mop around the base of the grandfather clock.

"Perhaps, although I wouldn't be too hopeful about that. There always seems to be a hiccup where Miss Sophia's concerned."

"I suppose it's her age."

"It's not just that." Mrs Craughton lowered her voice to a whisper. "She's one of the most ungrateful girls I've ever met! She has it all, yet she's never content with it. I don't understand her. She's marrying into the Lombard family, and they're exceptionally rich. You should see the house she and Master Lombard are to move into in Barnes! It's quite a place. I'm hopeful that marriage and children will refine her manners. It can't come too soon! You may have noticed that most of us in the household are impatient for their wedding day to arrive."

"What are the Lombards like?"

"They're held in high regard, and are good friends of Mr and Mrs Glenville. You'll meet them at the birthday celebration."

She peered into the bucket and pulled a disgusted face. "Haven't you noticed that the water needs changing?"

Lunch was a quick meal of bread and butter. I felt relieved to be able to sit down for a short while, even if it happened to be on an uncomfortable wooden chair at the kitchen table. As we ate, Mr Perrin continued to peruse his copy of the *Morning Express*. My fingers itched to pick it up and leaf through the stories.

"I've written a list of items which require cleaning in Mr Glenville's study," said Mrs Craughton, passing a sheet of paper to Maisie.

Maisie screwed up her eyes and peered at it, while biting her thumbnail.

"It needs to be completed this afternoon," added the housekeeper.

Maisie looked up at me and grimaced.

"Is something the matter, Maisie?" asked the housekeeper.

"You keeps forgettin' I can't read, Mrs Craughton."

The housekeeper sighed, took the paper from Maisie and thrust it in my direction. "I take it you can read, Flo?"

I nodded. "I can."

"You can clean the study this afternoon, and Maisie will work in the morning room."

"Can you write, an' all?" Maisie asked me.

"Yes."

"P'raps yer can learn me. I want ter read 'n' write."

"Maisie came from the workhouse," Mrs Craughton explained. "I think they should give children lessons in there. That way they'd have more chance of making something of themselves."

"I can teach you to read and write, Maisie," I said.

"Would yer?" She pulled her thumb away from her mouth and grinned widely. "Aw, thank you, Flo!"

"In your own time, though, please," urged Mrs Craughton. "No learning letters while you're supposed to be working."

"Of course not," I replied.

"Mr Perrin," the housekeeper said, turning to the butler. "I have prepared the menu for Saturday. Shall we discuss the wine?"

"Yes. I've already decided on Pommery 1876 for the champagne."

"That's your favourite, isn't it, Mr Perrin?"

"It's Mr Glenville's favourite, although I do enjoy a glass myself when the occasion allows it."

Mrs Craughton turned to me and Maisie, glaring at us as though we were no longer supposed to be there.

"What are you two waiting for?" she scolded. "Take yourselves off and get back to work."

On my way to Mr Glenville's study, I passed the girls who had slid with Sophia down the banister. They were better behaved now that they were under the care of their strict-looking governess.

I knocked at the door of the study and heard no reply. I slowly pushed the door open and was relieved to find the room empty. I felt wary of encountering Mr Glenville too often in case I accidentally said something which would give away my identity.

The room was gloomy, but not dark enough to justify lighting the gas lamps. I lit a candle so that I could read Mrs Craughton's list more easily. I had been instructed to light the fire so the room would be warm for Mr Glenville's use later that afternoon; once I had done so, the room felt more welcoming. A bookcase stood against one wall containing a number of leather-bound volumes, which included works by Dickens and Shakespeare.

A family portrait hung above the fireplace. It depicted Mr and Mrs Glenville with three small children, who I took to be Sophia, Maurice and Jane. Both Sophia and Maurice stared out of the picture with sullen faces and shocks of red hair. Jane was the pretty, dark-haired baby on her father's lap. The artist had flattered Mrs Glenville, and she looked quite a beauty. Mr Glenville's likeness was more accurate, except that the scar on his face had been omitted.

I set the candle on the desk, and it occurred to me that the multitude of drawers might contain something useful for James' investigation. I carefully pulled out the smaller drawers at the top of the desk and peered inside. I found writing paper, pots of ink, pens and a rubber stamp with 'Blundell & Co' marked on it.

I tried a larger drawer that was lower down in the desk, but it was locked. Distant footsteps cautioned me to concentrate on my cleaning work, so I referred to Mrs Craughton's list and opened the glass cabinet next to Mr Glenville's desk to begin cleaning the ornaments within it. It was an odd assortment: a pair of Etruscan-style vases, the bust of a Roman gentleman, bronze statuettes of warriors and goddesses, a table clock which had stopped working, and an odd-shaped stone, which was about the size of a house brick.

As I took each object out of the cabinet and wiped it with my cloth, I wondered how I could find out the information James required from me. Maisie didn't seem to know a great deal, and Mr Perrin had shown little interest in conversing with me so far. Mrs Craughton seemed the happiest to talk, and I hoped that she had some useful knowledge of the Glenvilles' affairs.

But how would I be able to ask relevant questions without her becoming suspicious? The solution would probably be to ask just a few questions each day. *But how long would it take me to find the answers I needed?* I desired my time here to be as short as possible.

"Mrs Craughton's got you cleaning the curios, then?"

The soft, deep voice behind me caused my heart to skip a beat. I spun around to see Mr Glenville in the centre of the room. I hadn't even heard him enter.

CHAPTER 12

"I'm so sorry, Flo. I didn't mean to alarm you!" Mr Glenville smiled apologetically.

"Oh, um, I can do this another time, sir," I said, flustered. "I didn't realise you required the use of this room now. I was told you would be using it later."

"Please don't worry." He gave a dismissive wave of his hand, then stepped closer to the cabinet and peered inside it. "These odd things have needed cleaning for a while. Continue as you are, and don't mind me. Goodness, I remember this."

He reached into the cabinet, picked up the odd-shaped stone and turned it over in his hands.

"It's one of the few things I have left of my mother's," he said. "One of the only things, in fact. She didn't have much. Do you know what it is?"

His eyes were like deep, dark pools, and he was close enough for me to smell his eau de cologne. It was an exotic scent, which brought to my mind the bright flowers and scented shrubs of Colombia my father had described in his diaries.

"I have no idea." My mouth felt dry. I felt sure he had guessed that I wasn't a real maid.

"It's an elephant's tooth!" He grinned. "My mother once worked for a nabob on his return from India. For some reason, he gave her this!"

"It's very large for a tooth," I said.

"Big creatures, though, aren't they? I'd very much like to see one in the wild."

"I'll be sure to take extra care with the tooth, sir."

"I'm sure you will, Flo."

I smiled meekly as he placed it back inside the cabinet, hoping that he would leave the room. My hopes were dashed as he walked over to his desk and seated himself there, only a few feet from where I was working. My heart pounded heavily, and my fingers felt clumsy.

Why did Mr Glenville create such a reaction in me?

"I feel I must apologise for my daughter," he said.

"Please don't, sir. There's no need," I replied, as I cleaned a statuette in an awkward manner. "She's simply a spirited young woman. She knows her own mind."

"She certainly does." He sighed.

"She strikes me as a clever girl," I said. "She has quite a future ahead of her."

"Oh, she's clever all right. Too clever for her own good. I swear she should have been born a boy."

He noticed the puzzled look on my face.

"My words sound odd, I know! But you understand what I mean, don't you? She's not a typical girl. Not like her sister Jane. Jane's just like her mother. Sadly, I think Sophia is rather like me." He smiled. "If only Maurice were like her, everything would be rather different."

"I'm not quite sure what you mean."

"Despite having six children, I have no heir," he replied.

"Maurice is the only boy, and he lacks the ability to inherit the business, as I'm sure you've already noticed."

I nodded uneasily.

"Everyone told us to put him in an institution as soon as he was born. Could you ever do that to your own child?"

"No, I don't think I could."

"Even now the boy's twenty years old, people still say it. What do they know? I can't deny that Camilla and I were disappointed as his weakness grew more obvious. And for a long time we hoped to have another boy. But things are the way they are, and we love him just as much as his sisters. It's impossible not to, isn't it? Do you have children, Flo?"

"No."

"Perhaps you'll understand one day."

"I might understand quite a bit already."

"I'm sure you do." He smiled, and there was a warm twinkle in his eyes.

I glanced at the jagged scar on his face and wondered how the injury had occurred.

"You're rather sharp, aren't you?" he continued. "Not the usual calibre of maid."

I felt my heart skip another beat. *Did he suspect me?*

Nervous perspiration caused my spectacles to slip down my nose. I pushed them back up, cleared my throat and decided to change the subject.

"I hear you've been at Blundell's a long time, sir."

"You've heard correctly. Yes, I was ten when I began work there. It's been almost forty years now. Can you believe that? Forty years!"

"I can't at all, sir."

"I was the smallest boy there, so I was the one they would send under the machines to clean. I fitted into the small spaces easily, and that's how I lost this thing." He shrugged the shoulder of his missing arm. "It was caught in a line shaft."

"Ow!" I winced.

"I didn't know anything about it, of course, I lost consciousness the moment it happened."

"And you continued to work there after that?"

"Well, there wasn't a lot else I could do. Mother didn't have any money, and school was out of the question for a boy like me. I had to work. Fortunately, Thomas Blundell thought a one-armed boy could still be of some use!" He laughed. "He saw the potential in everybody, that man. It's no secret that the workers in my factory have been complaining about their lot. And most of them have the use of all their limbs. They don't realise how much safer the factory is now than it used to be. These people encourage them to complain, you see."

"Which people?"

"The likes of Dorothea Heale. I'm afraid that's why I lost my temper when Sophia mentioned her at the breakfast table this morning. Dorothea and her friends lurk around the gates of my factory and encourage dissent. If I were to ask the workers coming out of any factory in this city after a long shift what they thought of the place, I would no doubt soon be surrounded by a crowd of whinging people encouraging each other in their complaints. Don't you agree, Flo?"

"It sounds quite likely."

"Exactly. Once someone starts to complain about something, it puts the idea into someone else's head, and then they realise they all want to be complaining about it. It spreads like a disease! Don't ever get pulled into that trap. Very few people possess independent thought. Have you noticed that? We all wish to be paid more, don't we? And we all wish to work a little less. Although I think reform is extremely important, these sentiments can sometimes be appropriated by troublemakers."

I felt myself beginning to relax in Mr Glenville's company as his manner was surprisingly informal. As I listened to him and methodically cleaned each object in the cabinet, I wondered if the factory owner was as unpleasant as the rumours about him suggested.

James had called him slippery and untrustworthy. *Was I right to believe his opinion?*

"This country relies on its workers," Mr Glenville continued. "They're not just responsible for the output of their factories each day. Oh no, it's much more than that. Great Britain is so named because of its industry. It's the backbone of the British Empire! We should all take pride in our work, Flo. From the ten-year-old boy who cleans under the machines to the men on the company's board of directors. We all do our bit, and look what we can achieve together. Life is about work and industry. This is why I won't tolerate complaining. If a worker has a genuine grievance, I'm more than happy to listen. But when it comes to general grumbling and moaning, which often goes hand in hand with complacency, I have no tolerance for it whatsoever."

I liked the manner in which Mr Glenville addressed me. He spoke to me as an equal, rather than as a member of his staff.

"I have considered taking legal proceedings against Mrs Heale," he continued. "But I'm not sure it's a worthwhile use of my time and money. Hopefully she'll realise that harassing people who are fortunate to have steady, paid work is also a waste of her time. There are countless other issues in this city which need addressing, aren't there? The slums, for example. And crime. Hopefully she'll direct her attention towards those in the future."

"What about workers' pay?" I asked.

"What do you mean, Flo?" His eyebrows drew closer together.

"Perhaps if you paid the workers more they would complain less."

He laughed. "If only it worked like that. Do you think that if I gave each worker an extra shilling a week they would be content? Not to mention the fact that it would bankrupt my business. It's a business I run, not a charity."

"You bought Albert Archdale's factory, didn't you?"

He gave an impressed nod. "You really do know a few things about me, don't you?"

One corner of his mouth lifted into a smile and I realised I was close to giving away my identity. I cursed myself inwardly for continuing this discussion with him.

"Yes, I bought Archdale's, and the rate of accidents has decreased dramatically since I did so. Archdale couldn't have cared less about his workers. There haven't been any complaints about me yet at the Bermondsey factory. Mrs Heale has yet to loiter beside the gates there!"

Mr Glenville got up from his seat.

"Well, I've talked at you for long enough. Thank you for all your work with these curios this afternoon." He stepped toward the cabinet again and admired them. "They look much better now. Isn't it funny how attached you can become to such silly things? Each one is a memento, I suppose."

"A memento of what, sir?"

He turned to me and I found it difficult to remove my eyes from his. He looked at my face so intently that I felt sure he hadn't blinked for some time.

Did he look at everyone this way?

I felt a prickling sensation at the back of my neck.

"Perhaps I shall tell you one day," he said softly. "Each one of these objects has its own story. Much like people, I suppose. We all have our own stories, don't we?"

"We do. And some have more than one." I wasn't sure

where my words had come from; I had intended to remain silent.

"Interesting!" A smile spread across his face. "I like that thought very much." Still his eyes didn't blink. "Complicated creatures, aren't we?" He grinned and turned to leave the room.

"See you later, Flo," he called back over his shoulder.

"Goodbye, sir."

I remained standing where I was as he closed the study door behind him. His scent lingered in the air, and it felt as though the shadows in the room had deepened. The more I got to know Mr Glenville, the less I knew what to make of him.

By the time I retired to my attic room that evening, my body was aching from the physical work. I should have felt pleased that I had managed to convince everyone I was a maid, but instead I felt dissatisfied that I had made no progress with James' investigation. Moreover, there was a niggling worry in my mind that perhaps I hadn't been so convincing after all. I thought about the comments Mr Glenville had made.

'Not your usual maid' was how he had described me. *What had he meant by 'complicated creatures'? Had he been referring to me or himself? Or had it simply been a turn of phrase, which I was dwelling upon too much?*

My mind felt almost as weary as my body as I changed into my nightdress, and it was only then that I noticed someone had been in my room. The neat pile of writing paper wasn't exactly as I had left it on the dressing table. It had been moved slightly to the left, as if someone had leafed through it. There was nothing obviously out of place, but I could sense that things had been shifted and put back clumsily. I hurriedly dropped to my knees and checked the trunk under my bed. I was relieved to see that it had remained in the exact position in which I had left it.

Or had it? Had the intruder cleverly left it just as he or she had found it?

I leapt up and moved the chair over to the wardrobe so I could check that the key to my trunk was in its original hiding place.

Thankfully, it was.

I knew that Mrs Glenville and Mrs Craughton were entitled to check my room and ensure that it was tidy. My door didn't have a lock on it, and I couldn't expect complete privacy.

I returned to my trunk and tried its lid. It was firmly locked. Then something else under the bed caught my eye. It looked like a crumpled piece of cloth. I picked it up and found that it was a white handkerchief with a lace trim. Three initials were embroidered in one corner: CDC.

I hadn't remembered seeing it under the bed before, and it was free of dust. It occurred to me that it must have been dropped there recently. *Who in the household had the initials CDC?* The first and last name began with a 'C'. The only person I could think of was Mrs Craughton. *Was this Mrs Craughton's handkerchief in my hand?*

I couldn't think how it had found its way under the bed. *Perhaps it had ended up there while she was preparing the room for my arrival.* That was the most likely explanation I could think of. However, I didn't recall seeing it when I first placed the trunk under my bed. *Had Mrs Craughton entered my room and looked through the papers on the dressing table? Had she tried to open the trunk?*

If Mrs Craughton wanted to look through my belongings, she could have simply asked my permission. *Why had she been secretive about it? And could I be sure that she was the mystery intruder?*

CHAPTER 13

Maisie's knock at my door the following morning came as an unwelcome interruption. Having lain awake worrying about who had been in my room, I had fallen into a deep slumber only shortly before dawn.

Maisie chuckled when she saw me. "Yer want to be back in bed, don't yer, Flo? I know that feelin'."

Once again, we crept around the quiet house and prepared the fires.

"Does Mrs Craughton check your room?" I whispered as we prepared to go into the nursery.

"No," replied Maisie with a look of surprise. "She ain't been in yer room, 'as she?"

"I think so. I can't be sure."

"I can't be sure, neither. P'raps she does check it and I don't know nuffink about it."

Mrs Craughton handed me a letter at breakfast time. I wondered if I would ever be brave enough to ask her about the handkerchief she had dropped in my room.

Would it cause embarrassment? Would she even admit it? I decided to wait a while before broaching the subject.

The letter had been forwarded to Florence Parker from my Milton Street address, which had been heavily inked out. I was grateful to Mrs Garnett for helping me hide my identity.

"A letter already," said Mrs Craughton. "You must be popular."

"It's probably from my sister," I replied. "I sent her my new address, but she still posted it to the old one!"

Thankfully, this explanation seemed to satisfy Mrs Craughton as I opened the envelope and held the letter up close to my spectacles so that no one else could read it.

My Dear Madam,

Thank you for your delightful letter, and may I say how flattered I am that the daughter of the eminent plant-hunter, Mr. F. B. Green, should wish to make contact with me.

Writing a book about your father's life is an admirable undertaking, and I wish you the best of luck with the endeavour. As an author of many books myself, I can attest that it is no small task! You will no doubt find my own texts on the subject of plant-hunting to be of great assistance in your toils, and I am confident that you shall achieve the end result with aplomb.

I would be more than delighted to meet with you, and to discuss your father's life and work. You are welcome to visit me at my home at the above address at a time and date convenient to yourself.

Do please note that my next round of travels will take me to the Himalayas, and I shall be departing London in July. You will no doubt wish to make an appointment with me before then.

Do please contact my secretary, Mrs Bowes, to arrange a suitable time.

I eagerly anticipate our forthcoming rendezvous.

Yours very truly,
  Mr. Isaac Fox-Stirling

I looked forward to hearing what Mr Fox-Stirling would be able to tell me about his expedition to find my father. I hoped he would have some new information about his disappearance.

Perhaps there was a clue about what had happened to him, which nobody had followed up on or considered significant.

My immediate problem was finding a time when I could visit Mr Fox-Stirling. Maisie mentioned that we would usually be permitted leave on alternate Wednesday afternoons, but I hadn't yet confirmed this with Mrs Craughton.

"You're to help Maisie in the conservatory this morning," said the housekeeper.

I folded the letter away and finished my last few mouthfuls of bread and butter.

"I haven't shown you the conservatory yet," she continued. "It's Mrs Glenville's pride and joy. You must be extremely careful with the hothouse plants. Many of them are extremely delicate tropical specimens."

"I know quite a bit about tropical plants, Mrs Craughton."

"Do you? Did Mrs Fothergill have a conservatory?"

"No." I wished I hadn't volunteered the information. "But my father did," I added, giving her a smile which I hoped was convincing.

The sight of the broad-leaved palms, bromeliads and orchids immediately brought a lump to my throat. Plants such as these had been lovingly described in my father's letters and diaries, and he had also made many sketches of them. *Perhaps some of the species I was looking at had been brought to England by him.*

As the sun streamed through the glass and filtered between the layers of thick foliage, I felt as though I were in another land. I breathed in the warm scent of the lush vegetation and wished my father could be there to see this place with me.

"Yer a'right Flo?" asked Maisie.

"I'm fine, thank you, Maisie. Tell me what needs doing."

"Well, all I knows is that they 'ad a load o' lice in 'ere. Plant lice. I thought it were just people 'n' dogs what got lice, but turns out plants get 'em an' all. Anyways, they got 'em killed off. There's a posh word what describes it. Fume summink."

"Fumigate?"

"Yeah, that's the one. Kills the lice but don't kill the plants. Pretty, ain't they?"

"They're beautiful. I didn't realise this conservatory was here. Goodness, look at that!" I stepped over to an orchid with a profuse spray of white and orange flowers. "I do believe that's a type of Oncidium."

"A what now?"

"It's an orchid."

"Yeah, but you said summink else. Not orchid. You said *sidum* or summink."

I laughed. "Don't worry, Maisie. I read something about it in a book once. Hand me that broom and I'll start sweeping the floor."

"I wish I could read books. Yer s'posed to be teachin' me."

"Shall we look at some letters this evening?"

"Yeah, I'd like that, I would."

Maisie and I chatted as we worked, happily immersed in our own little tropical paradise.

CHAPTER 14

"How are you finding the work here, Flo?" asked Mrs Glenville as she worked on her embroidery in the morning room.

"I'm enjoying it very much, my lady."

"Good. Well, we're very pleased to have you here." She looked up and gave me a brief smile, then returned to her work.

I forced a smile in return. "Thank you, my lady."

It was my third day in the Glenville household, and I was thoroughly tired of waiting on people and tending to their every need. I suddenly felt a great deal of sympathy for people who worked in service. They were expected to keep themselves hidden unless they were needed, and few people were interested in anything they thought or said. I wasn't sure I could continue with this work for much longer. I missed writing, and my work colleagues, and my cat Tiger. I even missed Mrs Garnett.

I rested a hand against my chest to feel the ring beneath my uniform. It felt as though I would never see James again. It was as if I had been condemned to this place for eternity.

"Would you like sugar in your tea, my lady?"

"No, thank you. Fetch me Mrs Craughton, would you?"

I left the room feeling resentful towards Mrs Glenville for the dismissive way she had spoken to me. I didn't dislike her. She seemed a pleasant enough lady, but I wasn't used to being spoken to like a servant.

I walked to Mrs Craughton's office and felt my resentment spread to Mr Conway and Mr Sherman. They were the ones who had put me in this position.

Why had they thought this a good idea? I had come across nothing which would help with James' investigation. The only possibility I could foresee was getting into the locked drawers in Mr Glenville's study. I would need to find the key to open them first.

I knocked at Mrs Craughton's door and passed on Mrs Glenville's message. As the housekeeper acknowledged me, I looked past her shoulder at the keys hanging from the neat rows of hooks on the wall. *Could the key to Mr Glenville's desk be one of them?* Each key was clearly labelled, but there was no time to look.

Mrs Craughton stepped straight out of her office and shut the door behind her.

"You and Maisie are to tidy and dust the library this afternoon," she said. "You both did well with the conservatory yesterday. Mrs Glenville commented on its cleanliness."

"Thank you, Mrs Craughton."

I met Maisie on the servants' staircase as we descended to the kitchen for our lunch.

"'A' is for apple," chanted Maisie. "I still remembers 'ow to write it."

"Good! Another lesson this evening?" I asked.

"Can't do this evenin'."

I wondered what else she had planned.

"Perhaps tomorrow, then?"

"Yeah, I can do tomorra."

Mr Perrin was already in the kitchen.

"Perrin. That's a 'P', ain't it?"

The butler gave us a rare smile and quickly returned to his newspaper. I wondered if I could locate his old copies of the *Morning Express* so that I might sneak a look at them. I was unaccustomed to having so little idea of what was taking place in the outside world.

"'Ow d'yer write 'P'?" asked Maisie.

"We can practise in the next lesson."

"But that's tomorra!"

"You told me you were too busy for a lesson this evening, Maisie."

"Oh yeah, I forgot."

"Who are these two?"

I had seen the portrait of the twin girls during my previous visits to the library, but this was the first chance I'd had to ask someone about them. The girls were aged about three or four, and stood hand-in-hand in a gloomy, woodland setting. They both had long red curls and wore pale-coloured dresses. Their large, wide eyes stared out of their flawless white faces.

"Dunno. They're from Mrs Glenville's fambly," replied Maisie. "All the pictures are of 'er fambly."

"They're identical, aren't they?" I commented. "And almost phantom-like. They're ghost children."

"Don't say that!" Maisie jumped with horror. "That'll scare me, it will! I don't like ghost children!"

"I was only joking, Maisie. They're not ghosts, are they? They're Mrs Glenville's ancestors. Maybe one of them is her mother."

I peered at the bottom of the picture, looking for an

inscription which could tell me more about the painting, but all I could see was a year: 1826.

"They looks like ghosts ter me," said Maisie. "I never thought of it till yer said it, but they looks like 'em, don't they? I don't never want ter be in this room on me own now. What if they climbs out the picture at night and goes walkin' round the 'ouse?"

I shivered and wished I had never mentioned the picture.

"Look at all these books, Maisie," I said brightly. I waved my feather duster in the direction of the four walls, which were lined from floor to ceiling with bookshelves. "Soon you'll be able to read them all!"

"Yeah, and it'll take me an 'ole lifetime, an' all."

"Choose the best ones first," I said, running my duster over the countless volumes. "When you know your letters better, you'll be able to read the titles on the bindings and decide which books seem the most interesting."

"Do they 'ave pictures in 'em?"

"I'm sure some of them will have."

I noticed a newspaper rack in the corner of the room, and to my delight I discovered that it contained an edition of the *Morning Express* for each day of the past week.

"I'm so 'appy you've came 'ere, Flo."

I stepped away from the newspapers and saw Maisie standing with her hand resting on the back of a chair, regarding me with her large blue eyes. I felt a pang of guilt.

"Really?"

"Yeah. I misses Betsy, but I'm glad you've came."

"Thank you, Maisie."

I smiled, but I felt a bitter taste in my mouth. I was deceiving the girl about who I really was. I turned from her honest, trusting gaze and occupied myself with work.

Before retiring that evening, I thought about the newspaper rack in the library.

The butler was permitted to read the newspapers, so surely an interested maid was also permitted to do so?

While the rest of the household slept, I took my candle into the library, avoided the gaze of the ghost twins and took the most recent copy of the *Morning Express* from the newspaper rack. I sat at a round, mahogany table and opened out the paper, keen to read all that had been happening beyond the walls of the Glenville house.

The candlelight flickered onto the news stories about the advancing British troops in Egypt, obstruction tactics in the House of Commons and the peace treaty negotiations between Chile and Peru. I also read that the experiment of closing public houses in Wales on Sundays had failed to reduce levels of drunkenness. Instead, men were buying more liquor on Saturdays and drinking it at home on Sundays with their wives and children.

"Are you unable to sleep, Flo?"

My heart jumped into my mouth, and I spluttered as I tried to reply.

"Mr Glenville!"

He stood in the doorway, and I could just about see his smile in the candlelight. Although I felt uneasy, I also felt pleased to see him for some strange reason.

"I'm so sorry to have startled you again," he said softly. His eyes seemed even darker in the dim light.

"You move about very quietly, sir," I replied. "I thought everyone was in bed."

"So did I!" He laughed and walked over to the table.

"I'm not supposed to be here, am I?" I said. "I'm sorry." I folded up the newspaper.

"No, stay! Of course I don't mind you being here. I must

say that I don't know many women who take an interest in the newspaper."

"I like to find out what's happening in the world."

"Admirable. Very admirable. And why shouldn't you? Sophia would say something similar. She also has an inquiring mind; always questioning everything. Do you question everything, Flo?"

"I suppose I do. In fact, I know I do."

He laughed and, to my great dismay, took a seat at the table with me. My entire body felt tense. The exotic eau de cologne hung in the air once again.

"You've heard Sophia talk about women's suffrage, haven't you? Camilla can't bear to hear about it as she comes from a family with traditional views. I keep quiet when they discuss the matter, but privately I would say that I agree with the cause. I see intelligent women like you and Sophia, and I realise how foolish our society is not to give you a say in how our country is run. Currently, some men who are permitted to vote have a far inferior intellect to women like you. Actually, most of the House of Commons, I should say!" He laughed again. "Do you ever feel trapped in your woman's body, Flo?"

He noticed my perplexed expression and chuckled. "Goodness, I phrased that in an odd way, didn't I? I'm so sorry. What I mean to say is that it must be difficult to be a woman with the intelligence of a man. We treat you so differently from ourselves, don't we? And much of the time we assume you don't have the mental strength we have. But you're the same sort of person inside, aren't you? We've got it wrong, all wrong. I've known a lot of remarkable women in my life, but the one I always held in the highest regard was my mother. She was the most selfless person I have ever met. And to think of what I put her through! On the day of my accident..." He pointed at his missing arm. "On that day, she was..."

As his voice trailed off, I could see that his eyes were moist. "It almost destroyed her. She thought my life was over."

Silence descended.

"But it wasn't," I said quietly.

"No, it wasn't! It was just the beginning. Because from that moment onwards, I was determined to show her what a twelve-year-old boy, even one who lived in poverty, could do. And I did it as well. I did it." He took a handkerchief from his pocket and dabbed at his eyes.

"Goodness, why did I begin talking about that?" He grinned. "I went quite off the topic there. My mind wanders when I'm tired. I should get to bed. The problem with you, Flo, is that you're a good listener. You encourage a man to talk."

"But I've barely said a thing!"

"Exactly! You listened instead."

"Oh yes, I see what you mean."

I laughed, and he got up from his chair.

"Well, goodnight. Don't stay up reading too late. I hope you don't mind me saying so, but your time is wasted as a maid. You should be doing something else with that brain of yours."

"Oh I do, sir."

"Do you indeed?"

I nodded, unsure how to elaborate.

"Perhaps you can tell me about it when we speak next. It's good to have discovered another night owl! Good night."

"Good night, sir."

I watched him leave the room before opening up the newspaper again. The ghost twins stared down at me and, despite the late hour, my mind felt wide awake. I tried to read an article about mining companies infringing the Explosives Act whilst forming an opinion about Mr Glenville.

Why did he seem so different from the way people had described him?

CHAPTER 15

The grandfather clock in the hallway struck one as I climbed the servants' staircase with the candle in my hand. My conversations with Mr Glenville had yielded nothing useful for James' investigation. I needed to find out if there was a key to his desk hanging on the wall of Mrs Craughton's office. If there was, I would have to take it, unlock the desk drawers and look through them without anyone noticing.

It seemed an impossible task.

I was beginning to wonder if there would be anything of interest in Mr Glenville's desk at all. Upon reflection, I decided the investigation could be based on little more than a personal grudge on the part of Mr Conway.

Perhaps even Dorothea Heale had been mistaken. It was possible that she had encouraged Mr Glenville's staff to concoct stories about the supposedly terrible conditions at the factory. Perhaps some of the stories were based on fact, but maybe others were merely gossip and hearsay. I had been reading and listening to other people's opinions, but I needed to establish the facts.

Was Mr Glenville a criminal? Or was Mr Conway merely pursuing a vendetta against him?

I stopped suddenly, certain that I had heard someone on the staircase above me. Large shadows flickered on the walls, and my ears strained to listen.

Everything was silent.

I took another step, and as I did so I felt sure I heard someone else move.

Was it Mr Glenville again?

"Hello?" I called out, my voice wavering in the silence.

I felt sure that someone was hiding from me. I bent down and carefully slipped off my boots. Then I slowly crept up a few more stairs. There was no further sound until the other person must have realised how close I had come. Then there was a clattering of boots and a rustle of skirts as the woman tried to get away. I leapt up a few stairs in one go and saw a pale face staring down at me, framed by the hood of a cloak.

Sophia.

"Wait!" I whispered, not wishing her to leave. "What are you doing here?"

"I could ask the same of you," Sophia whispered in reply. She continued up the stairs to the third storey, pausing by the door to the corridor.

"Where are you going?" I asked, looking at her thick woollen cloak.

"To my room."

"Using this staircase?"

"It's so that I don't wake anybody. You mustn't say that you've seen me here. Please don't tell anyone!"

"You've been out this evening? What if your mother and father find out?"

"They won't find out. I've done it many times. You won't tell anyone, will you?"

Her large, dark eyes were just like her father's.

"I won't tell anyone, Miss Sophia."

"Promise?" She seemed frightened.

"All right, I promise. But I hope you haven't been putting yourself in danger. It's not safe for a young woman out there on her own."

My mind was cast back to the St Giles murders, and I shivered.

"I wasn't on my own."

"Who were you with?"

"That's none of your business. And I don't mean that rudely; I just mean that it's no one's business. I'm almost eighteen. I know what I'm doing."

"I hope so. Your mother and father would be devastated if anything happened to you."

"You needn't worry. I was safe."

"Is he a man of good character?" I ventured.

"How do you know it was a man?" she snapped.

"Why else would you be so secretive?"

"He looks after me very well."

"It's not my business to ask what your reason for doing this might be, but perhaps you should discuss it with your parents."

"Never! They wouldn't understand."

"You might be surprised."

"They have never understood what I want. They've already decided how my future should be."

"I think you need to speak to them, Miss Sophia. You can't just creep out of the house at night, hoping that the situation will somehow improve. What of Dudley Lombard?"

"Don't mention his name to me!" she hissed. "If you mention a single detail to anyone else in this house, I shall do something far worse to you, just wait and see!"

"Please don't worry, Miss Sophia, I won't say anything. And there's no need to be angry with me. I have no wish to upset you. But please speak to your mother and father about your concerns regarding Mr Lombard. They wouldn't want you to be unhappy."

"How do you know what they want? How long have you been working here? A few days, is it not?"

"It hasn't been long, but I'm already developing an understanding of your family, Miss Sophia. I have an idea of what interests and motivates you. I heard you mention Dorothea Heale at breakfast earlier this week. My sister knows her."

"Does she?" Her face softened and she turned her head to one side, as if interested to hear more.

"Yes. Don't tell anyone this, but my sister is the chair of the West London Women's Society. Perhaps you would like to join them? She will be attending the march this weekend."

"I've heard of them! Your sister is Mrs Billington-Grieg?"

I nodded slowly, aware that I had given too much away. "I'll keep your secret, and you can keep mine."

"But why is it a secret that she's your sister? I should think you'd be very proud of her!"

"I am, but she's not particularly proud of me."

"Why not?"

"I'm a maid, and she's a lady. Our family is rather complicated, I'm afraid. I try not to talk about it. You will keep it to yourself, won't you?"

I felt angry with myself for the risk I had taken in my efforts to befriend her.

"Do we have an agreement that neither of us says anything?" I asked.

"Yes." She sighed. "Thank you for keeping quiet about this. Perhaps I can explain the situation to you a little better sometime soon."

"Please let me know if there's anything I can do to help, Miss Sophia."

"I'm not sure there is, but thank you for your kind thoughts."

She pulled the hood of her cloak down onto her shoulders, prompting untidy strands of red hair to fall around her face.

"Have you ever felt trapped, Flo?"

"Yes."

"And how did you get out?"

"I had to listen to my head instead of my heart."

"I'm not sure how that would help me."

I sighed, trying to think how I could explain myself better. "Your heart will only tell you what is best for today and tomorrow. Your head will tell you what is best for the years ahead."

"I will think about that. Good night." She turned to the door and pushed it open.

"Be careful, Miss Sophia," I whispered after her, but she didn't seem to hear me.

The door closed behind her.

I readied myself for bed and felt grateful that everything in my room appeared to be as I had left it earlier that evening. I hoped that Mrs Craughton hadn't been snooping around a second time.

I thought about Sophia and felt sorry that she was betrothed to a man she didn't love. And to worsen matters, there seemed to be another man whom she truly loved. I felt sure that her furtive, late-night excursions would only lead to trouble.

And what of the man who was wooing her, and leading her astray? It was rather irresponsible of him to encourage her to act in this way. Surely he was encouraging her into even more trouble.

I wondered what Mr and Mrs Glenville would make of

their daughter's predicament. *Would they show some understanding if she told them she had no wish to marry Dudley Lombard? It would thwart their plans to unite the Glenville and Lombard businesses, but would they not value their daughter's happiness above that?*

Despite what I had heard about Alexander Glenville, he struck me as a caring father. *Did I have a duty, as their employee, to inform them that I had encountered Sophia on the stairs late at night?* I felt I shouldn't, as I had told her I would keep it a secret.

But was it the right thing to have done?

I climbed into bed and blew out the candle. As I lay there in the dark, I thought I heard someone creeping up the stairs. I held my breath, my entire body becoming as stiff as a board.

Could it be Sophia again?

I sat up and strained to listen in the dark. *Who could it be?* The only other room on my floor was Maisie's.

I heard the slow creak of floorboards in the corridor outside. It sounded as though the wanderer was walking about in stockinged feet. As I readied myself for a tap at my door, I heard someone turn the handle of Maisie's.

Then the door quietly clicked closed again.

CHAPTER 16

"Were you awake late last night?" I asked Maisie as we tidied the drawing room.

"Last night?" She paused to think about it. "Nah, I'm never awake late. I'm the first one up in the mornin' ain't I?"

"That's odd," I replied as I dusted the china plates on the mantelpiece. "I thought I heard your door open and close last night. Early this morning, actually."

"What time?"

"The clock had just chimed one."

"One? Nah, you're 'earin' things, Flo. I ain't never awake at that time."

"It's rather strange, because I was sure I also heard footsteps."

I wondered if I should tell Maisie that I had encountered Sophia on the stairs, but I remembered that I needed to keep to my word and not mention it to anyone.

"Footsteps?" said Maisie, pausing her dusting of the cabinet. "Now yer just scarin' me with them ghost stories again!" She shuddered.

"There's no ghost. I feel sure there were footsteps, and then your door opened and closed."

"Stop sayin' it! Yer fright'nin' me!"

"I wonder whom it might have been."

"It can't of been no one. All I can think about now's them ghost girls in that picture. What if they comes out of it and walks round the 'ouse at night?"

"That's not possible, is it, Maisie? What nonsense! There's no need to be frightened of the twins."

Despite my confident manner, I recalled that I had purposefully averted my eyes from their portrait in the library the previous evening.

"Mrs Craughton told me ter clean the china in 'ere," said Maisie, peering into the cabinet. "This one's locked. I'll 'ave to go and get the key from 'er office."

"I'll go," I said quickly, mindful that I could look for the key to Mr Glenville's desk while I was there.

As I left the room, I wondered whether Maisie was telling the truth about the previous evening. *If it hadn't been her opening and closing the door to her room, whom might it have been?*

"That drawing room needs to be perfect," said Mrs Craughton, handing me the key to the cabinet. "And once it's done, the dining room will need to be thoroughly cleaned in time for Saturday."

I glanced again at the other keys on the wall as she spoke. *Where were the study keys kept?* I wondered.

"Not that Miss Sophia will thank you for your hard work. I can tell you now that she won't give any thought to the preparation taking place for her birthday celebration. She has no idea of the work that goes into these things."

I saw a large key and three smaller ones, each labelled 'Study'. *The desk key had to be one of those.*

"I have to go and see Cook about this menu again," continued the housekeeper. "Miss Sophia has decided that she no longer wishes to have oysters served. Is there another key you require?" She fixed me with her slow-moving grey eyes.

This was my chance to ask for the key to Mr Glenville's desk drawer. *But how could I justify asking for it? What reason could I give?* I could think of none.

"No, only this one. Thank you, Mrs Craughton."

I took my leave of her and felt angry with myself for missing the opportunity.

The next chance to borrow the key presented itself on Saturday morning. I passed Mrs Craughton's office and saw that the door was ajar. I knew she had taken something to Mrs Glenville and, unusually for her, had forgotten to lock the door.

Checking that no one else was nearby, I slipped into the office and peered at the keys on the wall. The only light available for me to see by was the dim lamplight of the hallway, but despite the gloom I managed to locate the study keys.

The largest of the four was presumably for the door to the room. Of the other three, I decided the smallest would most likely be the one to open the drawers of a desk. I quickly removed it from its hook and pushed it into the large pocket at the front of my apron.

Back in the corridor, I saw that there was still no one else around. I strolled towards the study humming a nonchalant tune to myself. The study was usually unlocked during the day. I reached the open door and saw that the room was empty. Checking around me once again, I slipped inside and tiptoed over to the desk.

My heartbeat thundered so loudly in my ears that I

worried I would be unable to hear any other sound. I glanced over my shoulder, moved back towards the door and quietly closed it. Then I skipped over to the desk once again and hurriedly pushed the key into the lock of one of the drawers. It twisted satisfactorily and the drawer slid open. My stomach flipped with excitement as I peered inside. A small, leather-bound book rested on a pile of correspondence.

Surely there was something in this book which would be useful to James.

My fingers trembled as I reached into the drawer and lifted the book out. I flicked through the pages, which were filled with dense, sloping handwriting.

What was I to do with this? It would take a long time to read. Could I remove it for a few days without Mr Glenville noticing?

I turned to the back of the book and saw that it contained a list of names and addresses. *Were these the people Mr Conway wanted to know about? Did the answer to the investigation lie within my hands?*

I didn't have time to lock the drawer as I heard the handle of the door turning. I sprung over to the fireplace and fell to my knees, as if examining the recently laid fire.

"Flo!" exclaimed Mr Glenville. "What are you doing in here with the door closed?"

"Oh, hello, sir." I stood to my feet and hoped that the book wasn't visible in the pocket of my apron. "I couldn't remember if Maisie and I had arranged the fire in here this morning."

He stared at me as if he were unsure that I was telling the truth. I felt an uncomfortable heat seeping into my face and prayed that he wouldn't notice. He glanced around the room, and I didn't dare look at the desk to check that the drawer was properly closed. He looked back at the fireplace.

"It looks like a well-laid fire to me."

"It does, doesn't it, sir? Would you like it lit?"

"Not yet, thank you. I came in here to fetch something."

I tried to swallow the lump in my throat. *What if he'd come for the book and found that it wasn't there? What had I done?*

I began to feel light-headed.

"Very well, sir. I shall leave you to it."

"Thank you, Flo."

I walked out of the room on unsteady legs. *If he discovered that the book was missing, he would know that I had taken it. There would be a confrontation and I would be found out. The entire investigation would be ruined.*

I made my way along the corridor and hummed the nonchalant tune again. It was so off-key that I sounded like a person who was beginning to lose her mind.

CHAPTER 17

The Lombard family arrived at seven o'clock that evening. The guests gathered in the drawing room, providing my first opportunity to catch sight of Sophia's suitor. I found myself sympathising with the poor girl. Dudley Lombard looked to be about thirty-five, with pale, wispy, mutton-chop whiskers covering his saggy cheeks. His eyes and lower lip drooped a little, and he removed his top hat to reveal a scant layer of mousy hair. He seemed pleasant and convivial, however. For Sophia's sake, I hoped that what he lacked in appearance, he compensated for in personality.

His father, Ralph Lombard, was a tall, broad man with a large stomach and a huge nose. Thin hair seemed to run in the family. His own was swept towards his face to create the impression that he had more than he actually did. He had a commanding presence, and was so well-practised in his manners that I imagined he had conducted himself in this way since he had been old enough to walk.

His wife, Mary Lombard, was also tall, and a weak smile was fixed permanently to her long face. She had large, violet

96

eyes, which flicked adoringly between her son and the long-haired, white dog which she carried under one arm. Her dress was of rustling turquoise silk, trimmed with lace where it was cut low at her ample bosom.

"Where's the birthday girl?" asked Ralph Lombard in a loud voice.

"She's still getting ready," replied Mrs Glenville with a smile.

She was resplendent in a gold and white dress, which was tightly laced with a large bustle. Her red hair was pinned neatly on top of her head and decorated with little gold and white bows. With her arched, painted eyebrows, she bore a passing resemblance to Queen Elizabeth.

I couldn't deny that there was something rather handsome about Mr Glenville that evening. He wore a black frock coat over a dark red velvet waistcoat, and a red silk cravat was knotted around his upright collar. The jagged scar somehow complimented rather than detracted from his looks. His dark eyes surveyed the room, and he was the only person who acknowledged me as I stood by the servants' door with my hands clasped nervously in front of me.

The missing book hadn't been mentioned. *Had Mr Glenville noticed that it wasn't in the desk drawer? Had he noticed that the drawer was unlocked?*

My plan was to read through the book that night and return it early the next morning. I hoped it would provide the answers needed for Mr Conway's investigation so that my job at the Glenville residence would be complete.

Mr Perrin announced Viscount Wyndham, and a short, jovial man bustled into the room accompanied by a petite, wan-faced wife. With them was Maurice Glenville, who was leaning on his walking sticks for support.

"Wyndham! What a surprise!" boomed Ralph Lombard.

The men shook hands heartily, and the dog under Mary Lombard's arm barked enthusiastically.

"Quiet, Tipsy!" she scolded.

"What a fine dog!" said Wyndham, his chest puffed up like a pigeon's. "Although I must admit to preferring mine a little larger. He's smaller than a rat!"

"*She*," corrected Mary Lombard, but Wyndham appeared not to hear as he helped Maurice to a chair.

"Maurice and I have had a fine day in the dark room, haven't we, Maurice?"

Maurice nodded and Wyndham rested the boy's walking sticks against the back of his chair. I admired Wyndham's avuncular manner towards the boy.

"We took some photographs in the garden and developed quite a number of them," Wyndham continued.

"You're quite the photographer now then, Wyndham?" commented Mr Glenville.

"It keeps me out of trouble," he replied with a chuckle. "My next plan is to set up a photographer's studio. Then I can photograph my beautiful wife reclining on a chaise longue. You know those pictures, don't you, Glenville? Where she's dressed in some sort of floaty attire, looking like a sylph-like nymph!"

He slapped his thigh and laughed. Lady Wyndham seated herself and rolled her eyes. Her fair hair was swept back from her pale, heart-shaped face, and she wore a dress of rose pink and lace. She appeared to be ten or fifteen years younger than her husband.

"You'll have to find another nymph for your photographs, Napier," she said haughtily. "I shall do nothing of the sort."

"Darn it. Camilla, perhaps?" said Wyndham with an infectious laugh that made me smile.

"Never!" replied Mrs Glenville frostily.

I recalled Mr Sherman telling me that Mr Glenville and

Viscount Wyndham were estranged, so I wondered what manner of change had come about in their relationship.

"Here she is!" shouted Ralph Lombard as Sophia entered the room with her sister Jane. Sophia wore a simple, green satin dress and smiled politely as she greeted her guests. However, all eyes in the room were on Jane, whose flowing scarlet dress was covered in all manner of elaborate ruffles and bows. Her dark hair had been curled and pinned up, and sparkled with tiny jewels. She grinned broadly from ear to ear, and I felt sure that her appearance had been designed to diminish that of her sister.

Mr Perrin poured out glasses of champagne and everyone drank a toast to Miss Sophia. For a brief moment, she caught my eye and we exchanged a smile. She seemed grateful that I hadn't mentioned her night-time excursion to anyone in the household.

The three younger Glenville daughters were accompanied into the drawing room by the governess and nurse. Much fuss was made of them before they were taken back to the nursery.

I kept expecting friends of Sophia's to arrive, but as everyone moved into the dining room for dinner I realised that the number of guests was complete.

CHAPTER 18

"I've had to take on an extra hundred workers over the past year," said Ralph Lombard. "There's no room on the premises for any more, so I'm looking at a new site in Fulham."

"It will be a terrible shame if you move the distillery there. It's extremely convenient having you so near to Blundell's," replied Mr Glenville.

They were dining on turbot with lobster sauce.

"But Fulham is near Dudley and Sophia in Barnes," replied Lombard. "It's important to be always thinking about the future. Perhaps you could move Blundell's out there. You could consolidate the Bermondsey and Vauxhall factories into one. It would help you economise."

Maisie and I walked around the table, collecting up plates and dishes which were no longer required. As I passed Lady Wyndham, I noticed that she held her glass of wine on her lap and was pouring a few drops of something into it from a small bottle. I recalled an aunt of mine who had a habit of doing something similar, and wondered whether Lady Wyndham was a laudanum addict as my aunt had been.

"Don't forget the costs, Lombard," said Mr Glenville. "You speak as though I can conjure up the necessary funds from nowhere."

"Don't worry about that," Wyndham interrupted. "I'll talk to Burroughs at Coutts again. They'd be more than happy to lend you the money."

I committed the name to memory. *Was Mr Burroughs at Coutts bank one of Glenville's friends in high places?*

"Very generous of you, Wyndham," said Mr Glenville.

"Don't mention it, Alexander," replied Wyndham.

Mary Lombard leaned forward to address Jane. "Your mother has told us all about your beautiful voice, Miss Jane. We must hear it after dinner."

Jane's face flushed almost as red as her dress. "Thank you. I must confess I am a little shy to sing in front of an audience."

"Oh, come, don't be shy," replied Mrs Lombard. "We shall be an extremely appreciative audience."

"How about piano?" piped up Ralph Lombard. "You're quite adept at that as well, I hear, Miss Jane. Perhaps we can hear a short recital."

I watched Sophia, wondering if she felt envious of the attention her sister was receiving. Her face belied no sign of it. Instead, she picked at her meal with a countenance that suggested boredom.

Dudley Lombard wiped his droopy lower lip with his serviette.

"Miss Sophia," he said. "Ma would like you to visit the house next week to choose the wallpaper."

"Oh, I'm sure any wallpaper will do," she replied sulkily.

I noticed that Mrs Glenville shot Mrs Lombard an apologetic glance.

"Miss Sophia, you are to be the lady of the house," said Mrs Lombard as she fed a piece of bread to Tipsy on her lap.

"I know you are unaccustomed to choosing wallpaper, but it is one of the privileges a lady has, among many others of course. The house must be decorated in the colours you like!"

"Not red," said Sophia, giving her sister a fleeting glance. "I don't like red."

Dudley Lombard wiped a piece of bread around the lobster sauce on his plate and watched his fiancée rather sadly.

"To think that the next time Sophia and Dudley dine together they will be married!" said Mrs Glenville with forced cheer.

"Indeed! The wedding day is almost upon us!" Ralph Lombard cried.

I noticed Lady Wyndham had a little more colour in her cheeks. Maisie walked behind her and Lady Wyndham seemed to pass her something, which the maid swiftly put into the pocket of her apron. I felt puzzled by this.

"I remember our wedding day as though it were only yesterday, Lily," said Wyndham, grinning at his wife across the table.

She smiled demurely and took a large gulp of her wine.

"The house will be so empty without you, Dudley darling," sighed Mary Lombard.

"You'll just have to get some more dogs!" said Wyndham with a loud laugh.

"I'm sure I will. But dogs are no replacement for a child, are they? We only have the one, and he is so very precious." Her violet eyes rested adoringly on her son once again.

"Better one than none at all," said Wyndham. "Still, perhaps we can adopt young Maurice!" He grinned at Master Glenville.

"There is no need for that," replied Mrs Glenville stiffly. "He has a perfectly suitable home here."

"He's not going to inherit anything, though, is he?" said Wyndham.

"Napier..." his wife warned.

"Wyndham, we've discussed this before, haven't we?" said Mr Glenville. "Now let's leave that conversation well alone and remember why we're all here."

He stood and raised a glass to his daughter.

"Happy birthday to my darling Sophia!"

The tension which had been building in the room dissolved away as everyone stood and raised their glasses.

"Happy birthday, Sophia!"

Mrs Craughton instructed me and Maisie to accompany the ladies into the drawing room while the men remained in the dining room. Most of the conversation was about the wedding, but I noticed Sophia hadn't joined in. Instead, she made a great fuss of Tipsy, who enjoyed lying on her back and having her underbelly tickled. A large vase of lilies filled the room with a scent which was almost cloying.

The men entered the room a short while later, and Jane was called upon to sing and play the piano. Among her repertoire were the parlour song favourites, including 'I'll Sing Thee Songs of Araby', 'It was a Dream' and 'Oh Mother! Take the Wheel Away'. Dudley Lombard watched her with an expression of rapture on his face, the drink in his hand untouched. I realised that he quite possibly longed to marry the younger daughter instead of Sophia.

Sophia sat next to Maurice and watched her sister with vague interest, stifling a yawn at times. I wondered if she had managed to attend the women's suffrage march in Hyde Park earlier that day. Eliza would have expected to see me there, but I knew there would have been little chance of me being granted leave to attend. I had accomplished something, however. I had one of Mr Glenville's notebooks to read, and I was pleased that the birthday celebration soon would be over so I could escape to my room to peruse it.

My hopes were dashed when Mr Glenville instructed Mr Perrin to bring out more champagne glasses and fill them for his guests.

"Well, that was a marvellous piece of entertainment. Thank you, Jane!" cried Viscount Wyndham, his cheeks red from the good food and fine wine. "Who will entertain us next?"

"I've heard the dog has a few tricks up her sleeve," said Mr Glenville.

"Does she now? A dog with sleeves is a trick in itself!" laughed Wyndham.

"She can indeed do a few tricks," said Mary Lombard.

"Show them what Tipsy can do, Ma!" her son said encouragingly.

"I've heard she can walk on her hind l-legs," said Maurice.

"The dog walks on its hind legs?" asked Wyndham. "This has to be seen!"

"Show them, Ma!" Dudley Lombard cheered.

With plenty of encouragement, whooping and clapping, Mrs Lombard managed to get her little dog waddling along the rug on her hind legs. Everybody cheered and laughed, including Maisie and myself. Mrs Craughton applauded, and even Mr Perrin managed a smile.

Sophia also found it funny, but then I heard her make an odd noise which wasn't laughter. I looked at her and saw that her face was quite red, as if she were struggling to breathe.

"Miss Sophia?" I said quietly, dashing to her side.

I knelt beside her and held her hands. She pulled them away and clutched at her throat, her dark eyes fixed on mine.

The laughter at the sight of the little dog subsided as everyone began to notice that something was wrong.

"What's the matter?" asked Dudley Lombard.

Mrs Glenville stood up. "Sophia?"

Mr Glenville dashed over to us.

"Is she choking?" he asked me.

Sophia let out a cry and slumped down off her chair. Mr Glenville and I just about caught her between us, but she seemed quite unable to breathe.

We laid her on the floor. Her eyes were wide with terror as she stared first at her father and then her mother, who had flung herself down by her daughter's side.

"Sophia!" she screamed, slapping her daughter's cheek. "Help!" she cried out. "What can we do?"

I stepped back so that Mr and Mrs Glenville could get closer to their daughter. Jane joined them and Maurice stood over them all, looking concerned.

"Good grief! What's happening?" entreated Dudley Lombard.

Tipsy yapped and Mary Lombard tried to quieten her.

"She needs some air! Give her air!" Mr Glenville cried out.

"Here, give her my salts!" Mary Lombard pulled out a little bottle from her purse.

I stood back, unsure what to do. I could barely see Sophia now that she was surrounded by people. The room felt too warm, and I wanted some cool air on my face. I fought an urge to open the heavy velvet curtains and pull up one of the windows.

Maisie looked up at me, her eyes welling with tears. I put my arm around her shoulder to comfort her.

"Fetch a doctor!" shouted Mr Glenville.

Mrs Craughton and Mr Perrin ran out of the room.

Mrs Glenville cradled her daughter's head while Mr Glenville paced the room, wiping his face with his hand.

"She'll be all right, old boy," said Wyndham, giving him a comforting pat on the back.

"I hope so. Good God, I hope so," said Mr Glenville. "I don't understand it."

Dudley Lombard sobbed openly. His mother clung onto his arm, her face white.

Lady Wyndham seemed to be stuck to her seat, her delicate features frozen in horror.

"Where is the doctor?" barked Glenville. "This is taking too long!"

Mrs Glenville rocked her daughter and sobbed, the skirts of Sophia's green silk dress spread in a crumpled pool around her. The salts had produced no effect, and I knew that a fainting fit would have come to an end by now.

It was probably only ten minutes before the doctor arrived, but it seemed like an eternity. He was a portly, grey-whiskered man, and he dashed into the room with a large leather bag in one hand. He knelt beside Sophia and tried to rouse her, but there was no response.

"Has she eaten or drunk anything recently?" he asked.

"We've just had dinner and drinks," said Mrs Glenville in an urgent, shrill voice.

Everyone else stood silently as the doctor attended to Sophia. I was unsure whether to watch or avert my eyes. Then he sat back on his heels before slowly getting to his feet. My legs felt weakened by a horrible sense of dread.

"I'm sorry." The doctor's voice was quiet and sombre. "I'm afraid we've lost her."

Mrs Craughton and I rushed to Mrs Glenville's aid as she fell to the floor.

CHAPTER 19

W e helped Mrs Glenville onto a chair and the doctor attended to Sophia for a short while longer. Then he asked for a blanket. Maisie quickly fetched one and the doctor carefully draped it over Sophia's body.

My eyes filled with tears and my spectacles misted over. I removed them and wiped my face with my apron. *Surely this was nothing more than a bad dream?*

Mrs Glenville flung herself down by her daughter's side again, sobbing uncontrollably. Mr Glenville stood silent and unmoving by the fireplace, his face drained of all colour. Everyone else had moved to one side of the room, looking on in horrified silence.

I felt myself trembling. *Surely the doctor was mistaken. There must have been something more he could have done. Sophia had to be given another chance at life.*

I stared at the cream woollen blanket beneath which she lay, and I willed it to move. *Surely she would come round and wonder what all the fuss had been about.*

"Stop all the clocks, please, Mr Perrin," said Mr Glenville, his voice tremulous.

The doctor seemed puzzled by something, and rubbed his grey whiskers while he processed his thoughts.

"Please can someone show me the glass from which Miss Sophia was drinking?" he asked.

"It was this one," I said, pointing to the glass on the occasional table next to the chair she had sat on. There was only a small amount of champagne left in it.

The doctor picked up the glass and sniffed its contents. Then he dipped his little finger into the remainder of the champagne before carefully placing his finger on the tip of his tongue. He closed his eyes and made a smacking noise with his lips for a moment.

We all watched him intently.

"Oh dear. This is most worrying," he said.

"What is?" asked Mr Glenville. "What's the matter, Doctor Dalglish?"

Mrs Glenville lifted her head and tried to calm her sobs so that she could listen.

"I'm afraid I can detect the taste and smell of bitter almonds," replied the doctor. "I fear that your daughter may have been poisoned by potassium of cyanide."

"Poisoned?" Mrs Glenville cried out.

"That's impossible!" said Mr Glenville. "How? By whom?"

"Never!" Dudley Lombard shouted.

Everyone began talking all at once. Mary Lombard held her face in her hands and began to cry. Jane buried her face in Maurice's chest and he held on to her, his expression wretched.

"The police will need to be involved," continued Dr Dalglish. "You'll need to send someone down to Church Court police station."

"The police?" said Mrs Glenville.

"Cyanide," muttered Mr Glenville. "Where would cyanide have come from? I think you're mistaken, Doctor."

"If only I were," replied the doctor.

"May I have a look at that glass?" Mr Glenville asked.

Dr Dalglish gave it to him. "I would caution you to be careful with that, Mr Glenville. Please don't make any attempt to drink it."

Mr Glenville held the glass up to his nose and inhaled deeply several times. "I can't smell anything, damn it!"

"Not everyone is able to detect the smell of cyanide," replied the doctor.

"Well that's darned convenient, isn't it?" Mr Glenville replied scornfully.

"I'm not sure what you mean by *convenient*."

"How do we know that the cause is cyanide if no one else can smell it?"

Dr Dalglish held up his hands apologetically. "Perhaps someone else in this room will be able to detect the smell. I can only report on what I find, Mr Glenville, and sadly I deduce that someone has poisoned your daughter with cyanide. It is not for me to comment any further. The police must be called, and if they require my help I shall be happy to assist them."

Mr Glenville walked over to his wife and bent down to hold the glass under her nose. "Can you smell cyanide?" he asked.

She sniffed at the champagne.

"What does it smell like?" she asked.

"Almonds, the doctor said."

"Bitter almonds," corrected Dr Dalglish.

"Well, there's a smell of something," replied Mrs Glenville. "I can't say I know what bitter almonds smell like, but there is a smell of something other than champagne, I think."

"But *cyanide?*" Mr Glenville asked his wife incredulously. "You really think it could be poison in there?"

"Oh, darling, I don't know." Tears sprung into her eyes again. "It was something, that's for sure, and now our daughter is dead!"

Inspector Herbert Trotter was a barrel-shaped man with a long, wide chin and a light brown moustache. He stood in front of the fireplace in a grey suit with his pipe in his mouth, taking down notes as the doctor explained his suspicions.

The inspector nodded and glanced at each of us in the room in turn as he listened. Then the doctor took him over to the body of poor Sophia beneath the blanket. I looked away as the doctor lifted it for the inspector to see her body. Once the doctor had finished giving his explanation, the inspector spoke. He had a lisp.

"Doctor Dalglish informs me that Miss Sophia Glenville has died from suspected cyanide poisoning. Consequently, I shall need to interview everyone in the house about the events of this most unfortunate evening. Mr Glenville, would you have the honour of speaking to me in private first?"

"Now hold on, Inspector. You're not going to waste time discussing this with me, are you? We need to catch the chap who's poisoned my daughter!"

Mr Glenville's appearance had become quite dishevelled. His hair was untidy, and he had removed his cravat and unbuttoned his collar.

"I need to interview everyone who was in Miss Sophia's company today," continued the inspector. "It's imperative that I establish the facts of this evening's events."

"Well, I'm sure my guests and staff will be more than happy to help you, but I can't bear to have precious time wasted, Inspector. He could strike again!"

"And may I ask what causes you to think that, Mr Glenville?"

"Someone may be planning to poison the lot of us!"

"If that is the case, Mr Glenville, I am sure you would agree that it is most urgent that I interview everyone who is in the house. It seems likely to me that the culprit is under your roof at this very moment! Unless one or more guests were here earlier this evening and have since departed, that is. Has anyone visited today and since left?"

Mr Glenville scratched the back of his neck. "Not this evening. No, there were no other guests. We receive deliveries and visitors during the day, I can't specifically remember any in particular, but then I've not been home for the entire day, so you'd need to ask the servants about all the comings and goings."

"In summary, then, if I understand you correctly, Mr Glenville, there were no other guests invited this evening who have since left?"

"No," said Mrs Glenville. Her eyes were circled with grey where the kohl liner had smudged. "There has been no one else here, has there, Alexander?"

I glanced around the room. *Could the person responsible for Sophia's death be one of these people here now?* I wondered. I studied their faces for any sign of guilt, but saw none. *What about the staff?* I looked at Mr Perrin, Mrs Craughton and Maisie. *It couldn't be one of them, either.* I couldn't understand it.

"If I manage to establish that everyone in this house is innocent," said Inspector Trotter, "then there is only one further option, which is rather a distressing one to consider."

"She took her own life!" interjected Mrs Glenville.

Everyone in the room looked at her, clearly as surprised by her comment as I was. Her face was taut and pale, her lips thin.

"It's something to consider, isn't it, Inspector?" continued

Mrs Glenville. "I don't wish to think that's what happened, but I know that you must consider all possibilities."

Mr Glenville shook his head. "No, Camilla. Sophia would never have done that. She wouldn't, she couldn't..."

"If she had intended to do such a thing, she would have done it privately," said Mrs Lombard. "People who commit such a heinous crime rarely do it in full view of others. I know it is terribly distressing for you to hear us discuss it in this manner, Alexander and Camilla, but I'm sure you'd agree that this dreadful event requires frank and honest discussion if we are to discover the truth. The girl would never have taken her own life."

"In which case we're investigating a murder," said Inspector Trotter.

Everyone glanced around the room at one another. Suddenly, each person had become a suspect.

"Perhaps it was an accident."

The words came out of my mouth before I had time to consider whether or not it was appropriate for me to speak up. I felt all eyes in the room on me.

"An accident?" Mrs Glenville snapped. "How could poison have found its way into Sophia's glass *by accident?*"

"I'm sorry. I don't know, my lady. My thought was that everything should be considered, no matter how preposterous it may sound."

"It is a fair point," said Inspector Trotter with a nod. "No possibilities should be dismissed at this stage." He checked his watch. "The hour is late and everyone is in need of a rest, I am sure. Myself included! I shall return in the morning and commence my interviews. Is there a suitable room in the house I can occupy tomorrow, Mr Glenville?"

"You may use the library, Inspector."

"Thank you. I would like to request that your guests

remain here for the night, Mrs Glenville. Do you have room to accommodate them?"

"Yes, we do. Mrs Craughton and Mr Perrin will look after them quite well."

"Thank you. I don't wish to detain anyone here any longer than is necessary, but if we allow the guests to leave it becomes significantly more troublesome to arrange interviews with them. I would like to speak to everyone as quickly as possible, as I'm sure you can all appreciate."

CHAPTER 20

"I can't sleep Flo," said Maisie, who sat red-eyed on my bed. "I dunno 'ow I'll ever sleep again."

"You will, Maisie."

"We saw 'er die! She just died right in front of us. She didn't deserve it, Flo. It ain't right. I don't believe it's 'appened."

I gave Maisie a hug and we sat there until the grey daylight brightened the curtain at the little window.

We were given black uniforms and caps to wear. They were old-fashioned and smelt rather musty from their time in storage. Maisie and I covered the mirrors with black crepe, and the curtains remained closed. We were instructed to stay out of the drawing room until Inspector Trotter had examined it.

A casket was brought for Sophia during the night, and flowers were delivered the following morning. Mrs Craughton helped Mrs Glenville wash and dress her daughter, and then we visited her in the morning room. Sophia lay in the satin-lined casket with her arms folded across her chest. Her porcelain face was peaceful, and her hair had been pinned far more neatly than I had ever seen it before. The bodice of her cream dress was swathed with light silk and trimmed with pale pink roses in the same fabric. Bouquets of flowers had been placed in and around her casket, filling the air with a heady scent.

Maisie sobbed as we stood by the casket, but I felt overcome by a strange numbness. I stared at poor Sophia and couldn't stop thinking about her last few moments of life. The memory looped around in my mind, and I wished I could push it away. My limbs felt oddly numb, as if they were somehow disconnected from my body. I didn't feel part of this scene; I felt as though I were an observer.

We moved about the house as quietly as possible, speaking only in whispers. There was little noise to suppress the dreadful sound of Mrs Glenville sobbing behind closed doors.

Inspector Trotter arrived shortly after breakfast and promptly installed himself in the library. Mrs Craughton took him coffee and toast, and Mr Glenville was the first to be interviewed. He wore a black shirt and tie, and there were large, dark circles under his eyes.

"Good morning, Flo," he said when he saw me.

"My deepest condolences, sir," I replied. "I'm struggling to believe that it can be true."

"Me too." He managed a slight smile, then opened the door to the library.

Staff from the Lombard and Wyndham households brought mourning clothes and other personal belongings to the house. At breakfast, Lady Wyndham and Mary Lombard cried into their handkerchiefs, and poor Dudley Lombard looked bereft. Sophia might not have cared much for him, but he looked distraught at her loss.

I did my best to wait on everyone, and offer a sympathetic glance or word when required. The whole group seemed upset, but there was a possibility that, for one individual, the grief was a mere pretence. I watched everyone carefully, wondering if I could find any lack of conviction in their conduct.

I knew there was no need for me to stay in the Glenville household any longer. Sophia's death surely meant that Mr Conway's investigation would have to be postponed. The book I had taken from Mr Glenville's drawer still lay locked away in the trunk under my bed. I had lost all interest in its contents. Mr Glenville's business affairs were of little importance now that such tragedy had struck.

I wanted to leave my employment, but I was worried about leaving Maisie, who seemed reliant on me for consolation. I hoped the shock would lift in a day or two, presenting me with an opportunity to quit the house. I comforted myself with the thought that I could remain in contact with her, but this also presented a problem. *Would she forgive me when she discovered I had been lying about who I truly was?*

A telegram was delivered to me that morning. The envelope was addressed to Florence Parker, but no attempt had been made by Mr Sherman to disguise my identity in the message. The instruction was for me to write about Sophia's death for the *Morning Express,* complete with the assurance that a boy would call at the house early that evening to collect the article.

Fortunately, Mrs Craughton, normally an inquisitive lady, was far too distracted to ask me any questions about the telegram. I resolved to find some time that afternoon to quickly write down what had happened. Mr Sherman would have to edit it into something more coherent when he received it.

Several news reporters called at the door, and Mr Perrin hurriedly shooed them away. I mindlessly dusted and swept. As I passed the library in the course of my chores, Mary Lombard's voice drifted through the door.

"Marriage is what the girl needed!" she exclaimed.

I paused close to the door and continued to listen as I attended to a mark on the floor.

"She was an intelligent girl. I suppose you could say the brains went to her instead of her brother. Unfortunately, she was a little too intelligent for her own good. She became one of these 'free thinkers'. Instead of conforming to the conduct expected of her, she excited herself with thoughts and ideas beyond the realm of a lady. I suspect she became bored. It's not uncommon in girls with lively minds."

The dog gave a few short yaps. "Quiet, Tipsy! I shan't be much longer now. Mother's speaking to the inspector. Where was I? Oh yes, marriage and motherhood would have occupied her, and there would have been little time for her to distract herself with matters that didn't concern her. She would have been the lady of the house with responsibility for staff, children, meals, furnishings, entertaining and socialising. Had she been married sooner, none of this would have happened. I did ask for the date to be brought forward, but Alexander found some excuse not to. I don't think he understood her. The Glenvilles are good friends of ours, but I hope you will be discreet if I say that they didn't know how to manage her at all. It's odd when you consider it. They could care for an idiot, but not a daughter! There's something rather strange about that, if you ask me."

I heard footsteps approaching, so I rose to my feet and continued on past the library.

"Flo!" came a harsh whisper from behind me.

"Yes, Mrs Craughton?"

I turned toward the housekeeper, remembering with a sickening turn in my stomach that I hadn't yet returned the key for Mr Glenville's desk to her office.

"The drawing room will require tidying after..." Her eyes dampened. "I can't bring myself to go in there. The inspector has finished examining the room now."

"I'll see to it, Mrs Craughton," I replied, relieved that she hadn't asked me about the missing key.

I took an oil lamp into the drawing room, which was as dark as a tomb with the heavy velvet curtains pulled across the windows. The air felt close, harbouring a mixture of perfume and perspiration. Mingled with it was another smell which I couldn't quite identify. *Was it the scent of bitter almonds?* I shivered and told myself it couldn't be so.

It was considered profligate to light the gasolier to clean a room; however, I could see so little by the light of my oil lamp that I had to pull one of the curtains open slightly to reveal an inch-wide gap. Weak daylight seeped in and I peered out, expecting to see the street. Instead, a thick, grimy fog the colour of tea caressed the windowpane. I let out a small cry. *Was there even another world out there any more?*

My throat and chest began to tighten. *I was trapped in this house. Would I ever get out and return to my normal life?*

My breath felt shallow, and I tried to calm myself by inhaling more deeply. I told myself I could walk out of the front door any time it suited me. I was only staying for Maisie. Besides, I had a news article to write. I knew that my work at the house would soon be complete, and then I would be free to leave. I could go back to my garret room with the temperamental stove and my stripy cat. I would see James again.

Everything would be normal again soon.

I comforted myself with these thoughts as I cleaned the fireplace and grate, and lay a new fire. Then I swept the floor and dusted the plates on the mantelpiece.

I was standing in the same room in which Sophia had died.

My skin prickled and I felt conscious of every move I made, as if someone were watching me. I stopped and looked over my shoulder once or twice, convinced I had felt someone's eyes resting upon me. But there was no one else here and everything was silent.

My last remaining task was to straighten the cushions on the chairs. Before I began, I stood in the place I had taken up the previous night. I looked at each of the chairs and remembered who had sat in which. The shaft of light from the curtains rested on the chair that had been Sophia's. Next to it was the table upon which her glass of champagne had stood. The only person I had seen near her glass was Mr Perrin.

Sophia had sat in that very chair during the last few moments of her life. She hadn't known what was about to happen to her, but I felt sure someone in the room had. Whoever it was had managed to conceal his or her true thoughts extremely well.

How had the culprit managed to remain so calm? How had they managed to feign grief?

I went to each chair and patted every cushion into shape. Particles of dust floated in the ray of grey daylight. As I was replacing the cushion on the third chair, I noticed a small square of white tucked down the side of the seat.

It appeared to be a square of paper. As I retrieved the item, I realised it was a little packet, which had been torn open along its top. There was writing on one side of it, accompanied by a skull and crossbones. It read:

Cyanide. POISON.

The packet fell from my hand back onto the seat of the

chair. I took a step back, hurriedly wiping my hands on my apron.

My heart thudded in my throat. I couldn't take my eyes off the small packet that had once contained the poison which had killed Sophia.

The murderer must have hidden the packet behind the cushion after he or she had carried out the terrible deed. Still keeping my eyes on it, I walked past the chair and towards the door. Then I dashed quickly through it and ran along the corridor to find Inspector Trotter in the library.

I paused at the door before knocking.

"I'd been looking forward to her birthday party for weeks," I heard Dudley Lombard say through the thin wood.

I waited impatiently for a natural pause in the conversation. "She looked beautiful, of course," he continued. "Truly beautiful. And I could scarcely believe that she was to be my wife. What had I done to deserve her? I felt flattered and honoured, and I couldn't wait for our wedding day to arrive. She was to choose the furnishings for our house in Barnes. The wallpaper, the curtains... the furniture." His words were interrupted by a brief choking noise, and then his voice returned, more plaintive than before. "But what of our home now? I cannot possibly live there. I suppose Pa will have to sell it, but what a thought. I had been looking forward to such happiness."

I decided I could wait no longer. I hammered sharply on the door.

"Who is it?" Inspector Trotter called out.

I stumbled into the room without answering. My voice was breathless when I spoke.

"Yes?" He removed his pipe from his mouth, and gave me a quizzical look.

"I'm sorry to intrude, Inspector, but I've found something which I think you should come and have a look at."

CHAPTER 21

Word soon spread throughout the household, and before long almost everyone was in the drawing room looking at the chair upon which the cyanide packet had been found. The large gasolier in the centre of the ceiling had been lit, but with everyone dressed in black the room still felt gloomy.

Inspector Trotter held the packet of paper between his gloved thumb and forefinger.

"There is no doubt about it. This is the empty paper for the potassium of cyanide which has been used to poison Miss Sophia Glenville. We should have conducted a more thorough search of this room."

"Yes, you should," said Mr Glenville, scowling at the detective.

I had already explained how I had found the packet, and the position in which it had been discovered. The inspector agreed that the murderer had made attempts to conceal it, most likely while everyone else was distracted by Sophia being taken unwell.

"Who sat on this chair yesterday evening?" asked

Inspector Trotter, looking around the group.

I could remember who it was, but decided I would only speak if no one else did. I had no wish to cast empty aspersions.

Everyone glanced about them, their brows furrowed.

"Why, it was Wyndham!" exclaimed Dudley Lombard.

"Me?" replied Viscount Wyndham incredulously. "I didn't sit there! I was on the chair next to it." His chest was puffed up even more broadly than usual, straining at the buttons on his shirt.

"No, that's where Mrs Glenville sat. You were on this chair here," said Dudley Lombard.

Viscount Wyndham moved closer and surveyed the two chairs. Then he shook his head.

"Have any of the chairs been moved since yesterday evening?" asked the inspector.

"No," said Mr Perrin. "And I agree with the young man. It was Viscount Wyndham who sat on that chair yesterday evening. I remember refilling his glass, which was placed on the table just in front of the chair."

Viscount Wyndham glared at the butler, but said nothing.

"I must add that, after Miss Sophia was taken ill, the chair was occupied by Mrs Lombard," the butler said.

We all turned to look at Mrs Lombard, whose face began to colour from the attention.

"Now careful, everyone," said Ralph Lombard, stepping closer to his wife as if to protect her from the implications of Mr Perrin's words. "We can't be slinging accusations at one another, now. That would be very dangerous indeed. The detective must continue to gather as much information as he can. And that includes understanding where each of us was sitting last night. We must all do what we can to assist him, but we should avoid pointing the finger of blame at anyone until the inspector has finished his work."

He took his wife's arm and I saw that her violet eyes were watery. She looked frightened.

"Well said, Lombard," added Wyndham.

Dudley Lombard nodded in agreement, but Mr Glenville's scowl grew even deeper.

"Easily said when you haven't just lost your daughter," he muttered.

"Please rest assured that I will catch the culprit, Mr Glenville," said Inspector Trotter.

"You need to, and fast," replied Mr Glenville. "I will not tolerate speculation among my guests here. It will only result in people upsetting each other. Are you certain you're capable of managing this case on your own? You examined this room after my daughter's death, and yet you missed a crucial clue which my maid was able to discover! I want more men working on this, Inspector. How about we call in Scotland Yard?"

"With all due respect, Mr Glenville, there is no need to have the Yard involved," replied the inspector. "I am quite confident in my ability to conduct this investigation. It is, indeed, regrettable that such a crucial piece of evidence was missed. May I commend you on your attentive and helpful staff, sir. Please trust that I will find the culprit for you. It is likely that he or she stands before me at this very moment."

Lunch in the kitchen was cold leftovers from the dinner the night before. I struggled to eat any of the cold ham or mutton, with the terrible memories from the previous night weighing heavily on my mind.

"My lady of the house won't eat a thing," said Mrs Craughton. "She had no breakfast, nor would she take any pie just now. She won't even eat a piece of bread."

"Quite natural after a sudden death in the house," said Mr

Perrin. "Her appetite will return in due course. Do you have a bottle of Dr Cobbold's Remedy?"

"No. Is it an effective remedy?"

"You should always have some in the house for times such as these. Four doses a day will see her right."

"Thank you, Mr Perrin, I shall fetch some this afternoon. In fact, I should like to step out of the house for a short while. It is rather stifling in here, isn't it?"

"You may also want to give the maid some Cobbold's Remedy," said Mr Perrin, nodding over at Maisie.

The poor girl sat at the table, pale and trembling. Her food sat entirely untouched in front of her.

"Come on, Maisie, you need your strength!" said the housekeeper encouragingly.

"I can't. It won't stay down."

"A household is reliant on its staff, Maisie. If you don't eat, you won't be able to do your work. And then what will become of everyone?"

"Maybe Maisie could try to eat something later," I suggested. "It can be difficult when your stomach feels knotted up."

Mrs Craughton sighed and stood to her feet. "I'll leave you be. I'm off to the pharmacy to buy the remedy. What's it called again?"

"Dr Cobbold's."

"It will put everyone right again, I'm sure."

The Wyndhams and Lombards were permitted to leave after Inspector Trotter had spoken to them. While Mrs Craughton was out at the pharmacy, I escaped to my room, sat down at the dressing table and hurriedly wrote the article Mr Sherman had requested.

The daughter of Mr. and Mrs. Alexander Glenville, Miss Sophia Glenville, died tragically at her home in Hyde Park Gate yesterday evening. Doctor Dalglish, who attended to the young woman, stated that she had been poisoned by potassium of cyanide. It is speculated that a malicious person deliberately placed the fatal poison into Miss Glenville's glass of Pommery champagne while she was celebrating the occasion of her eighteenth birthday.

Inspector Herbert Trotter of T Division is currently investigating Miss Glenville's death, and serious foul play is suspected. No arrests have yet been made, but Inspector Trotter is interviewing all guests who were present at Miss Glenville's birthday celebration on the night of her death.

Mr. Alexander Glenville owns the Blundell & Co vinegar factory in Vauxhall and the Archdale vinegar factory in Bermondsey. His late daughter was engaged to be married to Master Dudley Lombard, the son of Mr. Ralph Lombard, who owns the Lombard gin distillery in Vauxhall.

I also wrote a note to my editor:

I assume Mr. Conway's investigation into Mr. Glenville's business dealings is now concluded. I will give the housekeeper notice of my resignation and return to the office either tomorrow or Tuesday.

I folded the two pieces of paper into an envelope, sealed it and hid it on top of my wardrobe, ready for the messenger boy to collect it. I couldn't yet think of an excuse to give Mrs Craughton if she asked me what the lad had come to collect. I sensed this would be a good opportunity to return the key to her office. I made my way downstairs, but was disappointed to find that the door was locked.

Further along the corridor, the door to the library opened and Inspector Trotter's head peered out.

"It's Florence Parker, isn't it?"

"That's right, sir."

"Can you step in here and answer some questions, please?"

CHAPTER 22

I followed the inspector into the library, where he had arranged his papers into neat piles on the mahogany table. The ghost twins stared down at me through a haze of pipe smoke. I sat at the table and wondered whether I should be truthful with the inspector about who I was. If I was honest, there was a danger that the rest of the household would soon discover the truth. *Then what would happen? The atmosphere in the house was difficult enough as it was.*

I decided to keep my cover for a day or two longer. *Then I would explain to the inspector and the Glenvilles who I truly was. And I would leave.*

Inspector Trotter sat opposite me, fidgeting for a moment with his pen and the pot of ink, and then his pipe. He reached for the teapot.

"Oh dear, it's gone cold. Please could you fetch me some more once we're finished here, Florence?"

I nodded.

"Right then, here we go." He leafed through his notebook to find a blank page. "So your name is Miss Florence Parker?"

"Yes," I replied.

He must have detected the lack of certainty in my voice, as his brow furrowed slightly and he looked at me more closely. I was lying to a police officer, and it felt as though I was doing something terribly wrong.

"And this is a question I must ask everyone, I'm afraid. What is your age?"

"Thirty-four."

"And you live here at this address. Mrs Craughton tells me you are a new member of staff here. Where did you live previously?"

I was about to reply with my Milton Street address, but just managed to correct myself to the address of my supposed previous employer in time.

"Berkeley Square."

"And the house number there?"

"I think it was number twenty. The home of Mrs Fothergill." I felt a cold perspiration under my arms. I would have been much more comfortable had I confessed to the inspector who I really was.

"And I understand that you were present when Miss Sophia met her unfortunate end." His lisp meant that he especially struggled with the words 'Miss Sophia'.

"Yes, I was."

"And can you give me your account of what you saw that evening, Florence?"

I told him what I could remember. He listened intently, puffing on his pipe and writing in his notebook. I noticed that his handwriting style was rather slow and laborious. I wondered why detectives didn't have to learn shorthand, as journalists did.

"And as you witnessed the distressing spectacle, Florence, what were your thoughts regarding the cause of Miss Sophia's death?"

"I didn't have the first clue. I could see that she was struggling to breathe. I thought she was choking for a moment, as she didn't seem able to get any air. I imagined that perhaps she had a sudden complication with her lungs or heart. I had never seen her unwell before. I couldn't believe it when the doctor said she had been poisoned with cyanide. I cannot understand how someone could have poisoned her, or why they should want to do so! She had never caused anyone any harm."

"Bear with me while I write this down. Oh, darn it! My nib has broken."

I waited impatiently as the inspector found another pen and painstakingly filled it with ink.

"There we go. Now, where were we? Ah yes. I think you pre-empted my next question, which is: are you aware of anyone who might bear animosity towards Miss Sophia?"

"I barely knew her. I have only been here for a week, so I'm sure other members of the household would be able to tell you more than I can. I witnessed some bickering in the family, but it struck me as entirely normal familial behaviour. She was a young woman with modern ideas, and as such it would inevitably bring her into conflict with her loved ones from time to time. But they spoke fondly of her to me, and Mr Glenville was rather proud of her intelligence. He told me she had inherited many of his traits."

"I must say you're rather well-spoken for a maid, Florence."

"Am I?" I felt a surge of heat rush up to my face. "I had a good upbringing, Inspector. My parents sent me to school."

He nodded and returned to his notebook. I wiped my damp palms on my apron and prayed that our interview would soon be concluded.

"Have you had many dealings with Miss Sophia over the past week?"

"Not many. I waited table while she was dining with her family."

"So mealtimes were the only times you encountered Miss Sophia during the past week?"

"Yes."

"And on each occasion there were other members of the household present?"

"Yes, both family and staff."

"And yesterday evening Miss Sophia seemed her usual self?"

"She did."

"How would you describe her mood?"

"If I were to speak honestly, I would say that she had looked rather bored at times. I don't think she was the sort of girl who enjoyed parties very much. But she seemed to have a pleasant enough evening. Until—"

"Did you see anyone interfere with her glass of champagne?"

"No."

"Do you think that could have been a possibility?"

"I suppose it could have been, but I didn't witness anyone do it. That's why I'm so surprised. I suppose if someone was determined to poison her, they would have found a way without drawing attention to themselves."

"This nib is rather scratchy." He held up his pen and examined it closely. "Pens simply aren't up to the task these days, are they? I'm sure they stain your fingers far more than they used to. Now, what did I have in mind to ask next?"

As he leafed through his notebook, I decided there was something rather amateurish about his conduct. I began to doubt that he was capable of catching Miss Sophia's murderer.

"Ah yes, here we are!" he said. "Who was Miss Sophia sitting closest to in the drawing room?"

"Master Lombard and Master Glenville."

"And who did you see sitting on the chair upon which the empty packet of cyanide was found?"

"I remember Viscount Wyndham sitting there, Inspector. And then there was some confusion while Miss Sophia..." I felt my throat tighten. "...As she struggled to breathe. We were all moving about the room, and I think by that stage many of us were standing. When I give it some thought, however, I can recall that Mary Lombard was sitting on that same chair by the time the doctor arrived."

There was another long pause as he wrote this down, tutting intermittently at the ink splashes from his pen.

"Is my account similar to the others you've heard so far, Inspector?" I asked.

"Fairly similar, yes." He dipped his pen into the ink pot and examined the nib again.

"And what will happen once you've interviewed everyone in the house? Presumably, one or more will give a false account. How do you decide who's telling the truth, Inspector?"

He looked up and smiled condescendingly. "That's the skill of a detective's work, Florence."

I had my doubts that Inspector Trotter was a skilled detective.

"Where did the murderer obtain the cyanide?" I asked. "Do you know if any such substance is kept in this house? I haven't come across any myself. And what if the murderer is one of the Wyndhams or the Lombards? They have left the house now, and could easily make their escape!"

Inspector Trotter removed his pipe from his mouth. "You have a lively mind."

"I'm sorry. I have an inquisitive nature." I stopped talking, aware that I was in danger of letting slip who I really was.

"Thank you, Florence. That will be all. Have you anything else you would like to tell me about?"

"That is all, Inspector. I've only been here a short while, so I have very little information to enlighten you with, I'm afraid. I only knew Miss Sophia briefly, but she was an extremely pleasant and likeable young lady who had a bright future ahead of her, and I... Oh, wait."

"What is it?"

I realised I had forgotten to tell Inspector Trotter about my encounter with Sophia on the servants' staircase. I described the incident to him, and he listened with a great deal of interest.

"Now this is rather intriguing," he said. "Miss Sophia didn't tell you where she'd been, or with whom?"

"No. I wanted to ask, but I didn't feel it was my place to do so. I certainly wish I had now. And I also wish I had mentioned it to Mr and Mrs Glenville. She made me promise not to tell them."

I realised her parents would most likely find out about the secret meeting now and would be angry with me for not having mentioned it.

"And you think this was something she did regularly?"

"That was the impression she gave. I can't say I'm right, however, as she didn't specifically mention that she had done so before."

The inspector sat back in his chair and inspected the bowl of his pipe. This was clearly new information to him. *Was I the only person to know that Sophia had done such a thing?*

"I must add something else which happened after I encountered Miss Sophia on the servants' staircase."

I told the inspector about the footsteps I'd heard, and the opening and closing of Maisie's door.

"Hmm. Also interesting," he said as he laboriously wrote it down. "And from the way Miss Sophia spoke with you that evening, do you think it's fair to assume that she had no wish to marry Master Lombard?"

"She seemed quite angry and upset at the mention of his name. I assumed at the time that she had just met with a man she truly loved."

"And you have no idea as to his identity?"

"None. She mentioned that she might be willing to tell me more in the future, but we never found a chance to have another conversation on the matter."

"So you think it would be fair to say that Miss Sophia was unhappy about her engagement to Master Lombard?"

"Her demeanour certainly suggested that to me."

"So it seems we have a young woman who appeared happy to those around her, but in reality harboured animosity towards the man who was to be her husband," said the inspector, his attention fixed on his notebook.

Then he looked up at me. "Did Miss Sophia explain why she didn't wish to marry Master Lombard?"

"Not at all. She refused to be drawn on the subject."

"Interesting. Very interesting. Thank you for your time, Florence. You've been most helpful. You are free to leave."

CHAPTER 23

I went to fetch Inspector Trotter some more tea, and when I returned to the library I could hear voices through the closed door.

"You have witnessed arguments between Miss Sophia and her brother and sister, Mr Perrin?" asked the inspector.

"I have, sir."

"Can you elaborate any further?"

"I would describe the arguments as little more than squabbling, sir. Quite natural, and not unusual among young people."

"So the arguments in the family didn't concern you?"

"No, sir."

"Did Miss Sophia argue much with her parents?"

"She squabbled with them as well, sir. The cause of the argument was usually a trivial matter. Miss Sophia was an opinionated young woman."

"So you had no concerns about Miss Sophia or her family before her death?"

"No sir. Only one incident springs to mind."

"And what was that, Mr Perrin?"

"Miss Sophia ran away from home."

"Did she, indeed? When?"

"It was Monday the eighteenth of February."

"You have a good memory for dates, Mr Perrin. How long was Miss Sophia absent from the family home?"

I heard footsteps on the tiled corridor, so I reluctantly knocked on the door to take the tea tray in. Neither the inspector nor Mr Perrin said anything further while I was in the room.

The footsteps I had heard in the corridor belonged to Mrs Glenville. I caught up with her at the foot of the stairs. She was dressed from head to toe in black crepe. The change in her face was quite alarming. Her eyes had a haunted look to them, and her cheeks were white and sunken.

"My lady," I said. "Are you quite well?"

"No, I'm not at all well," she replied in a distracted manner.

She didn't look at me, but instead gazed up at the grandfather clock.

"It hasn't stopped," she said. "Perrin told me he'd stopped it."

The time on the clock was incorrect, but I could hear it ticking.

"Mr Perrin is with the inspector at the moment, my lady. As soon as he's finished I'll ask him to stop the clock."

"Would you?" Her eyes finally rested on me. "Thank you, Flo. I know I can rely on you."

I forced a smile. "It's no problem, my lady. Is there anything I can get you?"

I felt the need to guide her to a chair and sit her down. She looked so frail and unsteady on her feet.

"No. I thought I would go and sit in the conservatory for

a while. I don't like to leave her, but I feel the need to have a change of air."

"That sounds like a sensible idea, my lady. I'm so sorry about Miss Sophia. In the short time I knew her, I could tell she was an intelligent young woman with an exciting future ahead of her. I am sure the inspector will do all he can to find the culprit. I still can't believe this has happened."

"I feel like I've died too, Flo."

"I can understand that feeling," I replied.

"Can you?" She looked at me, her eyes earnest. "Have you also lost a loved one?"

"Yes. My father died nine years ago." I prayed that she wouldn't ask me his name. I would have to invent one if she did.

She looked down at the black handkerchief she was twisting around her fingers. "I'm sorry to hear that. Was he a good man?"

"He was." I felt unsure of my reply. *What made a man good? Was a man who had carried out a massacre of natives in Colombia a good man?*

"To lose a child is..." she trailed off. "I lost two as infants, of course, and that was unbearable. But this feels different. Sophia was a young woman. I had pictured a life for her, but now it's gone. And needlessly!"

The knuckles of her hand turned white as she clenched the handkerchief in her fist. "Who did it, Flo? Who killed my daughter?"

"I wish I knew, my lady. The detective will find it out, I'm sure."

"It was one of the guests yesterday evening, wasn't it?"

"I suppose it must have been, but I cannot understand why."

"And neither can I! The thought that anyone in our household should intend to poison another person here is unfathomable. It simply doesn't make sense. These things don't happen to families like ours. They happen to other people. That's what I had always thought. Who could have brought cyanide into our home? And how?"

"The detective will find this all out, my lady. I have every confidence in him."

The truth was, I had no confidence in Inspector Trotter at all, but I had no wish to tell this to Mrs Glenville.

"It would be remiss of me to pretend that Sophia and I had the perfect relationship," she continued. "She was strong-willed, as you have witnessed! And although her strength of character tried my patience more often than I care to remember, I felt proud that she was becoming an outspoken woman. It is something which is becoming increasingly common among women of the next generation, isn't it? In my day, we were not expected to voice our thoughts or opinions in the company of men. But times are changing, and I suppose it is for the best. The world is becoming an increasingly challenging place, and Sophia was a girl of her generation. She was better educated than I ever was, and encouraged to develop her own character. I wish now that I had been more lenient with her. Although she was a difficult child, I admired her headstrong qualities. I often wonder if that's what got her into trouble."

"No, that can't be possible."

"No, I suppose not."

Mrs Glenville gave me a sad smile.

"I know she liked you, Flo. And you've helped Mrs Craughton so well, and all the staff speak highly of you. I can tell you're a hard worker. Thank you for everything you're doing. Our household needs people like you."

I thanked Mrs Glenville in return and she walked on towards the conservatory. As I watched her, I felt overwhelmed with guilt. I was lying to Mrs Glenville about who I was. And even in these desperate hours, she had praised and thanked me. The situation felt unbearable.

The messenger boy called round for my article at the end of the afternoon.

"What does he want?" asked Mrs Craughton.

"My grandfather sent him," I replied. It was a reply which I immediately regretted. I knew that I should have thought up a better story.

"Your *grandfather*?"

"Yes, he likes to correspond by message. He doesn't trust the postal system."

"That's understandable," she replied. "They're terribly good at losing letters. Is it your grandfather who sends you the telegrams?"

"No."

"I heard that you received a telegram this morning."

"Oh yes, it was him that time."

My mouth felt dry. I hated being interrogated in this manner.

Mrs Craughton frowned, but I felt relieved when she didn't ask me to elaborate further.

"Well, I suppose your grandfather has heard about all this dreadful business. It will be in the papers tomorrow, won't it? We've had reporters calling at the door and it's most distressing for everyone. But news reporters don't give a thought to that, do they?"

"Most of them likely do. It's probably only a few who don't care whom they upset."

"Well, it's reprehensible behaviour. When someone dies, it should remain a private matter."

I said nothing further. My head ached from trying to keep up the pretence of being a maid. Mr Sherman was making matters trickier by sending telegrams and messengers.

It was high time that I left the house. It would be difficult saying goodbye to Maisie, and Mr and Mrs Glenville, but I couldn't bear to stay in this place for another day.

When I returned to my room that evening, I felt sure someone had been in there again. The trunk and the key on top of the wardrobe remained as I had left them, but the papers on my dressing table had been disturbed again.

I shivered. I needed to leave first thing the following morning. Without further ado, I packed all my belongings into my trunk, ready for my departure. My heart sank when I saw Mr Glenville's notebook in the trunk. I had forgotten all about it during the day and would need to return it before I left. *But when could I do it?* I knew that he occupied his study most evenings.

I looked out of my window. It was dark, but much of the fog had cleared away. A movement in the street below caught my eye. As I watched more closely, I could discern the figure of a man. He was tall and slim, and appeared to be looking up at the house. I felt sure there was something familiar about him, but I couldn't think why. I held my breath and stood as still as a statue as I watched him. He must have remained standing there for another minute or so before turning and walking away.

Puzzled, I returned to my bed and decided to wait until later in the night, when I could be certain that Mrs Craughton had retired. Then I would creep down to the study and replace Mr Glenville's book.

While I waited for the early morning, I opened a letter which I hadn't found the time to read. It had arrived for Florence Parker the previous day.

Dear Penny

Or should that be Flo? I hope you are enjoying your undercover assignment. I have told Mother about it, and she is most interested! I am looking forward to hearing about it when you return to your proper work again. How much longer do you think you will be there?

I very much enjoyed our recent walk, despite the inclement weather! I should like to repeat the experience (albeit on a warmer day, although that cannot be guaranteed, of course!), and I hope you would be open to another outing.

The reading room is not quite the same without you. In quieter moments, I have been perusing the collection of books we hold on the United States of Colombia, and I believe I am now furnished with a most thorough knowledge of the country in which your father travelled. I am looking forward to sharing my findings with you.

Please do reply at your earliest convenience, and I hope you will agree to another meeting.

I remain
Your most truly
Mr Francis Edwards

Mr Edwards seemed to occupy a completely different world from me. *Had it really been just eight days since I had met him in Hyde Park?*

Although he had written the letter before Sophia's death, its convivial tone felt jarring. It wasn't Mr Edwards' fault, but the letter was ill-timed. There was nothing about the man which especially irritated or offended me, but likewise there was nothing about him which excited me either. At solitary times such as this, it was James to whom my thoughts turned, and not Mr Edwards.

CHAPTER 24

I woke to a bright light at my window. I had slept deeply, and had no idea of the time. There had been no knock at my door from Maisie that morning.

I had fallen asleep on my bed wearing the black uniform I had worn the day before. I splashed the water which sat in my washbasin onto my face and hurried down the servants' staircase. I was supposed to have remained awake and returned Mr Glenville's book. I would have to find a way somehow to do it before I left the house.

Mrs Craughton was scolding Maisie in the kitchen for waking up late. The poor girl was in tears, and she looked exhausted. Mrs Craughton turned her attention to me and berated me for the same misdemeanour. I apologised and felt my jaw clench as her finger wagged at the pair of us.

"There's no time for breakfast for either of you," she fumed. "Flo, take some coffee to the inspectors in the library."

"There's more than one now?" I asked.

"Yes. Another turned up this morning with Inspector Trotter."

"Come in!" said Inspector Trotter as I knocked on the library door. I entered with the tray of coffee.

Inspector Trotter sat at the table with his piles of paper, and another man was warming his back by the fireplace. Maisie and I had failed to light it that morning, so I guessed Mrs Craughton must have done it instead.

I placed the coffee tray on the table and was about to acknowledge the second inspector when he spoke.

"Good morning, Penny."

I jumped.

James!

He gave me a warm grin and I felt a smile break out across my face. Then I realised what he had done.

He had called me Penny. He had forgotten that I was supposed to be a maid.

I quickly assumed a sombre face. "My name is Florence Parker, Inspector," I said.

"You may relax, Penny. I've explained everything to Inspector Trotter."

"Really? Is that wise?" I looked nervously at Inspector Trotter to gauge his reaction, but he merely puffed away on his pipe. "I'm sorry, Inspector. I didn't want to admit who I was yesterday for fear of someone finding out."

He removed the pipe from his mouth. "That's quite all right, Miss Green. It seems the situation in this household is more complicated than I first thought."

"I'd like to speak to Miss Green in private for a few minutes, Inspector Trotter," said James. "Would that be possible?"

"I suppose so, but only for a few minutes. Glenville's growing increasingly irate at the lack of progress. I've a lot of work to do."

"Indeed, and we can assist you with that afterwards."

As soon as Inspector Trotter had left the room, James took a few steps closer to me. His suit was a deep blue with a subtle check, and he was wearing a star-shaped tiepin. We held each other's gaze, and I felt overwhelmed with relief.

"I can't tell you how happy I am to see you here!" I said. "It's been miserable. Thoroughly miserable!"

Tears spilled down my cheeks, and James handed me his handkerchief.

"No one could have had any idea that this would happen," he said, resting his hand on my shoulder as I dried my tears.

The handkerchief smelt of his familiar eau-de-cologne, and it felt comforting.

"It's good to see you again, Penny," he said fondly. Then he glanced at my black uniform. "It's a shame you have to be dressed as a maid. And a maid in mourning at that! You've coped admirably."

"I wouldn't say that. And you'll need to speak a little more softly. People can hear through the door, you know."

"Is that so? Have you been listening in?" He grinned.

"A little. I have to, seeing as I'm working undercover, don't I?"

"Indeed. Thank you for everything you've done so far, Penny. How are you? You look rather tired."

"I am. I haven't slept well here until last night, when I think it all caught up with me. I overslept this morning."

He gestured toward a chair and we both sat down.

"I told Trotter that I'm here to help him," said James.

"Does he want your help?"

"No. He wants the case all to himself, but I felt duty-bound to inform him of my existing investigations into Mr Glenville's business dealings. I don't think the chap quite has the measure of this case yet, so he has reluctantly agreed to accept my help."

"That's good news, James. Perhaps I can also be of help. I can't wait to get out of here and resume my normal work. I shan't be in a hurry to work undercover again."

James pursed his lips, as if I wouldn't like what he was about to say.

"I think that you would be of great help to the investigation if you were to remain here for the time being, Penny."

"No!" I felt my headache begin to return. "I can't! I can't bear it here. A girl has just died in this house, and it's awful. Truly awful. Besides, they're going to find out who I am."

"They haven't found out yet, and you've managed to last a week here! Not bad for someone who has never worked as a maid before. Would you consider staying here a week longer?"

My heart sank. "Another *week?*"

"You've been extremely helpful so far. Trotter tells me you found the empty packet of cyanide, and that you also encountered Miss Sophia as she returned from her secret rendezvous."

"But that's all. I don't see what else I can do to help."

"You're privy to the comings and goings in this house. You will see and hear far more than Trotter and I could ever manage ourselves. We can interview everyone several times over, but you have the opportunity to find out who they really are. This is a crucial time for us in finding clues as to what happened. The more time that passes after the event, the harder it is to spot something important."

"I think you're overstating my abilities, James."

"Penny, I know you. And I trust you. Please can you spend another week here?"

"It's not what I want. I'm a news reporter. I want to be *reporting* on the stories, not actually *living* them."

He sat back in his chair. "That's fine. I understand. I don't want to force the issue if you're not comfortable with it.

Trotter needs all the help he can get in building his case against Glenville."

"He thinks Mr Glenville did it?"

"That's his theory so far."

"But that's ridiculous! Why would Mr Glenville harm his own daughter?"

"I have no idea, but he's a deeply unpleasant man."

"Actually, I don't believe he is," I retorted. "He may have made himself unpopular with people in the world of business, but as a person he's not unpleasant at all. He's quite the opposite. I like him."

James gave me an incredulous look.

"What about the cyanide packet on Viscount Wyndham's chair?" I asked. "Perhaps he did it."

James was about to reply when Inspector Trotter re-entered the room.

"I'm sorry to interrupt, but may I get on with my work now, Blakely?"

"Of course."

James and I rose to our feet.

"Thank you, Penny," said James rather formally. "Please let me know if you change your mind."

CHAPTER 25

Was *I letting James down?* I pondered this as I brushed the carpet on the stairs. *Surely he was expecting too much from me.* I felt sorry that I had ever allowed myself to be talked into this undercover job.

I had no interest in helping with the case, given that Trotter seemed to have decided that Mr Glenville was to blame. *What was the basis for his accusation? Did he know the man at all?* Even James had no idea what the factory owner was really like.

I reached for the ring that still hung around my neck. I recalled the moment James had given it to me in the Museum Tavern and longed to be there with him again. We'd had small disagreements in the past, but at this moment I disagreed with him more than ever before. *Would it be possible to work with him again?*

Once I had completed my chore, I went to Mrs Craughton's office to inform her that I was leaving. I had with me the key to Mr Glenville's desk, which I would claim to have found on the staircase.

"You've met the inspector from the Yard, then?" said the housekeeper inquisitively.

"Er, yes. Inspector Blakely, or something or other." I glanced at the empty hook that usually housed the key I had secreted in my apron pocket.

"I don't think Mr Glenville knows he's here yet," continued Mrs Craughton. "I think he'll be pleased to hear it, however. Inspector Trotter needs all the help he can get. Sadly, Miss Sophia is causing as much trouble in death as she did in life."

"What makes you say that?"

"You saw what she was like, didn't you? You didn't know her for long, but I suspect you got the measure of her. She always had to be the centre of attention, didn't she?"

"Did she?"

"You know she did!"

She lowered her voice to a whisper and stared up at me with her grey eyes, which for some odd reason reminded me of a lizard's.

"I know we're not supposed to speak ill of the dead, but I hope the Lord forgives me for what I'm about to say. I was extremely fond of Miss Sophia, but she could test the patience of a saint. You should have heard the arguments she had with people. The strong-headedness. The blame lies with her parents. They indulged her. She never learned how to restrain herself."

"Are you suggesting that the person who has murdered her may have been justified in some way?"

"No." She shook her head vehemently. "No, she didn't deserve such a dreadful thing to be done to her. I have a terrible suspicion that the poor girl ingested the poison deliberately."

"You think she took her own life?"

The housekeeper nodded.

"No, I don't believe she would have done such a thing," I said. "Why would she? She was a young woman with her full life ahead of her."

"I don't think she intended self-murder. I think she merely wanted to draw everyone's attention. You saw how much attention Miss Jane received that evening, didn't you? Miss Sophia couldn't compete, so she found a different way. It simply didn't work out as she had planned it."

"That doesn't sound like something she would do."

"She wasn't a particularly happy child. She attempted to run away several times, but she never got very far. She was too accustomed to the comforts of home!"

"Did you know that Miss Sophia stayed out late one night without her parents' knowledge?"

The housekeeper's eyes narrowed. "I heard rumours that she did such things, but could never be certain that they were true. How do you know this?"

I told her about my encounter with Miss Sophia on the stairs.

"I wonder who it was she met with," Mrs Craughton said. "She didn't tell you?"

"No. And I wish now that I had told Mr and Mrs Glenville about the incident. She made me swear not to, but, with hindsight, my chief duty was to them."

"You kept your word to her, so you mustn't feel regretful now. I suspect she was meeting with someone she considered a more eligible suitor. Scores of girls would have given their right arm to be in her position, engaged to such a man as Dudley Lombard! As I've told you before, she was extremely ungrateful. I don't think she had any notion that it can be quite difficult for young women to find themselves a suitable husband."

"Do you think she was unhappy about the engagement?" I asked.

"Probably, yes. She was never happy unless she was grumbling about something. And when people began to ignore her grumbling she took the poison."

"You really think she did it herself?"

"Yes, and that's what I've communicated to the inspector. He has to consider it, you know."

"If she met another man the night that I saw her, what would Dudley Lombard have done had he found out?"

"He would have been exceptionally angry, and rightly so," replied the housekeeper. "The entire Lombard family would have been livid. Now, you must excuse me while I go and see to my lady. She spends far too much time in that room with her daughter. There are funeral arrangements to be made."

As we stepped out of the office and Mrs Craughton locked the door, I pondered over what she had told me. *Was it possible that Sophia had accidentally taken her own life? Or had the Lombards discovered her love affair and poisoned her as an act of revenge?*

"You remember me complaining about those reporters outside yesterday, don't you?" asked Mrs Craughton.

"Yes."

"Some of the newspapers are already carrying the news of Miss Sophia's death. Have a look at Mr Perrin's *Morning Express* on the kitchen table when you find the chance. It's not right, is it? The press should have left the Glenvilles alone. Is the fire in the study lit yet?"

"I'll see to it, Mrs Craughton." I noticed that my voice had an odd, strangulated tone when I spoke.

I had been so distracted by our conversation that I had forgotten to return the desk drawer key or give notice of my resignation.

On my way to the study I passed the governess and the nurse

with the younger Glenvilles. They were all wearing their over-coats, as if they were about to go out for a walk. *How could Sophia's death be explained to children who were so young?* My heart felt heavy at the thought.

The study was dark. *If only I had brought Mr Glenville's book with me I could have replaced it in his desk drawer. Instead, it was still lying in the trunk in my room.* I cursed my lack of organisation, placed my oil lamp on the hearth and lit the fire. I watched the flames burn brightly for a moment and enjoyed their warmth.

"That's better, isn't it, Flo?"

I leapt to my feet and spun around to see Mr Glenville's dimly lit form in the chair by his desk.

"Mr Glenville! You have a habit of startling me!"

I wondered why he had sat there for several minutes without informing me of his presence.

His eyes were wide and dark. *Was he about to confront me about the missing book?*

"You frighten easily, don't you? You look terrified," he said.

"I'm sorry, sir. I can't deny that Miss Sophia's death has shaken me rather."

"I'm not surprised," he said sadly. "I've often thought that the loss of a person has a sort of rippling effect, like dropping a stone into the middle of a still pond. The ripples move outwards." He slowly spread out his hands as he spoke. "And disturb everything in their wake. Does that make sense, or am I talking nonsense again? It's probably nonsense, you know. I haven't been sleeping at all well."

"No, it makes sense, sir."

"Thank you, Flo. I knew you'd understand. He smiled. "The inspector tells me you saw Sophia return to the house late one night."

"Yes, sir. I was desperate to tell you and Mrs Glenville

about it," I said, feeling flustered. "But Miss Sophia swore me to secrecy. She made me promise and I didn't want to betray her confidence. I had always planned to tell you, and she gave me her word that she would explain it to me in greater detail. I wanted to wait until then and hear the full explanation. Then I should have known whether or not it would have been appropriate to draw the matter to your attention. I'm so sorry that I didn't tell you about it. I certainly wish now that I had done so. More than anything, I wish I had! But sadly, it cannot be undone."

"It would certainly have been helpful if you'd mentioned it to us at the time," replied Mr Glenville. "Perhaps we could have intervened. But there's little use in dwelling on what might have been. That doesn't help us now, does it? We must leave it up to the two detectives."

I swallowed nervously. *What would Mr Glenville think if he knew that Trotter suspected him?*

"If truth be told, I'm completely thrown by this," he continued. "I have coped with many things in my life, but never something like this." His voice began to sound choked. "Being present in the room as she died, and being able to do nothing about it whatsoever..."

He pulled a handkerchief from his pocket and wiped his face with it. "I will never be able to explain to anyone what that's like. I'm her father. I should have been able to protect her, and yet I was helpless." He fixed me with his dark, damp eyes. "For the first time in my life, Flo, I felt helpless."

I felt deeply sorry for him and was unsure what to say. *How was a maid supposed to comfort her employer?*

"You did all you could have, sir. It's natural to feel helpless."

"Yes, I suppose it is. That poor boy Dudley is devastated. He doesn't know, by the way."

"Doesn't know what, sir?"

"That she went out that evening to meet someone else. That's the assumption, anyhow. Why else would she have been so secretive? I can only assume it was another man, and that's what the inspector also thinks."

He got up out of his chair, walked over to the fire and stared into the flames. As he stood closer to me, I could smell his exotic scent again.

"If Dudley ever found out it would destroy him," he said. "He was desperately in love with her. Perhaps I was naive, but I never expected anything to get in the way of their marriage."

He turned to me and fixed me with his dark gaze. "If she was meeting someone else, I'd like to know who that chap is. I wonder if he has any idea of the upset his actions have caused. What man in his right mind would encourage a young lady to leave her house late at night to meet with him? He has no scruples whatsoever. I wonder if he even knows what has happened to her."

I thought of the dark figure I had seen standing in the street the previous night, but chose not to mention it lest it angered Mr Glenville further.

"I think the inspector is making enquiries into the identity of the man."

"I hope he is able to find him. It doesn't help in the search for the murderer, though, does it? The more I consider it, the more I believe that the murderer may have been trying to harm me. I think Sophia's poisoning was a mistake."

"Why do you think someone should want to harm you?"

"There are numerous reasons, but I shan't bore you with them. There are many in the establishment who begrudge me my success. They cannot understand how a man who was born into poverty could rise through the ranks; especially a man with a scarred and broken body. It's not the done thing, is it?"

He held my gaze, and my eyes moved to the scar on his left cheek.

"How did you injure your face?" I asked.

"It happened when I was eighteen."

"In the factory?"

"No. Someone attacked me with a broken bottle."

I gasped, and he smiled at my concern.

"Don't worry, Flo. At least I survived to tell the tale. He almost finished me off, but not quite."

I found myself wondering what the scar would feel like if I were to reach up and touch his cheek with my fingertips. We watched each other silently and the ticklish sensation returned to my stomach. I pulled my eyes away from his and quickly turned to look at the fire, embarrassed and horrified that I had even entertained the thought of touching him.

"I shouldn't detain you any longer," he said very softly. "That Craughton creature will no doubt come looking for you shortly."

I felt heat in my face and knew that it wasn't just from the fire.

"I shall go and find the Craughton creature before she finds me," I replied with a meek smile.

CHAPTER 26

J ane's voice was so loud that I could hear it quite clearly through the library door.

"Sophia was never happy or content!"

I checked the corridor around me and then paused.

"And do you know what might have been the cause of her unhappiness?" I heard Inspector Trotter ask.

"She was born like that."

"So you're not aware of any particular reason for your sister's perceived discontent?"

"No."

"Did you get on well with her?"

"No, not really."

"Did she confide in you?"

"Never."

"May I ask the purpose of these questions, Inspector?" I heard Mrs Glenville ask. "I should think it obvious to anyone that my fifteen-year-old daughter cannot possibly be involved in her sister's death."

"Please bear with us, Mrs Glenville. We won't detain either of you any longer than is necessary," said James.

"You suggest that your sister was an unhappy individual, Miss Jane," Inspector Trotter continued. "Was she prone to upsetting other people?"

"I'd say!"

"Who exactly?"

"All of us! Her entire family!"

"It was her age, Inspector," explained Mrs Glenville. "Sophia was at a difficult age."

"She was a difficult age every year of her life, Ma."

"Some people are more difficult than others, dear."

"You mention, Miss Jane, that your sister upset everyone in your family. Is there anyone in particular she upset the most?"

"No. It was the same for all of us. She did it on purpose, you know."

"Thank you, Miss Jane."

I heard sobs, and then Jane's distressed voice. "I didn't like my sister, but that doesn't mean I'm happy she has died. She didn't deserve it. She would have changed when she got married, but he didn't give her the chance."

"Who didn't?" James asked.

"Master Lombard."

"What do you mean when you say that he didn't give her the chance."

"He wanted to marry me!"

"Jane!" scolded Mrs Glenville.

"It's true, Ma! He told me so!"

I walked away from the library door before someone caught me eavesdropping there. I had initially thought that Dudley Lombard was a harmless fool. *But could he have harmed Sophia in the hope that he could become betrothed to Jane?*

I encountered Maisie on the servants' staircase. She appeared to be loitering there.

"What's the matter, Maisie?"

"Everythin', Flo." There were tears on her freckled cheeks.

"Miss Sophia wouldn't have wanted you to be sad like this."

"But she ain't 'ere, is she? 'Ow does she know? I don't feel right. I feel like everythin's all twisted up inside me." She held her hands to her stomach. "I can't work or do nuffink, and Mrs Craughton keeps tellin' me what ter do, and I can't do none of it! I don't feel right at all!"

"Why don't you go to your room and get some rest, Maisie?"

"'Cause Mrs Craughton won't let me! She keeps givin' me things ter do. I can't do 'em."

"What has she asked you to do?"

"Fill up the coal buckets."

"I'll do that for you. Go and get some rest."

"But what about Mrs Craughton?"

"I'll tell her you're not well. Please don't worry. It's important that you get better."

"I ain't never gonna get better. I'm gonna feel like this forever, I know it. Miss Sophia ain't never comin' back again!"

"You'll feel more like yourself after some rest, Maisie. Go quickly before I change my mind about filling up the coal buckets for you."

She smiled weakly. "Thank you, Flo. You're good ter me, yer are."

I lifted the lid of the coal store in the yard, but there was no sign of the small shovel used to fill the buckets. It was a pleasant spring day with birdsong in the air, and the spreading branches of a nearby oak tree had new green leaves on them. I stood there for a moment, enjoying the sunshine on my face and listening to the horses whinnying in the mews.

"You're still here then, Flo?" I turned to see James in the yard behind me, filling his pipe. He gave me a wink and then grinned.

"Yes, I am, Inspector." I looked up at the windows of the house, hoping nobody could hear our conversation. "Has the future Mrs Blakely found out about your secret pipe smoking yet?"

"Not yet. Have you changed your mind about staying here?"

"No. I simply haven't had the opportunity to speak to Mrs Craughton as yet." I looked around for the shovel again and found it inside one of the buckets.

"You still won't consider one more week?" he asked.

There was something about the twinkle in James' blue eyes which made it difficult to maintain my stubbornness. Besides, I had already made a vow to myself that I would somehow prove Mr Glenville could not have been behind Sophia's death.

"Inspector Trotter is rather clumsy," he said as he lit his pipe.

"What does that have to do with me?" I dug the shovel into the coal and noisily tipped it into the bucket.

James waited for the sound to subside. "He spilled his coffee over his notebook," he said. "And I'm afraid some of it has spilled onto the chair and carpet. I've tried to mop up as best I can with blotting paper and my handkerchief, but we need someone to help clean it up."

I felt my jaw tighten. "You're asking me to clean up after you and Trotter?" I hissed. "You consider me a real maid now, do you?"

"Penny..."

"For the past week I have done nothing but fetch and carry and clean for other people. It's the most back-breaking, demeaning work I have ever done. I am a news reporter, James! I shouldn't even be here!"

"Shush," he said, glancing around nervously. "Someone will hear you."

"Quite frankly, James, I don't think I care any longer."

"Penny, you're missing the point of what I'm trying to tell you. Don't you see? Inspector Trotter's notebook is half-ruined by coffee. He needs to transcribe its contents onto dry paper."

"Good luck to him. I've seen how slowly he writes."

"If he were to find someone who could do that for him, he could get on with his detective work. It would need to be someone discreet and trustworthy, as the notes are highly confidential."

I began to listen more carefully.

"Yes, Penny, you could do it. You could find out what he knows so far and then you would be able to assist us with the case."

"You're assuming that I'll agree to stay here for another week."

"Well, won't you?"

I delayed my reply while I considered the matter.

"And as for the spilled coffee on the rug and chair, it will take some time to clean that up properly. The person attending to it will be in the room while the interviews are taking place. We can't just ask any member of the household to clean it up, you know."

I considered the thought that I might hear more of the interviews without having to listen through the door.

I watched James for a while, leaving him to wonder what my reply would be. Then I wiped my hands on my apron and picked up the coal bucket.

"I suppose another week won't be the complete ruin of me," I said eventually.

His face broke out into a smile.

"And it's possible that we may find the culprit during that time," I added.

"Thank you, Penny." James gave a relieved sigh. "I can't tell you how happy I am that you've agreed to do this. You'll be such a great help."

"I certainly hope so."

We exchanged a smile.

CHAPTER 27

"Here's Flo to the rescue!" announced James as I entered the library with a cloth and a bowl of water. Then he turned to Inspector Trotter and said in a whisper, "Penny is happy to rewrite your notes, Trotter."

Inspector Trotter removed his pipe from his mouth and gave me an appreciative nod. "Thank you, Miss Green," he lisped. "I don't suppose more coffee and toast is allowed, is it?"

"Let's get through these next few interviews first," said James.

Inspector Trotter was about to argue when a knock sounded at the door.

"That will be Maurice," said James. "Come in!" he called out.

Maurice Glenville walked slowly into the room, supported by his walking sticks.

"Can you understand what I'm saying, Master Glenville?" asked Inspector Trotter in a loud, careful voice.

"I understand you p-perfectly," replied Maurice, taking a seat at the table with them.

He gave me a puzzled look.

"Don't mind Flo, Master Glenville," said James. "She's clearing up after a spot of carelessness on Inspector Trotter's part. Everything you tell us will be kept confidential. I can assure you of that."

"I am going to ask you some questions about your sister's tragic death," bellowed Inspector Trotter.

"There's no need to speak so loudly, Trotter. The boy's not deaf," said James.

Inspector Trotter glared at him before continuing. "Please don't worry, Master Glenville. We'll keep this as short as possible and I'll ask you the questions quite directly, if that's all right. Please can you tell me what you did on the fateful day of Saturday the twenty-ninth of March?"

I got to my knees and began scrubbing the carpet under the watchful gaze of the ghost twins. In slurred and stuttering words, Maurice described his visit to Viscount Wyndham's home; how they had taken some photographs in the garden and developed them in the dark room. Inspector Trotter fidgeted with his pen as Maurice spoke, as if frustrated by his slow speech. James listened patiently and I slowly mopped the coffee stain on the rug.

"Thank you, Master Lombard," said Inspector Trotter when he had finished speaking. "Now, let us discuss what you saw at the party. Did you see anyone put anything into your sister's glass of champagne?"

"No."

"Can you think of anyone who would want to cause your sister harm?"

"Yes. I can think of lots of p-people."

"Really, Master Glenville? Is that so?"

"She was argum-mentative."

"Did you argue with your sister, Master Glenville?"

"Yes. M-many times."

"When was the last time you argued with Miss Sophia before her death?"

"The day b-before."

"And what was the argument about?"

"She was always upsetting M-Mother. I told her she did it on p-purpose."

"And why did she upset your mother?"

"She was unhappy. She d-did it out of spite."

"Do you know why your sister was unhappy, Master Glenville?"

"She d-didn't want to marry Lombard."

"Did she tell you that?"

"It was obvious."

"Do you think that was a factor in her death?"

"What do you m-mean?"

"Could the reason she didn't want to be married to Dudley Lombard help to explain her death?"

"It c-caused arguments in the family."

"Arguments with you?"

Maurice nodded.

"Master Lombard, as the son and eldest child of your parents, surely you harbour some resentment that you were not chosen to inherit your father's business?" conjectured Inspector Trotter.

"Why sh-should I?"

"Because you are the rightful heir."

"I never expected to inherit the b-business."

I glanced at his twisted body and felt a pang of pity.

"So you didn't bear any animosity toward your sister because she and her future husband, Dudley Lombard, were to inherit your father's empire?"

"No. I d-didn't like her because of what she did to M-

Mother."

"Interesting," said Inspector Trotter after Maurice had left the room. "Do you think a cripple is capable of murder? The boy has been described as an idiot, but he appears to be of sound mind. There's no doubt he could comprehend my questions."

"At this stage I don't think we should rule anything out,' said James.

"But what's the boy's motive? That he didn't like his sister?"

"People have killed for less exceptional reasons than that," replied James.

"I don't think he's a person of interest."

"Keep an open mind, Trotter."

"There's no need to tell me what to do with my mind, Blakely." Inspector Trotter puffed up his barrel chest. "This is my investigation, and you're merely assisting me."

"You're taking a long time to clear up a bit of spilled coffee," commented Mrs Craughton as I walked to the library with a fresh bowl of water.

"It's made a terrible mess of the seat and the carpet," I replied.

"But it's almost time for dinner."

Maisie approached me as I continued on my way.

"Are you feeling any better?" I asked.

"Sort of." Her face was still pale. "I've got ter speak to the 'spectors next. Are you in the room wiv 'em?"

"Yes, I'm cleaning up the coffee which was spilled."

"Can you stay in there when I talks to 'em? I'm frightened, Flo."

"Don't be frightened, Maisie. They're perfectly friendly."

"But they's the police!"

"They don't mean you any harm at all. They're simply trying to find out what happened to Miss Sophia, and they need everyone's help."

"I don't want 'em harrestin' me!" Maisie shivered.

"They'll do no such thing. Why should they arrest you?"

"Dunno."

"Come with me now and you'll see that they're perfectly fine. There's nothing to worry about."

Despite my reassurances, Maisie fidgeted and trembled during her interview. She kept wiping her eyes with the back of her hand, stuttering over her words.

"Have you any idea who would wish to harm Miss Sophia?" James asked her.

"No." Maisie's eyes were wide and earnest. "No, I can't think of no one what would of done it!"

"Had she upset anyone?"

Maisie paused before replying. "No. Sometimes she argued with 'er ma and pa. But that's normal, ain't it? She never meant nuffink by it."

I finished cleaning the carpet and began wiping the chair with my damp cloth.

"Was she upset about anything in particular? Do you know if there was something bothering her?" asked James.

Maisie wiped her face with her hands.

"No. But she wouldn't of told me about nuffink anyway. Betsy's the one she spoke to most."

"Betsy is a maid who once worked here, am I right?" asked James.

Maisie nodded.

"And Miss Sophia was friendly with Betsy?"

"Yeah, they was good friends."

"Do you know if Miss Sophia confided in Betsy?"

"I dunno what you mean, sir."

"Did Miss Sophia tell Betsy how she was feeling?"

"Yeah, I fink so."

"And when did Betsy leave this household?"

"End of Feb'ry."

"To your knowledge, did Miss Sophia confide in anyone else after Betsy's departure?"

"Tell someone 'ow she were feelin', you mean?"

"Yes."

"Dunno. I don't fink so."

"So in your opinion, Miss Sophia was a happy young lady looking forward to her marriage to Dudley Lombard."

"Yeah. I mean everyfink weren't perfect. No one's life's perfect, is it? But there weren't nuffink what would make me think she were unhappy or that made me fink someone else would kill 'er. I don't understand why they dunnit."

"Were you aware that Miss Sophia was out of the house late in the evening on Wednesday the twenty-sixth of March?"

"No, I weren't."

"Did you see her depart or return?"

"No."

"Have you ever known her leave the house secretly late at night?"

"No, never."

"You're sure you have no knowledge of her leaving the house that evening? Perhaps she went to meet someone?"

"I don't know nuffink about it."

"On that same evening, footsteps were heard near your door, and your door was heard to open and close. Were you awake at that time, Maisie? At about one o'clock?"

"No. I were fast asleep. I'm always asleep then!"

Maisie dissolved into tears and I slipped her my handkerchief. She took a while to compose herself.

"What a nervous girl," remarked Inspector Trotter after Maisie had left the room. He poked around in the bowl of his pipe with the end of his pen.

"She's frightened of the police," I said. "I don't know why. I tried to reassure her. Perhaps her family has had a bad experience with the law in the past."

"Well, it seems the young maid had nothing much of interest to tell us," said Inspector Trotter. "We must turn our attention back to the guests from that evening."

"Just a moment," said James. "We shouldn't just consider what Maisie told us. We should consider what she *didn't* tell us."

"And how on earth do we do that?" asked Inspector Trotter.

"The footsteps that were heard outside her door, and the sound of her door opening and closing. Penny told us about that, and we know she's telling the truth."

"Do we know that?" asked Inspector Trotter, resting his gaze on me.

"Of course! I know Penny well, and she's one of the most trustworthy people you'll ever meet."

I felt my face grow warm at the compliment.

"Maisie must know something about those footsteps," continued James. "And she certainly must have heard her door open and close at that hour! I'd say there is a high chance that she was responsible for the noise herself. Like Sophia Glenville, she stayed out late that night. Whether the two incidents are connected or not I can't say, but Maisie isn't being truthful with us."

"Well, that's rather inconvenient," said Inspector Trotter. "Why would she hide the truth?"

"Because she's frightened," replied James. "I'd say the girl is terrified of someone. Would you agree, Penny?"

"Now that you say it, I suppose she does seem overly frightened. She has certainly not been herself since Miss Sophia died. I had assumed it was the grief, but it could also be fear."

"Who do you think she may be frightened of, Penny?"

"I don't know, I really don't. I'll do my best to find out. Perhaps I could ask her directly."

"Be very careful about doing that," said James. "She's keeping quiet for a reason. You don't want to make the situation more dangerous for her."

I felt the back of my neck prickle. It hadn't occurred to me that Maisie might be in danger.

CHAPTER 28

Reassuring myself that I could manage just one more week, I unpacked my trunk that evening and returned my clothes to the wardrobe. Then I sat down at the dressing table with Inspector Trotter's coffee-soaked notebook. It was almost dry, and some of the pages were brown and crisp with coffee.

Before I began transcribing his notes, I penned a quick letter to Mr Fox-Stirling's secretary suggesting a date of Wednesday the ninth of April for our meeting regarding my father. It was ten days away. *I would surely be free of the Glenville house by then.*

I began to copy out the inspector's notes from the stained pages. It was interesting to read what Mrs Craughton had told him. The coffee had blurred a number of the words, but I managed to guess their meaning.

Mrs. Charlotte Diane Craughton. 53. Housekeeper.
Interview: Sunday 30th March 1884. Half past 11 o'clock.
Employed by Glenville Family since July 1882.

Enjoys work.

Knew victim well. Describes her as defiant and argumentative. Unappreciative of her circumstances. Says victim was spoilt, had everything she wanted. Mrs. C. liked victim and bore no resentment towards her.

Victim and Master Lombard were to live in Barnes after marriage. Victim choosing furnishings.

Not known if victim was happy about marriage to Master L. Mrs. C. states that victim "rarely seemed happy about anything".

Speculates that victim may have accidentally poisoned herself in a bid for attention.

Saw no one near victim's glass on night of poisoning other than Mr. Perrin, butler. Mr. Perrin refilled victim's glass with champagne. Victim seemed usual self, nothing unusual about her demeanour or bearing.

Victim fell unwell after drinking champagne. Sudden. Approx. half-past 9 o'clock. Doctor summoned immediately. Attempts made to save victim failed. Victim pronounced dead shortly before 10 o'clock. Occupants of room much distressed.

I read the notes through after I had written them, and realised how difficult it was for James and Inspector Trotter to glean any useful information from the witness accounts. I tried to imagine what Mrs Craughton hadn't said in the interview. *Was that more important?* Her thoughts seemed fairly thorough to me, but I wasn't sure I could be an effective judge of her account.

I began work on Mr Perrin's interview.

Mr. Samuel Perrin. 49. Butler.
Interview: Sunday 30th March 1884. A quarter to two o'clock.
Employed by Glenville Family since February 1880.

Enjoys work.

Describes victim as headstrong but pleasant. Victim ran away from home Monday 18th February, approx. 11 o'clock. Mr. P. sent to find her. Mr. P. called at victim's friend's house and discovered victim had just departed for Hyde Park. Found victim in Hyde Park approx. 4 o'clock, just before nightfall. Victim cold and unhappy. No reason given for leaving home. Believes victim confided in maid, Betsy, about reason for leaving. Betsy seen listening at library door when Mr. and Mrs. Glenville spoke to victim about her running away. Mr. P. admonished Betsy for eavesdropping. Mr. Glenville dismissed Betsy from household Friday 22nd February.

Betsy was...

I was disappointed that a large coffee stain had obliterated the writing for several lines. *Surely Betsy had some useful information. If Miss Sophia had confided in her the reason for running away, Betsy would have a good idea about Miss Sophia's state of mind.* I tried as hard as I could to discern what the writing had once said, but all I could see in this section of the page was a stain of dark ink mixed with coffee.

I turned the page and was able to read the following:

...ay 4th March.

Saturday 29th March. Evening: Mr. P. served wine with each course, poured by himself. No one else poured wine or champagne. Pommery 76. Nothing unusual about bottles. Nothing unusual about champagne glasses, which were kept in drawing room cabinet. All checked for cleanliness before champagne served. Nothing unusual noted.

Victim's glass was on table next to chair she was sitting in.

Below this was a blurred plan of the drawing room sketched by Mr Perrin. He had noted where everyone had been sitting that evening. I redrew the plan and added the annotations he had made. While I worked on it, I noticed that it wasn't entirely accurate. He had mistaken where Ralph Lombard had been sitting. Mr Perrin struck me as a thorough man, so I was surprised that he had made such a mistake. I would show James and Inspector Trotter my revised plan the following morning.

Mr. P recalls refilling victim's glass once. Possibility of twice. Recollection imperfect.

Victim taken ill at approx. quarter to ten o'clock. Doctor summoned. Victim passed away while being attended to in drawing room. Approx. ten o'clock.

Mr. P. refutes suggestion he administered any substance to victim's glass other than wine or champagne. Mr. P. refutes suggestion anyone asked him to administer a substance to victim's glass other than wine or champagne.

Of all those present that night, Mr Perrin was the one who had the easiest opportunity to put the poison in Sophia's glass. *Could he have done it? Could someone have asked him to do it?*

And what of Betsy?

She seemed to be the only person Sophia had confided in. *James needed to find her urgently.*

CHAPTER 29

The following morning I was in the hallway with Mrs Craughton when the grandfather clock chimed nine.

"What is wrong with that clock?" exclaimed the housekeeper. "It's supposed to have been stopped! I must ask Mr Perrin to look at it again." She turned to me. "You do realise the front steps didn't get scrubbed yesterday, Flo. Can you make time to do them today, please?"

"Yes Mrs Craughton. I will return these notes to Inspector Trotter and then start work on them."

"Good. Today will be busy. The Lombards are returning for further interviews with the police." She eyed the papers in my hand and frowned. "What have the inspectors tasked you with, exactly?"

"Inspector Trotter's notes need to be rewritten after he spilled coffee over his notebook."

"Doesn't he have someone else who can write them for him? You're busy with your household duties."

"It's not a problem at all, Mrs Craughton. I worked on them last night once my chores had been completed."

"You're good enough at writing then, are you?"

"I am told that I write well."

Her eyes narrowed suspiciously, and I realised I was holding my breath.

"And the inspector has permitted you to read all that he's written?" she asked. "It was supposed to be private, or at least that's what he told me."

"I have promised that I will keep every confidence."

"Found out anything interesting, has he?"

The housekeeper stepped forward, as if she hoped that I would show her some of the notes. I gripped the book and papers tightly in my hands.

"Surprisingly, no. Everyone's statements match up quite well so far. And they fit with my own recollections of the evening. But someone was responsible, I suppose, so one or more of the interviewees must be lying."

I fixed Mrs Craughton with my full gaze, assessing her reaction.

"Yes, I suppose someone must be."

She stared back at me with her reptilian grey eyes, then looked away and ran her finger along the wainscoting, checking for dust. "It's extremely clean in this part of the house. It's no coincidence, I would think, that it's right next to the library. The doors are rather thin, aren't they?"

I didn't like the stern look on Mrs Craughton's face, and I feared she had guessed that I had been listening to the conversations in the library.

"I shall take these papers into the library and then get on with my chores."

"Please do. In the meantime, I shall check with Mr Glenville that he's happy for you to be helping the police in this manner. I would put a stop to it myself, but I know he's keen that the investigation into his daughter's death should progress as quickly as possible. He is desperate to find out who the culprit is."

"We all are," I added.

"Indeed."

She gave me an odd look and turned away. I knocked on the library door and heard James' voice telling me to enter.

"It's why the negro maid was dismissed, you know," said Mrs Craughton, who had unexpectedly paused and turned to face me again.

"Who?" I asked.

"Betsy. For listening at doors."

"Where is Betsy now?" I asked.

She turned and walked away from me without giving a reply.

I entered the library feeling a little perturbed by my conversation with Mrs Craughton. I thought of her handkerchief I had found under my bed and shivered.

"Morning, Penny!" said James. "Are you all right?" He had noticed the bothered expression on my face.

"I don't know. I've just had an odd conversation with the housekeeper. She has become rather hostile towards me. I think it's because I'm helping you."

"I'm sure it is," said Inspector Trotter, lighting his pipe. "You've broken rank, you see. Servants are rather peculiar about that sort of thing."

I gave the inspector the notes I had written so far.

"Thank you, Miss Green. You have neat handwriting."

"You'll notice that I redrew the map Mr Perrin had sketched. His version wasn't quite accurate."

"Really?"

"He'd placed Ralph Lombard next to Sophia, when I can clearly recall that he was sitting beside Lady Wyndham."

"Is that right?" Inspector Trotter opened his beleaguered notebook and compared the two drawings.

"Interesting," he said. "And you are quite sure of your version of events, are you? There is no chance that you could be mistaken?"

"Obviously, I have only my memory to rely upon, but it's usually quite good. I am as clear as I possibly can be that this is how the guests were sitting that evening."

"I find it rather intriguing that the butler might have made a mistake in his plan," said Inspector Trotter. "He seems such a precise, accurate sort of man."

"Is he intentionally trying to mislead us?" asked James.

"He might be, but I doubt it. He doesn't seem the sort."

"The housekeeper told me that the Lombards are returning for further interviews today," I said.

"They are indeed," replied James.

"It will be interesting to hear what they have to say," I said. "And you need to find Betsy, James. I keep hearing her name mentioned, and I see that Mr Perrin also referred to her in his interview. Mrs Craughton told me just now that Betsy was dismissed for eavesdropping. I haven't met the girl because she left before I began my work here, but I understand she and Miss Sophia were close. Maisie says that Miss Sophia confided in her."

"Yes, it would be incredibly helpful to have her testimony," said James.

"Do you know where she is now? Inspector Trotter, there was a section of Mr Perrin's interview which I couldn't transcribe because it was blotted out by the spilled coffee. However, I imagine that it contained some more information about Betsy. The more I think about her, the more I believe she may hold some important information."

"She might indeed, if that were possible," replied Inspector Trotter.

"Did Mr Perrin tell you where you could find her?" I asked.

"He did. And he told me a little more than that, in fact."

"Perfect!" I said. "She will be extremely useful, I feel sure of it. There is nothing quite like a nosy maid to fill us in."

"Penny, I'm afraid that's not possible," said James, his face sombre. "I have already tried to find Betsy."

"Has she moved away?"

"No. I'm afraid she's dead."

I gripped the back of a nearby chair to steady myself.

"She can't be!"

"Do you recall that when I came to the *Morning Express* offices early last month you had just reported on the tragic murder of Elizabeth Wiggins?"

"Yes, the woman who was beaten by her husband."

"Indeed. Well it seems that Elizabeth Wiggins is the Betsy in question."

"The same woman?" I stared down at the carpet for a moment, which, despite my hard work, still bore a stain from the coffee spillage. "How do you know this?"

"When I asked Perrin where I could find Betsy, he told me that she had sadly lost her life," said Inspector Trotter. "When I questioned him further about the circumstances, he told me that she had been murdered by her husband in Battersea almost four weeks ago. He remembered the very day; the man seems to have a good memory for dates. The murder occurred on Tuesday the fourth of March."

"And you're sure it's the same woman?"

"Yes, I've confirmed with Mr Glenville that Betsy's surname was Wiggins," said Inspector Trotter.

"But that's dreadful! I only knew of her as Elizabeth. I had no idea she was also known as Betsy."

"Households often like to shorten maids' names, as you well know, Flo," said James.

My legs felt weak. I sat down in the chair I had been leaning against.

"Betsy would have known a good deal more about Miss Sophia," I lamented. "She would have been able to help us. Now there are some details which we will never discover."

CHAPTER 30

The Lombard family arrived at ten o'clock. I served them coffee in the dining room.

"Well, here we are again," said Ralph Lombard. "Another day being taken up by merely repeating to the police what we've already told them." He smoothed his thin hair into place.

"They have their reasons for doing these things, dear," said Mary Lombard. Tipsy sat on her lap and licked her chin.

Dudley Lombard's face was red and blotchy. "I wish to see her!" he demanded. "May I please see Sophia?" he asked Mrs Craughton more politely.

The housekeeper escorted him to the morning room, and a moment later Mr Glenville entered the room to greet the Lombards. Although there were still dark shadows beneath his eyes, he looked better than when I had seen him last. Tipsy jumped off Mary Lombard's lap and trotted over to him.

"How are you bearing up, old chap?" asked Ralph Lombard.

"I've been better," Mr Glenville replied.

"Is there any word yet on when the funeral will be held?" asked Mrs Lombard.

"Next week some time. Camilla and I are discussing the date with the vicar of St. Michael's. I'm so sorry you've been dragged back here again. Inspector Trotter has a detective from Scotland Yard helping him now, so hopefully we'll get to the bottom of Sophia's death quickly."

"Scotland Yard? Goodness, you must be important!" said Mary Lombard.

"How did you wrangle that one, Alexander?" her husband asked.

"I didn't, particularly. The chap just turned up." Mr Glenville bent down to make a fuss of Tipsy, whose tail wagged happily. "I can't deny that I'm pleased to have the Yard's assistance," he continued. "Where's Dudley?"

"He's gone to see her," said Mary Lombard quietly.

"Oh."

"Have you spent much time with her?" she half-whispered.

"Yes, I have. Not as much as Camilla. She has been reluctant to leave Sophia's side at all. It's understandable."

"She's spending time with her while she still can."

"Indeed." Mr Glenville's voice cracked slightly.

The door opened and Dudley Lombard entered the room. His face was pale and his droopy lower lip wobbled.

"You weren't in there long, darling," commented Mary Lombard.

"I couldn't bear it for long, Ma. She's so... still."

"Yes, of course, dear."

"Still and silent. She was never like that while she was alive!"

"No, she wasn't, darling."

"I think I prefer to remember her how she was."

"Yes, of course."

"Alive."

"Indeed, my dear."

Mrs Lombard took her son's arm and patted it reassuringly. He pushed his fingertips into his eyes, as if he were trying to stem the flow of tears.

"We were to be married in six weeks' time. Just six weeks!" said Dudley. "She was to have been my wife. I can't understand it. I cannot believe that she's no longer here. In fact, I'm certain that it cannot be true, I keep expecting her to walk into the room and look at me in the way she always looked at me, with those loving brown eyes. I called them puppy-dog eyes. She had that way of looking at me, and I remember feeling so proud that we were to be married. I feel certain this is just a bad dream from which I will soon wake. Indeed, it's more than a bad dream. It's a living nightmare. I cannot believe that it's true! I refuse to believe that it's true!"

Much as I sympathised with Dudley Lombard's grief, I couldn't help feeling an unexplained dislike for the boy. It seemed odd that I considered him a boy when he was my senior by a year. *How could Mr Glenville have considered this grown-up child a suitable future owner for his business?*

"Chin up, Dudley. Chin up," said Mr Glenville patting him on the shoulder. "Sophia wouldn't have wished to see you so distressed."

The mention of her name caused Dudley to emit another large sob.

"Dudley!" Ralph Lombard said reprovingly.

He gave me an awkward glance, as if he were embarrassed with regard to his son's display of emotion. I busied myself with refilling their cups of coffee.

Mrs Craughton entered the room and immediately approached Mr Glenville.

"May I speak to you, sir?" she asked.

"Of course. Please excuse me a moment," he said to the Lombards.

"*She* has to come too," said the housekeeper, pointing at me.

"Flo, you mean?" Glenville said. "Come on then, Flo."

I joined them in the corridor.

"I'm sorry to disturb you, sir," said the housekeeper, "but the Scotland Yard inspector has asked for Flo's help."

"Has he indeed?"

Mr Glenville gave an impressed nod and smiled at me. I felt a warmth in my face and struggled to pull my eyes away from his once again.

"But it's not convenient, sir," Mrs Craughton objected. "Flo has so many chores to do today."

"What's he asked Flo to help with?"

"He says she's good at writing, sir. She's been helping to rewrite Inspector Trotter's notes after he ruined his notebook by spilling coffee on it. And it seems they are so impressed that they require her to take down notes during the interviews they're conducting today."

I felt a skip of excitement in my chest. *James was involving me in the investigation as best he could.*

"They will be interviewing each of the Lombards today, sir," continued the housekeeper.

"Is it for today only?"

"I hope so! Flo is a maid, not a police officer! I have concerns about privacy, sir. I don't think it right that a maid should be privy to police matters."

"The inspectors clearly trust her. Who am I to question their judgement?"

"Quite so, sir. But it's simply not convenient."

I chose not to speak. Instead, I allowed them to make up their minds about me as if I wasn't present.

"Can't Maisie pull her weight a bit more today?" Mr

Glenville asked the housekeeper. "The girl's been hanging about like a wet blanket the past few days. I don't mind Flo writing notes for the inspectors. If the speed of their work can be increased by them not having to record the statements themselves, so be it. I won't expect the full range of usual chores to be completed today, Mrs Craughton."

"But it's terribly inconvenient, sir. It can only be for one day. She cannot possibly do it again tomorrow."

"I agree. Just one day, Mrs Craughton. Keep them well supplied with refreshments, if you please."

"Indeed I will, sir."

The housekeeper gave me a frosty stare and I felt immensely happy that I was to hear all that the Lombards had to say for themselves.

CHAPTER 31

Mr Glenville accompanied me into the library, where James and Inspector Trotter were preparing themselves for the interviews.

"A busy day for you inspectors, isn't it?" he said to them. "Let's hope that by the end of it you have a good idea of who may be responsible. It's unimaginable to think that any of these good friends of mine could have been behind it, but it's clear that someone I have previously trusted must have been. It's a bitter pill to swallow, let me tell you."

"Of course, Mr Glenville. It's an extremely difficult time for your family," James said.

I watched to see if James displayed any signs of his underlying dislike for Mr Glenville, but I saw none.

"I do wonder if someone made a terrible mistake," said Mr Glenville.

"What sort of mistake?" asked James.

"I believe the murderer may have intended to kill someone else."

"Such as whom?"

"The most obvious target is myself, isn't it? Much as I

would like everyone to adore me, I cannot pretend that they do. I'm aware that I have my critics. Loud, outspoken critics, who disagree with the way I run my factories. There are others who accuse me of financial misdemeanours. I don't understand why anyone would want to harm my daughter, but I understand why many people might want to harm *me*."

"Surely there is no one who wishes you dead, Mr Glenville?" asked James. "And your guests on the evening of Miss Sophia's birthday celebrations were your friends, were they not?"

"They were people I called friends, but you never know when someone might become a turncoat, do you, Inspector? It's no secret that Wyndham and I had our disagreements over the years. Someone in that room could have been instructed to poison me. Even paid to do it. It's not unheard of for servants to do such a thing, is it?"

"Not unheard of, no," James replied.

"All this is mere conjecture, but it's something I wanted to mention to you because I don't want it overlooked during your investigation. If you wish me to give you a list of my enemies, I'll happily provide it. It's quite long, I can tell you!"

Mr Glenville laughed, and James and Inspector Trotter smiled.

Then Mr Glenville's face turned serious and he lowered his voice. "When I discover who's behind this poisoning, I won't hold back."

"The strong arm of the law will deal with the culprit, Mr Glenville," James confirmed, seemingly unbothered by Mr Glenville's change in tone.

"But is the arm of the law strong enough, Inspector? With regard to what I have in mind for the culprit, I suspect not."

His eyes seemed to grow darker, and he watched each of our faces closely. No one spoke for a moment.

Then Mr Glenville appeared to brighten up. "Anyway, now

that has been said, I hope the interviews go well today. I'm pleased that Flo is able to assist you with them. I often think her active brain requires a more cerebral activity than menial maid's work."

He gave me a broad smile and left the room.

"Glenville likes you, doesn't he, Miss Green?" observed Inspector Trotter.

I shrugged, unsure how to answer him.

James sighed. "Those were some strong words from a man who may have committed the crime himself. There's something about him I don't like."

"You think he'd murder his own daughter?" I asked.

"It would be a cruel act. But I don't believe it's beyond him," replied James.

"You're only saying that because you have never liked him. But shouldn't you forget about your personal thoughts and consider him objectively?" I said.

"Yes, that's what we detectives are supposed to do. But what if a detective has a hunch?"

"Are hunches usually correct?" I asked.

"I think they are," Inspector Trotter interjected.

"For once I agree with Trotter," said James. "Hunches may be unscientific, but they can't be ignored."

"Well, I have a hunch that Mr Glenville isn't the culprit, so where does that leave us?" I retorted.

"We're the detectives, Miss Green," lisped Inspector Trotter.

"So your hunches are worthier than mine?" I asked.

"In a case such as this, I think they have to be," replied the inspector. "Now, isn't the housekeeper supposed to be bringing us more coffee?"

Their comments made me feel even more determined to

prove that someone other than Mr Glenville was behind Sophia's death.

James looked up at the portrait of the two children and grimaced. "That pair frightens me. Who are they?"

"I've no idea," I replied. "But I call them the ghost twins."

"That's a fair description," said James.

"Let's get on with the interviews, shall we?" suggested Inspector Trotter.

"Yes, let's," replied James. "Are you ready, Penny?"

I sat myself at the table with a pen, pot of ink and James' notebook.

"I think so."

"We need you to do more than just write," said James. "You were there when Miss Sophia died. While these people are talking, please consider how well their testimony matches up with your own recollections of the evening. Make a note of anything which doesn't seem right to you."

"I will do. And I've been thinking about Betsy. You could speak to her brother, you know. I interviewed him shortly after her death. If you can find a copy of the *Morning Express* from the fifth of March, you will see the article there. I can't quite remember his name. He's a dark-skinned man."

"Thank you, Penny, that's a good idea," replied James. "Battersea, isn't it?"

"Yes. Gonsalva Road, I remember that. It's close to Wandsworth Road Station."

"I know the area well. It's not far from where my grandfather lived. Right, we'll get Master Dudley Lombard in first, shall we, Trotter?"

Inspector Trotter nodded.

"I should warn you that Master Lombard was rather emotional just now," I said.

"Thank you, Penny," said James. "Extreme displays of

emotion can sometimes be used to cover up a person's true feelings, so we'll keep a close eye on this one."

Dudley Lombard sat in his chair looking desperately sorry for himself.

"She was as pretty as a picture that evening," he mumbled, fidgeting with his fingers. "She looked beautiful in her birthday gown. She only wanted a small celebration; that was Sophia for you. She didn't like a fuss. That was why we only had a small gathering. The dinner was very agreeable. And after that... I can't bring myself to even think about it."

"Did you see anyone else pick up Sophia's glass or put anything in it?" asked James.

"I cannot bear to think about it."

"I understand your distress, Master Lombard, but can you please bring yourself to think about it? You may have seen something which proves important in our investigation," James coaxed.

"I cannot bring myself to take my mind back to that terrible evening, sir!"

"Please Mr Lombard, for your fiancée's sake. She deserves justice. We need to find out who did this to her," said James.

Dudley Lombard scratched his neck.

"Very well," he replied. "No, I didn't see anyone else near her glass. I imagine the butler perhaps topped up her glass with champagne. That must have been done at some point during the evening. But I didn't see anyone doing anything suspicious. There. That is all I can bring myself to think about regarding the whole unfortunate incident."

"Three days before her death, Miss Sophia was seen returning to the house late one evening," said Inspector Trotter. "Were you with her on the evening of Wednesday the twenty-sixth of March?"

Dudley's droopy, red eyes widened. "She went out? Where?"

"That is what we're trying to find out, Mr Lombard," the inspector added.

"But she must have told someone where she was going, surely?"

"It appears that she didn't."

"But that's ridiculous! She wouldn't have been allowed out if she'd refused to tell anyone where she was going!"

"She left the house in secret, Master Lombard."

"But why?"

"That is what we're trying to establish. She didn't leave the house to meet you that evening?"

"No, she didn't. I think I was at the Garrick Club with Pa that evening. I didn't see Miss Sophia at all."

"Thank you, Master Lombard."

"But why would she leave the house like that? What was she doing?"

"As I have already said, Master Lombard, that is what we are still trying to discover," replied Inspector Trotter, losing patience with each response.

"You'll let me know as soon as you do, won't you?" said Dudley Lombard. "I cannot understand what the girl was up to." He shook his head in dismay. "I wonder..."

"You wonder what, Master Lombard?"

"Nothing. It's nothing. Just let me know what she was up to as soon as you find out. You don't think it could be connected to her death, do you?"

"Your guess is as good as ours," said James.

"Inspector, you have to find out who did this to her. She was to have been my wife!"

"Master Lombard, can I ask if you have ever harboured any affection for Miss Sophia's sister, Miss Jane?" asked James.

Dudley's face reddened. "No, of course not. What a ridiculous notion!"

"We have heard it reported that you propositioned her."

"Who said that?"

"It doesn't matter who said it, Master Lombard. Is it true?"

"Of course not! Why would I do such a thing? I loved Sophia! Marrying her would have made all my dreams come true!"

"Indeed," said James. "In the meantime, can you please draw a quick plan of the drawing room and add notations to explain who sat where?"

James passed him a piece of paper and a pencil.

"I can't remember that!"

"Please draw what you can remember, Master Lombard. Where did you sit?"

"By the window."

"Can you please draw that for us?"

"I can't remember where anyone else was."

"Please try your best."

Ralph Lombard was impatient and fidgety as he sat opposite the two inspectors.

"You'd like me to repeat *everything* I've already told you?" he asked Inspector Trotter.

"How long have you known the Glenville family?" asked James.

Ralph Lombard sighed with exasperation. "As I have already explained to your police colleague, I have known them both since Alexander and Camilla's engagement. My family and Camilla's have been close for a number of generations. I first met Alexander at their engagement party, and we got along from the very first moment we met. We're men of enterprise, you see. Our journeys to this point have been quite different, but here we both are doing similar work, and we have the same interests."

"Which interests are they?"

"As I say, Inspector, I'm a man of enterprise. I own a gin distillery in Vauxhall. I inherited it from my father, and my son Dudley will inherit it from me. He was to have run the place with Sophia..." He paused to wipe his forehead with his handkerchief. "She was a clever girl. A very clever girl. The two of them would have done a good job. I felt content knowing that the family business was to rest in their hands. The distillery and the vinegar factories; they would have been in charge of it all! It was the perfect match for both our families, and now... Well, now I have no idea what happens. Dudley will inherit my distillery regardless, but as for Blundell's, that's anyone's guess. Glenville can't possibly pass it on to the idiot boy. I suppose Jane will inherit it now, although they had plans for her to marry a baronet or similar. Alternatively, Glenville will have to consider one of the younger ones, and they're too young to—"

"My apologies for interrupting, Mr Lombard, but time is not on our side," said James. "I wish to discuss the events of the evening with you. Can you tell me what happened at the party?"

"We had a rather fine meal and everyone was in good spirits. In fact, there was not a cross word exchanged between Sophia and any of the guests. Had there been, my suspicions would fall upon the person with whom she had argued."

As I wrote his words down I recalled Sophia's sulky, disinterested face that evening.

"But there was no disagreement at all!" he continued. "Everyone was very pleasant, and it was a very enjoyable evening, until... I can't bear to relive it, I'm afraid, Inspector.

I daren't recall the terrible memory for fear of it embedding itself deeply into my mind. That poor girl."

"Did you witness anyone tampering with Miss Sophia's champagne glass, Mr Lombard?"

"No one! I don't understand it. Even if the girl had poisoned herself, someone surely would have witnessed her tipping the powder into her own glass."

"How was your relationship with Miss Sophia, Mr Lombard?" asked James.

"She was my future daughter-in-law! Mrs Lombard and I only have one child, Inspector. She was to become the daughter I had never had."

"You got along well with her, then?"

"Yes, of course."

"Did you see anyone attempting to hide the empty packet of cyanide on the chair which was occupied by Viscount Wyndham and your wife during the course of the evening?" asked James.

"No, I didn't; not a bit of it. It's a very strange business, that. The murderer might have planted it there later that evening, perhaps even the following day. It wasn't found until the next day, am I right?"

"You're correct, sir," said Inspector Trotter.

"There you go, you see. It could have been anyone. Even a member of the staff. Perhaps the maid who claims to have found it."

I felt him glance over at me, but I didn't lift my eyes from the page.

"This maid is your secretary now, is she, Inspectors?" He chuckled. "A woman of many talents, it seems. You do see my point about the packet of poison, though, don't you? There's no evidence that it was placed there at the time of Miss Sophia's death."

"However, it's rather a coincidence, isn't it Mr Lombard?" probed Inspector Trotter.

"Yes, which is why the murderer has presumably put it there intentionally. Any murderer worth his salt would never be so remiss as to hide it on his own chair, would he?"

"I don't know, Mr Lombard. I must always keep an open mind," said James. "Were you aware of Miss Sophia's attempts to leave home without her parents' permission? She ran away on one occasion, and on another she left the house secretly to meet with someone."

Mr Lombard's face darkened. "I wasn't aware of this at all. What was the girl up to?"

"That's what we'd like to find out."

"Well, I thought Glenville had tighter reins on her than that. It's not right that a young lady should go off as she pleases. A young lady, engaged to be married, out on her own. And in the evening, too, you say? How utterly shameful." He shook his head. "Shameful. I hope you get to the bottom of it, Inspector. The girl could be a bit of a handful like that. Much as I was fond of her, I found myself wishing at times that she were more like her sister, Jane."

James asked Mr Lombard to draw a plan of where everyone had been sitting that evening, and he obliged. Ralph Lombard also took great pains to reveal the fact that Viscount Wyndham had spent longer sitting on the chair upon which the cyanide packet had been found than Mary Lombard had.

CHAPTER 32

"Tipsy! Over here, my pretty! Leave the maid alone!"

Mary Lombard's interview was interrupted on frequent occasions by her dog. She had refuted any suggestion that she should leave the animal out in the corridor.

"I won't hear of it, Inspector! She would cry at the door terribly. She can't bear to let me out of her sight."

Mrs Lombard wore a black satin dress with a large gather of lace at her throat.

"Your husband tells us that you have known the Glenville family a long time," said Inspector Trotter.

"Yes, I've known Camilla since we were debutantes, and I met Alexander when she became engaged to him. A surprising choice for her, really, but I suppose Camilla had always been rather limited in her options. She only had her family name to recommend her. There was very little money left in the family by the time she married him. She was just what Alexander was looking for. The marriage gave them both what they needed."

"Can you give me your account of the evening, please, Mrs Lombard?" asked Inspector Trotter.

"Must I do so again?"

"If you would, please."

"But why?"

"Inspector James Blakely of Scotland Yard would also like to hear your account."

"Would he?" Mrs Lombard appeared rather flattered by this remark, and she recounted the entire evening as she remembered it, including the conversations that took place and what everyone had worn that night. As I wrote down her account, it seemed to be quite accurate.

"It was rather pleasant up until... well, I needn't elaborate," she said. "As I have told you before, Inspector Trotter, we should have married them sooner. This should never have happened if Dudley and Sophia had already been married."

"Mrs Lombard," said James. "Shortly before her death, Miss Sophia left this house late one evening, She did so of her own accord, and in secret. Have you any prior knowledge of this?"

"She left the house on her own? At night?" Her mouth hung open for a moment. "Why should I know anything about that? It seems most inappropriate to me. And dangerous. As I have said a number of times now, if she and Dudley had been already married it would never have happened. Quiet, Tipsy!"

The dog lay down at my feet.

"So you were not aware that Miss Sophia had left the house at night on that occasion, or on any other occasion?"

"No."

James sighed and sat back in his chair. His expression suggested that he was losing his patience.

"It really is a puzzle," he began. "For some time now we have been trying to understand why Miss Sophia might have left the house in that manner. Was she meeting someone? We're inclined to think that she was. But whom? Your son says he has no knowledge of the evening excursion either. Can it really be that no one knew what her intention was?"

Mrs Lombard shrugged her shoulders.

"You were a young woman once, Mrs Lombard," continued James. "What do you think a girl of almost eighteen is getting up to when she secretly leaves her home late in the evening?"

"I couldn't possibly say. I never did such a thing myself!"

"She must surely have been meeting someone, mustn't she? The question is, with whom was she meeting? As it was a secret rendezvous, I can only surmise that it was a person she wasn't at liberty to see in public. Do you think Miss Sophia was looking forward to marrying your son, Mrs Lombard?"

I clenched my teeth at the directness of the question.

"Of course she was! What nonsense are you suggesting here, Inspector?"

"I only ask because she confided to at least one person that she had no wish to marry him."

"Ridiculous!" A piece of spittle flew out from Mrs Lombard's mouth. "It was arranged many years ago that Miss Sophia and my son were to be married. They were both looking forward to their forthcoming nuptials. They were in love!"

"Were they really in love, Mrs Lombard?"

She glared at James, her violet eyes unblinking.

"Yes! They were sweethearts! There was never any question of them not marrying. I don't know to whom Miss Sophia spouted this nonsense, but she never expressed any reluctance to anyone in my family or her own."

"Can you be sure of that, Mrs Lombard?"

"What more can I say, Inspector? You've pushed this far

enough. You must leave the topic well alone now. This can do nothing to help solve the mystery of the poor girl's death."

"This is pure speculation on my part, Mrs Lombard, but I think Miss Sophia may have gone to meet a gentleman when she left the house late that evening. That was why she was so secretive. She was terrified that someone might find out about it."

Mrs Lombard remained silent.

"Is that theory nothing but wild speculation on my part, or do you suspect that there is an element of truth to it?" James asked.

"Mere speculation, I should say. It has nothing to do with the girl's death. Can I leave now, Inspector?" She stood and picked Tipsy up.

"Very shortly, yes. I shall quickly finish expressing my thoughts first, however, if you don't mind. I will have to speculate further, as I fear that I have not received honest answers from everyone I have spoken to so far—"

"How insulting!"

"Please do let me finish, Mrs Lombard, it won't take much longer. We're reaching the stage of the investigation at which speculation cannot get us any further. What we need now are some facts, and it's enormously frustrating when the people we question withhold them. I've spoken to you, your husband and your son this morning, Mrs Lombard, and I feel certain that at least one of you has some information which you haven't yet disclosed. In your minds it may not seem relevant to the murder inquiry, but Inspector Trotter and I should be the judge of that. So before you leave, Mrs Lombard, can I urge you to consider for *one last time* whether there is anything more you should tell us?"

"What do you think my husband and son might be concealing?"

She gripped the little dog tightly, but Tipsy didn't seem to mind.

"I'm asking *you*, Mrs Lombard. What are *you* not telling me?"

"Nothing whatsoever."

"A girl has lost her life, Mrs Lombard. This isn't the time for secrets. Rest assured that we will find out the true facts of this case eventually, and at that time it would be rather embarrassing for anyone who had refused to tell us something when initially asked. It wouldn't look good in a court of law, would it?"

"A court of law?"

"That's what I said."

"You cannot take me into a court of law!"

"You could be subpoenaed, Mrs Lombard, if needs be. As I say, it would be rather embarrassing—"

"All right, Inspector!" snapped Mary Lombard. "I've heard enough! There is only one small matter which I haven't told you. It's really not relevant at all, but I'll say it anyway, just so I can leave this stifling room. We knew about Miss Sophia. We knew there was another gentleman on the scene."

James slapped his palms down on the table with relief. "Thank you, Mrs Lombard. Thank you for being honest with me. When you say *we*, I assume you mean you, your husband and your son?"

"Not Dudley. Just Ralph and I. We didn't dare tell Dudley. It would have destroyed him."

"And may I ask how you knew of this assignation?"

"We received a letter."

"From whom?"

"It was anonymous."

"Why would someone send you such a letter anonymously?"

"I have no idea."

"Can you remember exactly when you received the letter?"

"It was about two months ago."

"And is it still in your possession?"

"No. We threw it into the fire. We refused to believe it, anyway. May I go now, Inspector? I really have had enough. I find all this terribly distressing."

"Did you discuss the letter with Mr and Mrs Glenville?"

"Of course not! The only people who read it were my husband and I. May I leave now?"

"Yes, Mrs Lombard. Thank you very much for your time and your honesty."

Mary Lombard swept out of the room with Tipsy under her arm.

"Time to call Ralph Lombard back in," said James.

"Oh no, must we?" I said. "Won't he be short-tempered with us?"

"Probably. But the man hasn't been honest with us, has he? He didn't mention that he knew of Miss Sophia's other suitor."

"What is it this time?" fumed Ralph Lombard as he marched into the library again. "When will I be able to leave this infernal house?"

I could certainly empathise with this sentiment.

"We won't detain you any longer than is necessary," said James.

He repeated to Ralph Lombard what his wife had just told us about the anonymous letter. As Ralph Lombard listened, his shoulders slumped a little, and then he sat down in a chair, wiping his face with his hands.

"Can you confirm, Mr Lombard, that your wife's account is correct?" asked James.

"Yes, I can confirm it," he replied meekly, running a hand through his thin hair.

"And you had no wish to tell us of this yourself?"

"I had my reasons, Inspector; the main one being pride. No one wishes it to become public knowledge that he has a cuckold for a son."

"I appreciate it is a sensitive matter, Mr Lombard. Have you ever discussed it with Mr Glenville?" Inspector Trotter asked.

"As a matter of fact, I did."

"Did you show the letter to him?"

"Yes."

"And did he have any idea who might have written it?"

"He said he couldn't be certain, but he suspected that it was the housekeeper's handwriting."

I accidentally blotted the page with ink when I heard this last part.

Mrs Craughton?

"You believe the housekeeper, Mrs Craughton, wrote you a letter to inform you that Miss Sophia was meeting with another prospective suitor?"

"Yes."

"Did you discuss it with her?"

"Not directly, no. Glenville told me he'd speak to her about it. Like me, he was rather embarrassed by the situation. The wedding had been arranged for such a long time, you see, and the future of our businesses depended on the union. I hoped that Glenville would sort it out. He clearly didn't, because the girl was off gallivanting again just last week, was she not?"

"Did you feel any anger towards Miss Sophia?"

"No."

"Mr Lombard, can I ask if you ever approached Mr and Mrs Glenville about your son marrying Miss Jane instead?" asked James.

Ralph Lombard reddened.

"Did you?" asked James again. "It would make sense, would it not, if the proposed marriage to Miss Sophia wasn't going to plan? After all, your ultimate goal was to unite your family businesses."

"It was a fleeting thought," admitted Ralph Lombard after a long pause.

"Did you discuss it with them?"

"Briefly. But they have other plans for Miss Jane. She is to marry a society man. She has this patroness, this elderly dowager, who has taken an interest in her future."

"But despite this, you made the request, Mr Lombard, because you were not convinced that Miss Sophia would be a suitable wife for your son. Is that an accurate appraisal?"

"No!"

CHAPTER 33

"Well done, Blakely," said Inspector Trotter once Ralph Lombard had left the room. "What made you so sure that the Lombards were holding something back?"

"I wasn't," replied James. "It was a bit of luck, really. I was getting tired of the rather dull replies to our questions. I decided it was worth a shot to find out whether they knew more about Miss Sophia than they had cared to admit."

"It paid off," I said. "Well done, James!"

"I don't think the Lombards cared which of the Glenville daughters their son married," continued James. "The important matter was that he was married into the Glenville family, so that their son's personal and professional future was secured. Perhaps Miss Sophia was proving to be too much of a troublemaker for their liking."

I considered this theory. It made sense.

Besides, hadn't Mrs Lombard sat in the chair upon which the empty packet of cyanide had been found?

"Now we will need to speak to Mrs Craughton again," said

James. "We need to ascertain why she sent such a letter to the Lombards."

The housekeeper refused to speak to James and Inspector Trotter with me in the room taking down the notes.

"The girl is my junior," she said, giving me a withering glance.

While Mrs Craughton was in the library, I went down to the kitchen to make some tea. Maisie stood at the table cleaning silver cutlery. She looked painfully thin and miserable.

"Are you sure you're all right, Maisie?" I asked. "I'm worried about you."

"Why?" She looked up at me, her eyes wide and fearful.

"You seem so sad."

"Yeah, well, Miss Sophia's dead and I'm worried it's 'cause of summink I done."

"Such as what, Maisie? What might you have done?"

She rubbed repeatedly at the handle of the fork in her hand.

"It was nuffink much. I didn't mean no 'arm by it. It's proberly nuffink to do with what 'appened."

"What is it you're trying to tell me, Maisie?"

"Nuffink. It's nuffink."

"But it must be something, because I can see that it's bothering you. Even something which seems small and irrelevant might be important. That's what Inspector Blakely and Inspector Trotter told me."

"I ain't tellin' 'em nuffink!"

"There's nothing to worry about. They need all the information they can get, that's all. They won't hold you responsible for anything you may have done."

"You don't understand 'ow it really is, Flo. You ain't been 'ere long enough ter understand."

Her face hardened, and I could tell that the moment when she had been ready to confide in me had passed.

"Maisie, it's important."

"But it ain't, though." She held up the fork to examine it, then rubbed at it furiously once again.

"Please, Maisie."

I realised that the more I pleaded with her, the more determined she was to keep from me what was on her mind.

Was she really in danger, as James suspected?

I knew that I would need to be careful if there was any truth to his suspicions.

"Thank you for your help today, Miss Green," said Inspector Trotter as I handed him the notes I had written down during the interviews. "I'll take these back to the station and have a read through them. Same time tomorrow, Blakely?"

"Indeed. See you then, Trotter. We have Viscount Wyndham and Lady Wyndham coming tomorrow."

Inspector Trotter quit the room, leaving me and James alone at the table in the library.

"How did you get on with the housekeeper?" I asked.

"She admits that she sent the letter to the Lombards. She said that she hadn't mentioned it sooner because she hadn't considered it relevant. As to why she sent it, I simply don't know. She says that she wanted the Lombards to know what Miss Sophia was really like. I don't think she held the girl in high regard, did she?"

"She didn't seem to. She has often called her ungrateful. I wonder if Mrs Craughton was even envious of Miss Sophia. She saw a clever young woman who had everything she could possibly want given to her, and yet she didn't seem at all happy with her lot. Mrs Craughton probably didn't understand it. I don't see why she felt the need to meddle in the proposed marriage, however."

"Exactly. And I don't know why she didn't tell us sooner that she knew Miss Sophia had another suitor. She didn't admit that to you, did she?"

"No."

"She sketched a plan of where everyone was sitting that evening. Does it appear accurate to you?"

I looked at the sketch. Mrs Craughton had clearly labelled each person.

"Yes, it looks about right to me," I said. "Do you still think Mr Glenville is behind this, James?"

"I believe so. But there's little evidence pointing to him at the moment."

"You still don't like him, do you?"

"I don't, I'm afraid."

"He gave me his permission to help you today."

"Yes, he did. That's something to be grateful for, isn't it?"

"There's more evidence connecting the Lombards to Miss Sophia's death than there is connecting Mr Glenville."

"That seems to be true at the moment, Penny, but let's wait and see. Oh, darn it! I meant to mention something about the cyanide packet to Trotter."

James leafed through his notebook and pulled out a small envelope. Inside it was the empty packet of poison.

"I was examining this yesterday evening as I mulled over the day's events," he said. "And look here. There's something interesting on one side of this packet."

He laid it in his palm and moved closer to me, so that I could see better. My heart skipped as I smelt the familiar scent of his eau de cologne.

"Look. On this side of the packet the paper is slightly

thinner, as if some of it has been torn away. And have you noticed this slight red stain?"

I peered more closely at the square of paper in the palm of his hand. "Where?"

"The light's not very bright in here, is it?"

James glanced around the room before walking over to the mantelpiece and fetching a candle.

"Here." He placed it on the table and lit it with the flint he normally used to light his pipe. "That's better."

He sat down next to me, even closer this time. "Now can you see it, Penny?"

I stared at the packet of poison in the bright, flickering candlelight. "Yes, I see it now."

There was a small patch of roughened paper, as if a part of it had been ripped off, and I could see the faint red mark James had mentioned.

"In fact, if I hold this up to the candle, you can see the light shines more brightly through the part where the paper is thinner. Lean in, Penny, so you can see better."

I lent in close, so that our shoulders pressed together. I didn't realise how near I was until my cheek brushed against his, and I was slightly startled by the roughness of his stubble against my face.

"I see now," I said quietly.

But I wasn't thinking about the empty packet of poison he was holding up. Instead, my thoughts were consumed by how close to him I was at that moment, and how I could hear his soft breath by my ear. I had kissed him once before, while under the influence of alcohol, and had regretted it deeply afterwards. This time I had no excuse to make a second attempt, so I resisted the urge and remained where I was, holding my breath and making the most of this rare moment of intimacy.

"Do you know what I think?" he asked softly.

"What?" I asked cautiously, wondering whether he would refer to the packet of poison or our inappropriate closeness to one another.

"I think this packet has been stuck to something."

James turned his face toward me and I felt his warm breath on my cheek. I didn't dare look at him because I felt sure that I would try to kiss him again. I reminded myself that he was engaged to be married, urging my heart to forget any attraction I felt toward him. I removed my spectacles and stared resolutely at the paper packet in his hand.

"Do you?" I practically whispered.

With the candle burning in front of us, the rest of the room dimmed into darkness. It seemed as if James and I were the only two people in the world.

"Yes. I think someone has attached this packet to something with a blob of wax," he said. "That's what the reddish mark is. Then they've pulled it off again, and some of the paper has been torn off by the wax. Somewhere there must be a piece of wax with some paper residue from this packet stuck to it."

"I think you may be right. I can't think of anything else which would leave such a mark on the packet. That's very clever of you, James."

"There's no need for flattery. I only reached this conclusion after studying the packet for a long time yesterday evening. I don't have much else to do in the evenings, you know."

"Don't you?"

I finally turned to face him. He was so close that I could see the candle flame reflected in his bright blue eyes. I felt conscious that our lips were extremely close.

"No."

"What about Charlotte?"

A flicker passed across his eyes.

"Charlotte?"

"The future Mrs Blakely. Does she not keep you company in the evenings?"

"She lives with her parents in Croydon."

"Oh yes, I remember now. Well, when you are married she will be with you in the evenings."

He looked away and I wished that I hadn't mentioned his fiancée. The air in the room felt slightly cooler all of a sudden.

"Perhaps you are one of those women who becomes rather excitable about weddings. I can't say I care much for them myself," he said.

"No, I don't care much for weddings. Or marriage either. Unless it's to the right person, of course."

He looked at me again and began to smile. "You do say some funny things, Penny! Of course marriage is supposed to be with the right person."

"Yes, it is. There's no use in considering it otherwise, is there?"

"No, there isn't."

His face became serious again as we held one another's gaze. *Did he truly believe that he was marrying the right person?*

A sharp knock at the door startled us so much that James dropped the cyanide packet and I almost fell off my chair as I leapt away from James' side. I smoothed down my apron as Mr Glenville strode in, and felt a cold perspiration on my forehead as he surveyed us both.

"The other chap's gone already, has he?" asked Mr Glenville, staring at me.

"Yes, Inspector Trotter has just left," replied James in a matter-of-fact tone. "Flo and I were just reading through the notes from our interviews with the Lombard family, weren't we, Flo?"

I nodded.

"I see," said Mr Glenville in a slightly reproachful tone.

I felt sure he suspected that something had passed between myself and James. He kept his dark eyes on me as he walked over to the table and joined us.

"Was anything of interest mentioned during the day?" he asked, finally turning his attention to James.

"It was all fairly unremarkable I'm afraid, sir, except for one thing." James leafed through the notes. "Here we are. Mr Lombard mentioned that he once asked you if there was a possibility of a betrothal between his son Dudley and your daughter Jane."

Mr Glenville frowned. "Why should he have told you that?"

"I'm not sure why, exactly. It was simply a piece of information he offered us. Is it correct?"

Mr Glenville sighed and laughed uncomfortably. "Yes, I'm afraid it is. I don't think the chap was ever really serious about Jane. He and Mrs Lombard had some nerves about the marriage as the wedding day grew closer. And Sophia was playing up a bit at the time, as you well know. Dudley is their only son, and they're extremely protective of him. This was the only marriage they would ever have been at liberty to arrange! It's rather different when you have several other children to consider. When compared with her sister, Jane does seem the docile type; however, I put that down to her age. I'm sure that in a few years' time she will be every bit as lively as Sophia was! I told Lombard that and it reassured him. Marriage would have been the making of Sophia. I have no doubt that she would have become a calm and devoted wife. And mother." His voice began to crack. "Sadly, that has all been taken away from us."

"It has indeed," said James. "Thank you, sir, for sharing your feelings on the matter."

"Not at all, my good man. Do please ask if anything else

requires clarification. I'm rather impatient to get this unpleasant business resolved before Sophia's funeral. I should so like her to rest in peace."

"We'll do our best, sir," said James.

"The Wyndhams are coming here tomorrow, aren't they?" said Mr Glenville. "You need a clear and honest answer from Wyndham as to why that empty packet of poison was found on his chair. I'd like to hear his explanation for that."

I readied myself for bed that evening with a range of emotions whirling through my mind. I had enjoyed spending time with James that day, even though Inspector Trotter had been present for much of it. My mind kept wandering back to the moment we had shared as we inspected the empty packet of cyanide. I hadn't wanted that moment to end.

There was no longer any use in denying the fact that I was attracted to James. I had pretended for several months that he was of no interest to me as a suitor. But it seemed that the more I pretended, the more drawn to him I became. I couldn't help myself.

As we shared that special moment in the library, I had felt that I belonged by his side. Although I knew that it was wrong, it hadn't felt wrong. The only matter which seemed incongruous was the fact he was engaged to be married to someone else.

What did he think of during the evenings he spent alone? Was he looking forward to his marriage? Or did he wonder whether he was making a terrible mistake? Was I underestimating his strength of feeling for Charlotte? Did he really care for her and simply pretend to me that he didn't?

I wished I knew the answers to my questions. The only solution was to ask him myself, but there never seemed to be an appropriate time to do so.

CHAPTER 34

Much to Mrs Craughton's consternation, I was permitted to take down the notes from the Wyndhams' interviews the following morning. Lady Wyndham was invited into the library first. Her pretty, heart-shaped face was creased with anguish and she wore a beautiful fitted dress of black silk. She sat down in the chair and immediately began to weep.

James cleared his throat and spoke.

"Are you all right, Lady Wyndham?"

"No. This is distressing; too distressing to discuss. Why won't you allow my husband to accompany me?"

"We won't detain you for long. We must question each guest alone to identify any differences between their versions of events."

"I should warn you that I'm not at my best without my husband by my side."

"We understand that. This isn't easy for anybody. However, it's important that we establish the facts of what happened on the evening of Miss Sophia's death. We're trying to find the person who harmed her."

"Of course." She dabbed at her red eyes with a lace hand-kerchief before giving her brief version of events.

"Did you witness any cross words between Miss Sophia and her siblings?" asked Inspector Trotter.

"No, none at all. It's no secret that she and Master Maurice have their differences, of course. And as for Miss Sophia and Miss Jane, you would never think they were sisters! They're not alike at all. The Glenvilles have had their differences, but I was pleased to see that they had been swept aside for the celebration of Miss Sophia's birthday."

"Did you see anyone pick up Miss Sophia's glass or put anything in it that evening?"

"No, I didn't. If I had, the case would be easily solved, wouldn't it? I can't bear to think about it, Inspector, I really can't." She dabbed at her eyes again. "One moment Miss Sophia was enjoying herself with her family and friends, and the next she was making that awful... Oh goodness, that noise. That *choking* noise!"

She dissolved into tears.

We waited for Lady Wyndham to compose herself.

"Your husband is a keen photographer, is that right, Lady Wyndham?" asked James.

"Yes, he is," she replied breathlessly.

"On the day of Miss Sophia's death, he and Master Maurice took some photographs and developed them in his dark room."

"Yes."

"Am I right in thinking that one of the many chemicals used to develop photographs is potassium of cyanide?"

She stared at James and I felt my skin prickle as I made the connection between Viscount Wyndham's hobby and the poison.

"I don't know anything about photography, I'm afraid. You would have to ask my husband," she replied sullenly.

Then she suddenly cried out and fresh tears began to flow. Her breathing became quick and shallow.

"Help me, dear!" she cried, stretching out her hand towards me.

I leapt up from my seat and hurried over to her. I took her hand, and noticed that her palm felt cold and clammy. Her eyes were large and watery, and she gasped like a fish.

"I need air!"

I began to feel alarmed, but I suspected that she probably needed her laudanum rather than air.

"Inspector Blakely, Inspector Trotter," I said. "I think we should postpone Lady Wyndham's interview for the time being."

After attending to his wife, Viscount Wyndham joined us in the library. Mrs Craughton brought in coffee and Inspector Trotter lit his pipe.

"How is your wife, Viscount Wyndham?" asked James. "I do apologise for any upset we may have caused. As you can appreciate, this is not an easy task."

"Don't apologise, Inspector! It cannot be helped. You're only doing your job. Lily suffers from a disorder of the nerves."

I had expected Viscount Wyndham to be angry that his wife was upset, but instead he seemed his usual jovial self.

"I believe the young maid, Maisie, is sitting with her at present."

"Thank you for your understanding, Viscount Wyndham," said James. "I know you have already spoken to my colleague, Inspector Trotter, but can you please retell your version of events on the night when Miss Sophia died for my benefit this time?"

"Yes, of course. It's truly dreadful, Inspector. A beautiful young lady having her life cut short in this manner. At the celebration of her birthday! I cannot understand who would commit such a terrible crime. A young, harmless woman. What has this world come to?"

Viscount Wyndham described the evening as I remembered it. His account was thorough, and it was clear that he endeavoured to be as helpful as possible.

"I understand that one of your hobbies is photography," said James.

"Yes, it's a pursuit I have enjoyed for a number of years. It's something Master Maurice is also becoming interested in, and he has visited my dark room a few times now. He needs something to occupy his time, doesn't he? No one will ever employ the poor fellow. While I salute the Glenvilles for not putting the chap into an institution, I do feel that he's rather overlooked much of the time."

"You mention your dark room. This is a facility you've set up in your home?" asked James.

"Yes, in the basement, next to the kitchens."

"Forgive me, Viscount Wyndham. I'm no expert in photography, but I assume the dark room is where you develop your photographs."

"Yes. Once the plates have been exposed, I take them into the dark room, whereupon they're washed with a variety of chemicals to produce the finished photograph."

"You must have in your possession a number of chemicals to produce the photographs. Is that correct?" asked James.

"Yes, that's correct."

"Including potassium of cyanide?"

I watched Viscount Wyndham intently as he cleared his throat. "Yes, including potassium of cyanide. You're quite correct, Inspector."

"And you are aware that cyanide was the cause of Miss Sophia's death."

"Yes, I'm aware of that, Inspector."

"Have you anything further to add in relation to this?"

"Only to say that it is a preposterous idea that I could have poisoned her." Wyndham's short, round frame grew tense. "Do you think for one moment that I would have retrieved a packet of potassium of cyanide from my dark room, brought it with me to the home of a good friend of mine and proceeded to tip the poison into the glass of his eldest daughter? *On her birthday?*"

"I am not accusing you of any crime, Viscount Wyndham," replied James. "I merely wished to highlight the coincidence. Is it possible that someone else might have taken the potassium of cyanide from your dark room without your knowledge and placed it in Miss Sophia's glass?"

"Such as who? Master Maurice? My wife? Quite ridiculous, Inspector. Quite ridiculous."

"We're not accusing anybody of the crime just yet," said James. "But please may I ask whether it's at all possible that someone could have taken the potassium of cyanide from your dark room without your knowledge? Do you keep it locked in a cabinet, or is it merely sitting on a shelf?"

"It's merely sitting on a shelf, Inspector, and it's still sitting there at this very moment. I invite you to visit my dark room and see for yourself!"

"Thank you, Viscount Wyndham, I may take you up on your offer. But how would we know that you did not possess more than one packet of the poison? One may still be sitting on a shelf, but perhaps another has been removed."

"You'd have to take my word for it that there is only one, and that it is safely stored in my dark room."

"Shall we imagine for a moment a scenario in which there were two packets of potassium of cyanide sitting on the shelf of your dark room, Viscount Wyndham?"

"But there has only ever been one!" He leant across the

table and glared at James. "Listen, old chap. I wish to be helpful, but your questions are becoming quite ridiculous!"

"Let's forget the facts for a moment and imagine there was more than one packet of cyanide," James continued without acknowledging the viscount's protests. "If the packets were sitting on the shelf and not under lock and key, could someone have entered your dark room and taken one of the packets without your knowledge?"

"I suppose they could, yes."

"Is the door to your dark room usually kept locked, Viscount Wyndham?"

"No."

"So there is a possibility that someone could have stolen something from the room without you realising?"

"Well, they'd have to get into the house first, and then make their way down to the basement. I haven't noticed anyone breaking into our home, Inspector."

"We can't escape the fact that the empty packet of cyanide used in Miss Sophia's poisoning was found hidden on the chair which you occupied that evening."

"Ah yes. I was wondering when you'd mention that," he sneered in reply.

"Can you explain how it came to be there?"

"No, I can't! I didn't even know it was there until the maid found it the following morning! And don't you forget that Mrs Lombard also sat on that same chair!"

"We haven't forgotten, sir. Do you believe that Master Maurice has the ability to run his father's business?"

"Of course he has! The boy's no fool. People believe he's an idiot because they've never taken a moment to sit down with the chap and realise that he's an extremely intelligent young fellow."

"And you've shared your feelings on this matter with Mr Glenville?"

"Of course! None of this is a secret to him. We've discussed the matter at length in the past."

"And this was the cause of the falling out between you?"

"There's no need to call it that. We disagreed over the matter. I said it then, and I'll say it again now. There is no need for the boy's inheritance to be overlooked. His limbs are subject to involuntary movement and his speech is sometimes difficult to understand. However, the boy should naturally inherit the business. I say that as a childless man who has become interested in the fortunes of the boy as if he were my own son. I think he is unfairly overlooked and, sadly, he is often mocked."

"So the fact that Master Maurice was bypassed in favour of his sister provoked a certain ire for you, Viscount Wyndham?"

"If truth be told, yes. But as I've already said, this is no great secret. Alexander and Camilla are fully aware of how my wife and I feel about the matter. I can't tell Alexander how to run his family, or his business for that matter, so instead I do what I can for the young fellow, and I hope he has grown up realising that there are one or two people out there who will always help him. It can be a cruel world for a boy like Maurice, Inspector."

"Thank you for your time, Viscount Wyndham. That is all we need to discuss with you for the time being," said James.

"Is that it? Don't you have any further questions about the evening? Instead of establishing the facts of what happened, you seem intent on preoccupying yourselves with the chemicals in my dark room! Don't you wish to ask me anything further? I was there the entire time, you know. I witnessed the poor girl's tragic demise first hand."

"That will be all for now, Viscount Wyndham. We shall need to speak to you again, I'm sure."

"Oh dear," I said once Viscount Wyndham had left the room. "He's a nice man and it seems a shame to have upset him."

James gave a hard laugh. "The nice people are often the ones you have to watch out for."

"Does that mean he could have poisoned Sophia?"

"It's a possibility. Although his motive doesn't seem as strong as the Lombards'. Thank you again for all your help, Penny. I'm sorry that you have to return to your maid duties this afternoon. In the meantime, I'll go down to Battersea and see if I can find this brother of Betsy the maid."

"I wish I could come with you," I said.

Inspector Trotter gave me a quizzical look.

Had he realised how I felt about James? I wondered.

"I miss my work as a reporter," I quickly added. "Being out and about is far preferable to being stuck in this house."

"It won't be for much longer," said James reassuringly. "You've been a big help. Let's try and get you out of here before the end of this week. Will you be content with that?"

"I certainly will!"

CHAPTER 35

Mrs Craughton instructed Maisie and me to clean the library that afternoon once the police inspectors had vacated it.

"'Ave they said who they fink done it yet?" asked Maisie as she polished the mahogany table.

"Do you mean the detectives, Maisie?"

"Yeah."

"No, there's a lot of work for them to do yet. But they'll find the killer, I'm sure of it."

I ran my feather duster along the rows of books.

"Will they need ter speak ter me again?"

"Why do you ask? Is there something you wish to tell them?"

My eye was suddenly drawn to a small piece of white paper between two leather-bound volumes.

"No! No, I don't want to tell 'em nuffink'. I was just wond'rin'."

I heard faint footsteps and I turned to see the black, ghostlike figure of Mrs Glenville as she stepped into the room. She moved slowly and her face was terribly thin. It was almost skull-like in appearance.

"My lady!" I exclaimed. "How are you?"

"I think I'm feeling a little brighter today," she said. A faint smile wrinkled her sunken cheeks. "I've decided I need to move about a bit more. I've been in there with her for too long." She sniffed the air. "It smells of pipe smoke in here."

"The police inspectors have been using this room for the past few days," I explained. "They've concluded most of their interviews now."

"Good. But they haven't discovered the culprit, have they?"

"Not yet, no."

She began to twist her black handkerchief around her fingers. "Oh dear," she said. "Oh dear, oh dear."

I became concerned by her distress. "Please come and sit down, my lady," I said, stepping towards her.

"No, I don't want to."

"Can I fetch you something to eat? Something to drink?"

"Thank you, Flo. I'll take care of my lady," said Mrs Craughton, who had suddenly appeared in the room and took Mrs Glenville's arm. "It's time for your next dose of Dr Cobbold's Remedy, my lady. You'll feel better after that."

The housekeeper guided her out of the library, comforting her as if she were a young child.

My attention returned to the small piece of paper I had seen. I pulled it out and saw that it was folded. Upon opening it, I discovered two words written upon it: *Cubby & Bunty*.

I stared at the words, which were written in blue ink with a sloping hand. It looked like Mrs Craughton's handwriting to me.

Cubby and Bunty. Were they nicknames? The names of two pets?

I would have dismissed the piece of paper as meaningless if someone hadn't clearly attempted to conceal it between the two books. The paper was crumpled, as if it had been pushed into place rather briskly.

"Maisie, have you ever heard of Cubby and Bunty?" I asked.

"I 'aven't. Why d'you ask?"

I showed her the piece of paper I had just found.

"Can't read it," she replied.

"This word says Cubby, and that one says Bunty."

"Oh yeah. I can see the 'C' and the 'B'." A rare smile spread across Maisie's face. "Them's funny words. Who wrote 'em?"

"I don't know for sure. I think it's Mrs Craughton's handwriting. But I think someone tried to hide it."

Maisie sniggered. "Why?"

I stared down at the paper again. "I wish I knew."

Mrs Craughton re-entered the room and my initial reaction was to hide the piece of paper, but I knew she had already seen me holding it.

"What's that you have there?" she asked.

"I found it in here. I thought you were with Mrs Glenville."

I was surprised by how quickly the housekeeper had reappeared.

"I was, but she has gone up to her room now. Thank goodness she has decided against returning to her daughter's side for the time being. What is that piece of paper in your hand?"

"I don't know. I think someone tried to hide it, but I cannot tell why."

"Let me see."

She took it from me.

"In fact, it looks like your handwriting, Mrs Craughton."

"It does look rather similar to mine, doesn't it? However, I can assure you that it isn't."

"Do you recognise the names?" I asked her.

"Oddly enough, they seem familiar, but I cannot think where I've heard them before. I'll ask around."

She tucked it into the pocket of her apron.

I wished I had been able to hold on to the scrap so that I could have shown it to James.

Would Mrs Craughton really ask anyone about the paper? Or did she know more about it than she was letting on? Perhaps she was hoping that I would forget about it.

I found it frustrating that I felt unable to fully believe or trust anyone in the house. This feeling was exacerbated because I was carrying out such a great deception myself. I felt I was part of one enormous pretence.

Later that afternoon, I encountered Maurice walking slowly towards the study. I couldn't resist asking him whether he had heard of the two names which had been written on the piece of paper.

"Yes, I kn-know them."

"Who are they?"

"Great-uncles of mine. B-Broderick and Snowdon. Their surname was Noel-J-Johnstone."

"Cubby and Bunty? Are you sure?"

My puzzled face encouraged him to clarify his assertion.

"Follow m-me," he said.

We made slow progress along the corridor, his sticks clicking on the floor as he walked. He stopped by the library.

"In here?" I asked.

Maurice nodded, and I opened the door for him. He walked into the centre of the room and stood facing the portrait of the ghost twins.

"There they are." He slowly raised one stick, which trembled as he pointed it toward the portrait.

"The twin girls?" I asked. "They're called Cubby and Bunty?"

"Boys," he replied. "They're b-boys."

I looked again at the portrait and realised I had made an incorrect assumption. The two young children wore the traditional clothing of boys before they were breeched. Perhaps the curls of their red hair had given them a more feminine appearance. But now I knew they were boys, I could see that the bodices of their dresses were not shaped by a corset as a girl's bodice would have been.

"Why Cubby and Bunty?"

"That's what M-Mother called them. They were n-nicknames her family used."

"They look very alike. Do you know which is Broderick and which is Snowdon?"

"No, I don't. P-perhaps I should!" He smiled and then staggered closer to the portrait. "I th-think this was painted in 1820 or th-thereabouts." He peered at the dark brushstrokes at the foot of the painting. "Yes, 1826."

I stared at the two boys and wondered why someone should want to write their names down on a piece of paper and then hide it between two books in the library. Now that I knew the identity of Cubby and Bunty, I felt even more confused.

"Do you know if they're still alive?" I asked Maurice.

"They're b-buried in the churchyard of St. Michael's. Th-that's where the family v-vault is."

"The Noel-Johnstone family?"

Maurice nodded.

The matter was most perplexing.

"Thank you for showing me, Master Maurice."

"My p-pleasure. You're not like the others, are you?"

My stomach flipped uncomfortably. "I don't know what you mean."

"You're not a usual m-maid. You sp-speak differently."

I worried that, while addressing Maurice, I had been speaking as myself rather than Flo.

"I went to a good school," I replied.

It was the only explanation I could think of whenever anyone pointed out this discrepancy. I wished I hadn't slipped out of character.

"You w-went to a good school and b-became a m-maid?" he asked. He was smiling, but I felt worried that his suspicions had been aroused.

"Yes, my family is quite poor and I had to find work as soon as possible. Besides, I enjoy working as a maid."

"R-really?"

"Perhaps one day I might become a housekeeper."

"I th-think you could do b-better than that."

"Thank you, Master Maurice. I should get on with my work."

"See you later, Flo."

I swiftly left the room and tried to busy myself with the rest of my chores. I only had a few days left, and I fervently prayed that I wouldn't be found out during that time.

CHAPTER 36

When I returned to my room late that evening, I felt sure someone had entered it in my absence once again. The belongings on my dressing table seemed to have been rearranged. I immediately pushed the chair toward the wardrobe and stood on it to feel around for the key.

It was where I had left it.

But not in the same position.

A nauseating weight lurched in my stomach. Each time I had placed the key on top of the wardrobe, I had ensured that the bit of the key faced toward the wall. This time, the bit was facing toward me.

Was it possible that I had placed the key there in that position? I thought about the last time I had hidden it, and felt sure that I had placed it in the same way. It had become a habit of mine.

I picked up the key, stepped down from the chair and dashed over to the trunk beneath my bed. Thankfully, I found it locked. My fingers stumbled as I tried to turn the key in the lock. I pulled the trunk out from underneath my bed and my heart pounded in my ears as I lifted up the lid.

Someone had looked through my papers.

And Mr Glenville's notebook was no longer here.

I wiped my face with my hands and cursed myself for being such a fool. *Why had I not returned the notebook sooner?*

Now someone had gone through my belongings. *But who?*

My papers weren't in complete disarray, but they had been moved about and rearranged in a way that was not my usual habit. The letter from Mr Edwards had been pulled out of its envelope and clumsily pushed back in. *Someone had looked through my papers in a hurry. What had they read? Had they taken anything else?*

My entire body trembled as I sat back on my heels.

Someone in the house knew who I was. It had to be Mrs Craughton, whose handkerchief I had found under my bed. Perhaps I should have confronted her about it sooner. Perhaps if I had returned it to her she would have known I had discovered that she had been poking around in my room.

I imagined her explaining to Mr Glenville that she had found his book in my trunk. I imagined her telling him who I really was.

What would he think of me then? He had liked me. He had trusted me.

Perhaps it wouldn't be as bad as I feared.

My other thought was that perhaps Maisie had been in my room. *Was that what she had wanted to confess to me in the kitchen the previous day?*

I comforted myself with the thought that the intruder might have been Maisie. As she was unable to read, she wouldn't have found out who I really was.

I felt faint. I had to prepare what I might say if confronted by someone who might have discovered my identity. *How could I begin to explain why I had taken Mr Glenville's notebook?*

I regretted agreeing to undertake this undercover assignment more than ever before. The stress and responsibility had felt too great for me to bear. I wished I could run away and escape it all. *If I ran, I would never have to face my accuser. I wouldn't have to pretend any longer. I should have left when I had decided to, and ignored James' entreaties.*

I began to pack my belongings into the trunk for a second time. I would leave at first light; hopefully before the household rose for the day.

As I packed my things away, I thought I heard footsteps in the corridor outside. I quietly opened my door and looked out. I was just in time to see Maisie's door close with a quiet click. I decided to ask her if she had been in my room.

Taking my candle with me, I walked over to her door and knocked gently.

There was no reply.

I knocked again and spoke loudly enough for her to hear me, but quietly enough so that I wouldn't disturb anyone else.

"Maisie? It's me, Flo. Can I speak to you?"

There was still no reply. I tried knocking a few more times, but no answer came. For some reason, Maisie didn't wish to speak to me.

I would be gone before she got up in the morning, and I hadn't found the chance to say goodbye.

With a heavy heart, I returned to my room and finished packing up my belongings. I would have to stay awake until first light, which would be shortly before six o'clock.

I sat on my bed and my eyelids soon felt heavy. I reluctantly made myself get up again, and paced up and down the length of my room to keep myself awake.

I heard the grandfather clock downstairs strike midnight. Mr Perrin had still been unable to stop it.

Then I heard Maisie's door open again. *What was she doing?*

I crept over to my door and put one hand on the handle, ready to turn it. I heard another door close, which I presumed to be the one which led to the servants' staircase. There was silence for a moment, and then there was a cry followed by a horrible echoing thud. I was startled by the sound. Then I heard hurried footsteps.

Something was wrong.

I picked up my candle and flung open my door.

"Maisie?" I called out.

I was met with complete silence.

I knocked at Maisie's door again, but still there was no answer. Feeling increasingly worried, I turned the handle. Her room was dark inside, but I could smell that a candle had recently been snuffed out.

"Maisie?" I said quietly.

As I stepped into the small room and looked around, I could see she wasn't inside it. A piece of paper and a pencil lay next to the extinguished candle on her dressing table. There was also an empty bottle of laudanum. On the piece of paper, in a very clumsy hand, the following words were written:

Sorry. God Forgive Me.

I heard a shriek, and realised after a few seconds that the noise had come from me.

What had she done?

The sound of the thud came back to my mind.

The steep stairs. The steep servants' staircase.

I ran out of Maisie's room and pushed the door to the staircase open. The flame of my candle quivered as I held it out over the stairwell, afraid of what I might find. I peered cautiously over the banister into the darkness below.

"Maisie!" My voice echoed in the silence, and I felt

nauseous as I became increasingly convinced about the origin of the thud I had heard.

I slowly descended the stairs, holding my candle out in front of me. It felt as though the silence and darkness were trying to close in around me. After waiting a while, I held my candle up over the banisters. As I looked down into the depths, I could see that my worst fears had been confirmed.

The pale form of a person lay at the very bottom of the stairwell. The limbs were twisted into such a position that I couldn't imagine the poor individual might still be alive.

Short, sharp breaths raked at my chest. I felt as though I had left my own body as I descended the staircase toward the terrible, white, twisted figure at the bottom.

When I reached the foot of the stairs, I looked at the white form again and saw Maisie's eyes staring up at me, wide and black.

CHAPTER 37

"What was the girl thinking of?" Mr Glenville exclaimed.

He sat at the table in the dining room, and had clearly dressed in a hurry. He hadn't had time to pin back the sleeve of his right arm, which hung limply at his side, and there was stubble on his chin.

Mrs Glenville sat beside him, her face masked by a mourning veil. Maurice and Jane were also seated at the table, along with Mrs Craughton, whose face was red, her eyes sore from crying.

I had woken Mrs Craughton as soon as I had found Maisie, and she had roused the rest of the household.

James and Inspector Trotter had joined us. James hadn't found a chance to shave that morning, either. His face was sombre, and he wore a dark blue suit. Inspector Trotter stood beside him, laboriously writing in his notebook as James asked everyone in the room for their version of events.

"Self-murder," said Mrs Glenville, shaking her head. "We did get her from the workhouse, didn't we, Alexander? I suppose we were asking for it."

"Let me summarise what we know so far," said James. I stood next to Mr Perrin at the back of the room. I felt so very cold and sad, and longed for the terrible events of the night to somehow be reversed.

"Miss Parker," James said, nodding in my direction, "heard Maisie's door open and close shortly after midnight. Can you confirm that Miss Parker?"

"Yes, Inspector Blakely."

I felt everyone's eyes resting on me and wondered who was aware of my true identity. I avoided Mrs Craughton's gaze. *Surely she knew. She had to know.*

"But you didn't see Maisie herself?"

"No."

"And you say that you knocked at her door a short while before then, but there was no answer."

"Yes."

"Why did you knock at her door?"

I had wanted to ask Maisie if she had been inside my room, but how could I admit that in front of the others?

"I had been concerned about her ever since Miss Sophia's death," I said. "She seemed to be worried or frightened about something. And it was unusual for her to be up late, so I wanted to make sure she was quite well."

"I certainly agree with that," said Mrs Craughton. "The girl was exceptionally upset over Miss Sophia's death, and I don't think she ever recovered. That must be why she took her own life. She simply couldn't cope."

"Mr and Mrs Glenville, is that what you think?" asked James. "Do you agree that Maisie struggled to cope after Miss Sophia's death?"

"Absolutely," said Mrs Glenville. "The girl had a weak mind. People with weak minds are particularly affected by grief."

Mr Glenville nodded solemnly.

"So the best possible explanation we have for Maisie's death is that she struggled to cope with the passing of Miss Sophia, and four days after the tragic event the maid took her own life," commented James.

There seemed to be general assent from around the room.

I chose this moment to speak. "Except there is something which we have overlooked, Inspector Blakely."

"What's that, Miss Parker?"

"Maisie left a note. I saw it on her dressing table. I suppose it is what you might describe as a note someone would write before they take their own life."

"That's right," said James. "It was only a very short note, written in pencil. And the pencil was left lying next to it."

"There's something which bothers me about it."

"What is it?"

"Maisie couldn't read or write," I said. "So how did she manage to write a suicide note?"

"It was crudely written," said Mrs Craughton. "Maisie knew how to write a few simple words."

"I don't think she did," I quibbled. "I had been teaching Maisie her letters, but she wouldn't have been able to write words."

"So what are you saying, F-Flo?" asked Maurice. "Are you s-suggesting that she c-couldn't have written it?"

"Yes. I saw the handwriting, and it was very crudely written, as Mrs Craughton describes. I think someone must have helped her to write it."

"Really?" said Inspector Trotter.

"Yes, they told her what to write and probably guided her hand. That would account for the untidiness."

Mr Glenville snorted. "If someone helped her write her suicide note, that means they would have known what she was about to do. They wouldn't have helped her and then left her to it. They would have stopped her!"

"I know what Miss Parker is suggesting here," said James. "Someone encouraged Maisie to write that note because they wanted her death to appear as a suicide. If that's what happened, her death cannot be ruled a suicide. It must have been a murder."

"No!" Mrs Glenville shrieked.

"Maisie was murdered?" cried Mrs Craughton. "How ridiculous! Why would she be?"

"First my sister and now the maid," said Jane sorrowfully. "I cannot believe that both may have been murdered!"

"Now hold on a minute, Blakely," said Mr Glenville. "Two murders under one roof within a few days?"

"It's possible, Mr Glenville. We cannot be certain."

"Cannot be certain?" said Mr Glenville. "That suggests there's an alternative and plausible explanation for both deaths."

"Both may have been suicides," said Jane.

"Your sister would never have done such a thing," said Mr Glenville. "The maid might have, but Sophia wouldn't. Now let me tell you, Inspector, what I really think happened here. My daughter was poisoned by mistake. The poisoner attempted to poison me, but somehow my glass was accidentally confused with Sophia's. For some unknown reason, the maid has taken her own life."

"How do you explain her ability to write the note?" asked James.

"I haven't seen it, but I hear that it is not well written. Perhaps she found a way to practise her writing. As my wife has said, we found her in the workhouse and wanted to give her a better life than she had there. Perhaps we failed to realise how feeble-minded she was. The question is, why did she do it? I don't think any of us can answer that. Perhaps she was rejected by a suitor. We cannot know what goes on in a girl's mind. Especially a girl who was brought from the workhouse."

"If she did write the note, why should she say she was sorry?" asked James.

"For taking her own life, one would presume," said Mrs Glenville. "It's a sinful act."

"And perhaps she meant to apologise for causing more upset within a grieving household?" added Mrs Craughton. "It is a rather selfish act, if you ask me."

"But it's also terribly tragic, and another death which could have been avoided," said James.

"Not if she was determined to do it," Jane argued.

James sighed. "Well, thank you everyone for your time this morning. Inspector Trotter and I will need to speak to each of you in turn—"

"Not again!" Mrs Glenville cried out.

"I apologise, Madam, but when someone dies in suspicious circumstances we must do our best to investigate as thoroughly as possible."

"But it's not at all suspicious!" said Jane. "She threw herself down the stairwell!"

"We will conduct our interviews as quickly as possible, Miss Jane."

Mr Glenville stood to his feet and glowered at James. "There will be no more of your darned interviews for the time being, Blakely. I'm sick and tired of them."

He turned to face me, and I didn't like the darkness I saw in his eyes.

"They say that in many cases the person who found the body is the one who is responsible."

He spoke so calmly and quietly that I could barely believe what I was hearing.

Everyone turned to stare at me.

"Mr Glenville, no," I said. "I only ran out when I heard—"

"Yes, I'm sure you did. But we only have your word for it, don't we, *Miss Green?*"

I opened my mouth to reply, but stopped when I realised what he had called me.

My secret was out.

"Miss Parker, you mean," James said in an attempt to correct him.

"Parker, eh?" Mr Glenville spun round to glare at him. "You really think so, do you, Blakely?"

The tension in the room had become unbearable.

"Did you know, Blakely, that this woman is a *news reporter?*" Mr Glenville continued.

"I must say that I wasn't aware of this at all, Mr Glenville. A news reporter, you say?"

Glenville's dark eyes narrowed. "Are you certain you didn't know, Blakely? If you were a half-decent detective you'd have seen through her by now. And you too, Trotter."

Inspector Trotter appeared to have decided that it was best to say nothing at all.

"A news reporter posing as a maid," said Mr Glenville, turning back to face me. "And to think that I trusted you." His voice remained low. There was more sadness than anger in it.

"I'm sorry, sir," I began. "It was well intentioned, I promise—"

"Spinning a web of lies while you live and work under my roof is *well intentioned*, is it, Miss Green? Stealing my own belongings from my desk is well intentioned?"

He pulled the notebook from the pocket of his jacket and held it up for all to see. I heard gasps from around the room.

"Mr Glenville," I pleaded. "I can understand why you are angry. If I can just explain—"

"There's nothing to explain, Miss Green," he replied. His lower lip trembled slightly, then he turned his back on me. "If you're still in my house five minutes from now I shall summon the police!"

"But we *are* the police, sir," said James.

"That may be the case, but either you're so inept at your job that you failed to spot who this woman truly was, or you colluded with her. Either way, you're not fit to run the investigation into my daughter's death," said Mr Glenville. "I want the both of you out of my home immediately. I'll call in some detectives who actually know what they're doing. And I'm sure they'll be extremely interested to speak to you about poor, unfortunate Maisie, Miss Green."

Hot tears pricked the backs of my eyes. I glanced at Mrs Glenville but was unable to discern her reaction beneath her veil. I wanted to apologise again and explain my behaviour, but I could see that Mr Glenville had no wish to hear any more. I felt Mrs Craughton's fearsome gaze upon me, so I took pains not to look at her.

"Of course, Mr Glenville," said James convivially. "It's a great shame you no longer wish us to find your daughter's killer, but I feel certain my superior at the yard will continue the work we have begun. As this is a house of mourning, I have no wish to cause any further upset. Shall I ask Chief Inspector Cullen to call round later today?"

Mr Glenville nodded. "I want to catch my daughter's killer. This Cullen chap needs to find him before we hold her funeral next week."

CHAPTER 38

I sat with James and Inspector Trotter in the restaurant of the Carlingford Hotel on Kensington Road. It was a small, comfortable place, and the white tablecloths gleamed brightly in the morning sunshine, which came flooding through the paned window.

Inspector Trotter tucked into his breakfast of mutton chops, but I could muster no appetite. Instead, I sipped at my coffee and watched James spread marmalade onto his toast. I still wore my black maid's uniform, and my trunk was upright on the floor beside my chair.

"I didn't have the chance to tell you that someone found the key to my trunk and discovered my true identity last night," I said.

"I suppose you were bound to be found out at some stage. You lasted a decent length of time," said James, poking about in the marmalade pot with his knife. "Look on the bright side, Penny. At least you've escaped the house!"

"I have." I breathed deeply and tried to enjoy the sense of freedom. "Although Mr Glenville is extremely upset with me, isn't he?"

"He's upset with all three of us," said James. "But please don't worry, Penny. You did everything we asked of you."

I removed my spectacles and wiped my eyes with my handkerchief. I felt a lump in my throat.

"Poor Maisie. I can't stop thinking about her," I said. "You were right, James. She was in danger. Did you see the bottle of laudanum next to her note?"

"Yes, I spotted that. It was empty."

"I wish I could understand what has happened. How on earth are we going to find out what befell Sophia and Maisie now? It feels as though I've thrown everything away. I was careless. I should never have taken that book. I was going to give it to you as part of your investigation on behalf of Mr Conway. But when Sophia died I forgot all about it. I've been so foolish."

"I have a feeling that someone suspected you weren't who you said you were right from the start," said James. "That's why they continued to search your room. It was only a matter of time before they found the key to your trunk. You did well to stick it out for as long as you did. And you did enough for the investigation, so please don't worry any more about it. Cullen will do a good job of picking this up with Glenville."

He bit into his toast.

"I hope so. Cullen won't want my help, though, will he? We've had too many disagreements in the past."

James laughed. "He doesn't bear grudges. Now, would you like to cheer yourself up with a slice of toast? I'll put some marmalade on it for you, if you like?"

I smiled. "Thank you, James."

Inspector Trotter finished off his mutton chops, then wiped his mouth and fingers on the starched serviette.

"It's all very well handing over this case to Cullen," he said. "But where does that leave T Division? I'm supposed to be the chap investigating Miss Glenville's death."

"This is where we can be clever, Trotter," said James. "We give Glenville the impression that Cullen is now looking after the case, but in reality we continue with our investigations. It won't be difficult to speak to the Lombards and the Wyndhams again. The only difficulty we have is our inability to look for clues within the Glenville home."

"The important thing is that this continues as a joint investigation between T Division and the Yard."

"Absolutely, Trotter. You have my word."

"So what do we do now?" asked Inspector Trotter.

"Good question," said James. "We need to formulate a plan."

"Did you have any success in finding Betsy's brother?" I asked.

I wiped my spectacles with my serviette and put them back on. James passed me a slice of toast and marmalade.

"Mr John Morrison? Yes, I have," he said. "I had to promise him my discretion, though. He has rather a lot to hide."

"Such as what?"

"He's a married man."

"What does being married have to do with anything?"

"He is the man Sophia Glenville had been with the evening you encountered her on the staircase."

I almost dropped my toast. "Her secret suitor? Betsy's brother?"

"Yes. They were in love. Despite him being married to another woman, who is currently expecting their second child."

"What a rat! So, if I understand this correctly, Sophia was good friends with Betsy the maid. And then she began a love affair with Betsy's brother, John?"

"Yes. Apparently, they began meeting secretly in the summer of last year."

"Did Sophia know he was married?"

"I believe she did, yes."

"And do you think he loved Sophia?"

"Yes, I'm fairly certain that he did. He seems utterly devastated by her death. According to John, she wanted to elope, but he told her he couldn't leave his wife."

"It sounds as though John Morrison needed to make a decision about which woman he was to remain with," I said.

I thought of the dark figure I had seen in the street staring up at the house after Sophia's death. *Had it been him?*

"I assume John Morrison knew of Miss Sophia's murder before you spoke to him," I said.

"Yes. I don't know where he heard the sad news. Perhaps he read the newspaper reports."

"And he's had to grieve in private. Presumably he has been forced to hide his feelings from his wife. That's a sad thought. It sounds as though they really did love each other, but he had already married the wrong person. What a terrible thing to happen."

"Indeed." James held my gaze before distracting himself with another slice of toast.

"That Glenville fellow is slippery," Inspector Trotter interjected. "I know he's behind all this, yet we can't find anything on him!"

"Perhaps because he didn't do it," I suggested.

"He has to be the culprit though, doesn't he, Blakely?" said Inspector Trotter, pouring more coffee into his cup. "There's something about him. Or do you think he's ''armless'?"

Inspector Trotter laughed at his own quip. "Did you get what I meant there? The fellow only has one arm!"

"I found out who the ghost twins are," I said to James, deliberately ignoring Inspector Trotter's joke.

"Who are they?"

"Uncles of Mrs Glenville. They were called Broderick and Snowdon Noel-Johnstone, but they had interesting nicknames."

I explained about the piece of paper I had found secreted between the books the previous day, and he listened with interest.

"And Mrs Craughton has the piece of paper now?" he asked.

"Yes. She told me she would find out what it referred to, but she had neither the time nor inclination to tell me. I asked Maurice Glenville in the end."

"So why would the ghost twins' nicknames be written on a piece of paper and hidden between two books?" said James. "It has to be a message, doesn't it?"

"It didn't look like much of a message."

"Whatever it was, I can imagine the housekeeper has destroyed it by now," said James. "She seems the type to do that sort of thing."

CHAPTER 39

I was overjoyed to see Tiger again, although she pretended not to notice me. I knew it was her means of punishing me for having gone away.

"How did you get on with doing a proper day's work?" my landlady, Mrs Garnett, asked.

"It was tiring," I replied.

I felt relieved to be home. I could finally be myself again and spread my papers out over the writing desk without worrying that someone would find and read them. I certainly wouldn't miss the physical work, and I was pleased not to be wearing a maid's uniform any more. I no longer had to obey orders and I felt independent again. It was a sensation I relished.

But Maisie's death overshadowed my joy. I still struggled to believe that it had happened. The events of the previous evening turned over in my mind as I unpacked my belongings. I changed my clothes and remembered that the maid's mourning uniform belonged to the Glenvilles.

I would have to return it to them fairly soon. But not too soon.

That afternoon, I went in to the *Morning Express* offices. Pleased to be no longer restricted by a uniform, I wore a fitted mauve jacket over a cream silk blouse and a dark blue woollen skirt.

"Miss Green!" Edgar Fish grinned from ear to ear. "You've returned to us!"

"Thank you, Edgar. You actually seem pleased to see me."

"I'm always pleased to see you, Miss Green. We've missed you, haven't we, Frederick?"

Frederick Potter gave me a nod. "Welcome back, Miss Green."

Mr Sherman marched in, slamming the door behind him.

"Good afternoon, Miss Green. How did you find it?"

"It was interesting. And rather tragic."

"Two deaths while you were there, eh?" said Mr Sherman with a smirk. "Did you bring a curse to the household? Or perhaps you had a hand in it yourself?"

"I wish I could see the humorous side, Mr Sherman, but it's been so terribly sad. Inspector Blakely and I—"

"Blakely? Of course!" interjected Edgar. "That inspector's never far away from you, is he, Miss Green?"

"Inspector Blakely and I worked with Inspector Trotter of T Division," I continued. "We made some progress in the search for Miss Sophia Glenville's murderer, but now we have no chance of finding the culprit. And the terribly sad death of the maid means there is a great deal of work to do. I suppose I always knew that my time there would be limited, but I hoped we would find the person responsible for Sophia's death. Sadly, we didn't. And we made no progress at all with the investigation for Mr Conway."

"It's a shame you were found out," said Mr Sherman.

"I wasn't a very convincing maid, I'm afraid."

"Never mind. It's the first time you've worked undercover.

Edgar's an old hand at it, of course. Anyway, Miss Green, you may have been evicted from the Glenville household, but that doesn't mean you can't report on the story now that you have returned."

"Please don't ask me to go back there."

"I won't, but do what you can to report on developments. We need to find out whether this maid took her own life, or whether someone caused her some mischief. Is her death linked to the daughter's, do you think?"

"I think it must be. Maisie seemed frightened of someone, but I have no idea whom she feared."

"Well, keep talking to the police and ensure that they tell you everything they know. Can I have a quick report on the maid's death by deadline today, please? And you'll need to get down to the inquest."

I sat at the typewriter and began my work.

Police are trying to establish the facts behind the tragic death of a housemaid at the home of Mr. Alexander Glenville in Hyde Park Gate. Maisie Brown, 14, fell down the stairwell of the servants' staircase in the early hours of Thursday morning.

Maisie Brown's death occurred four days after that of Mr. and Mrs. Alexander Glenville' daughter, Miss Sophia Glenville, who died from a poisoning incident. Kensington T Division and Scotland Yard are continuing their search for the culprit.

Mr. Alexander Glenville is the owner of the Blundell & Co vinegar factory in Vauxhall and the Archdale vinegar factory in Bermondsey.

I felt a lump in my throat as I worked at the typewriter. The language in the article was impersonal. I had written it as if I'd never known Maisie. But in my mind, I saw the small, freckle-faced girl who had been so cheery and helpful during my first day at the Glenville house. I had never been able to explain to Maisie who I really was, and the guilt I felt at having deceived her weighed heavily in my heart.

CHAPTER 40

The inquest into Maisie's death was opened and quickly adjourned as the coroner awaited further evidence of what had happened to her on the night she had died. I sat beneath the familiar dome of the reading room and contemplated the task James had ahead of him.

How would he be able to piece everything together if Mr Glenville wouldn't allow him inside the house? Would Inspector Cullen be of any assistance at all? I hadn't found him helpful in the past.

Meanwhile, my meeting with Mr Fox-Stirling was drawing near and I had to remind myself of my father's last known location so that I would have the right questions in mind.

The last letter I received from my father had arrived exactly nine years previously, dated April 1875. The final line had read:

Tomorrow I plan to ride twenty miles southwest of Bogota to the falls of Tequendama. I have heard much of the orchids and tropical birds there, and am looking forward to the spectacle of the River Funza plunging from a height of five hundred feet. It must be quite a sight to behold!

I had not received the letter until the May of that year. By the time it arrived, he had already supposedly vanished. His last diary entry had been written at about the same time as the letter. It detailed a walk he had taken around Bogota and a dinner he had eaten with a German merchant. I wrote down a summary of the events I wished to speak to Mr Fox-Stirling about:

April 1875: Last known letter which Father sent. Last known location: Tequendama Falls.

June 1875: Father's expedition returns without him.

March 1876: Mr. Isaac Fox-Stirling embarks on search party to find Father.

September 1876: Mr. Isaac Fox-Stirling returns from Colombia having found a hut where Father had stayed, and some of his sketches and drawings. No trace of Father.

I wondered if Mr Fox-Stirling had heard about the massacre in which my father had been caught up. Perhaps he had been involved in a similar skirmish himself?

"I've found another useful book for you, Miss Green," whispered Mr Edwards, placing it on top of the pile on my desk.

"Thank you, Mr Edwards. I will only be here for a short while. I don't have enough time to read through all of these today."

"I'm sorry, Miss Green. Perhaps I have been a little over-enthusiastic, I'm rather pleased to see you again, you understand."

He pushed his hair off his spectacles and smiled.

"You speak as if I'd spent a year overseas in India or somewhere similar."

"Penelope!"

My sister's loud greeting echoed across the quiet library. Before I could respond, I was caught up in her embrace.

"You have to whisper in here, Ellie!" I muttered into the folds of her jacket.

"Sorry, Penelope, I forgot." She took a step back. "Goodness, you look even thinner. You're lucky you weren't murdered!" she said in a loud whisper.

I had telegrammed Eliza to let her know that I had left the Glenville house. In reply, she had suggested that we meet for afternoon tea at The Holborn Restaurant. I gathered up my papers as Eliza exchanged whispered pleasantries with Mr Edwards. The red-whiskered man sitting opposite me scowled at the disturbance.

"How was it with the Glenville family?" asked Eliza as she bounced her bicycle down the steps outside the British Museum. The sky was grey, but there was a spring warmth in the air.

"Not much good, I'm afraid."

"Two people dead! Did both die in mysterious circumstances?"

"Yes."

"And the killers haven't yet been apprehended?"

"No. James was working on the case with another inspector, but Mr Glenville found out my true identity and we were asked to leave."

"Oh dear. How embarrassing for you! I suppose it was rather a foolhardy undertaking from the outset. Not the sort of thing you'd do if you were—"

"Married? A mother?"

"Exactly, Penelope. You knew what I was going to say, didn't you? I've said it many times before, but there's no harm in repeating it just in case you had failed to listen on previous occasions. Married women simply don't get themselves into these scrapes. Speaking of which, I confess I am rather taken with the pleasant Mr Edwards. What a delightful gentleman, and so extremely knowledgeable about all manner of things. I know some people consider his type a bore, but I find bookish people most interesting, don't you, Penelope?"

"He works in the British Library, so I suppose he would be rather knowledgeable."

"Exactly! And what a safe and sensible occupation, he has Penelope. It's perfect!"

"Perfect for what?"

"Being safe and sensible. The Lord knows you need it. You wouldn't find Mr Edwards living in a house in which people get murdered. Or getting shot at, or attacked with a knife."

"You'd be surprised, Ellie. There are a good few cut-throats in the reading room."

"Really?"

"I'm joking. I think the most serious danger Mr Edwards might encounter would be a heavy book dropping onto his toe, or being shouted at by a visitor when the electric lights fail."

Eliza laughed. "And I suppose there is a risk he might fall off the small wooden ladder they use for retrieving books from the highest shelves."

"Yes, there's that as well."

"If I had to choose between that and getting shot at, I know what I would plump for," said Eliza. "Anyway, I must say I'm looking forward to hearing what Mr Glenville is like. Dorothea Heale has told me so many terrible things about him."

"Has Dorothea ever met him?" I asked.

"I can't say that I know."

"Because if she did, and she gave him the chance to explain how he runs his factories, I think she would understand him a little better. He's not as bad as people say. In fact, I rather like him."

Eliza stopped pushing her bicycle and stared at me. "Penelope! Really?"

"Really."

"But the man is so horrible to his workers!"

"Do you know that for certain?"

"Yes! Dorothea wrote all about it. You've read her articles, haven't you? Do you think she has made it all up?"

"No, not all of it. But perhaps there has been some misunderstanding along the way."

"What nonsense, Penelope. This isn't like you at all. I believe he's hoodwinked you. I hear he's quite handsome if you can overlook the scar on his face."

"And what's that supposed to mean?" I retorted.

Eliza seemed startled by my angry response. "It wasn't supposed to mean anything. I think we should go and have some tea and cake without further ado."

CHAPTER 41

S ophia Glenville was dead. Maisie Brown was dead. And so was Betsy Wiggins, who had once worked in the Glenville household. Perhaps it was a coincidence. But with all three deaths occurring within the space of five weeks, I felt sure there had to be a connection.

I sat at my writing desk in my room and thought back to the grey, rainy morning when I had stood outside Elizabeth Wiggins' home and spoken to her grieving brother. The man who transpired to have been Sophia Glenville's lover. I leafed through the papers in front of me and found my report on the coroner's inquest into Elizabeth's death. There was something which hadn't seemed right back then, and it still bothered me now. I reread the deposition of one of Betsy's neighbours:

The Coroner heard that, after a night of drinking, Mr Wiggins had returned to the home he shared with his wife in Gonsalva Road, and an argument had immediately ensued. Their neighbour, Mrs Violet

O'Donnell, told the coroner that she had heard shouts late in the evening at approximately 11 o'clock.

Coroner: Were you accustomed to hearing shouting of this manner between Mr and Mrs Wiggins?

Mrs O'Donnell: Until that evening I never heard a cross word between them.

Coroner: To your knowledge, was Mr Wiggins a drinker?

Mrs O'Donnell: Not to my knowledge. He may have been, sir, but I never heard a racket like that before.

Mrs O'Donnell's statement suggested to me that Mr Wiggins' behaviour on the night he had murdered his wife was somewhat out of character. Perhaps I was clutching at straws, but it seemed to me that the nature of Betsy's death needed to be investigated.

I had visited James in his drab, smoky office in Scotland Yard once before. Today I approached his desk as police officers strode in and out of the room with their piles of books and papers.

Writing furiously at a nearby desk was Chief Inspector Cullen, who had silver-rimmed spectacles, a thick grey moustache and a bulbous nose.

"Penny!" said James as I approached him. "This is a surprise!"

He got up from his chair and I noticed that Cullen gave me a cursory glance.

"What brings you here?" asked James.

"Do you have some time today to visit Battersea again?" I asked.

"Well, I suppose I could make time." He consulted the diary which lay on his desk.

"It's regarding the Sophia Glenville case," I said. "And Maisie Brown and Elizabeth Wiggins, for that matter. I wonder if we can find something to connect their deaths."

"An interesting thought, Penny."

Cullen put down his pen and glared at me. "This ink slinger fancies herself as a detective again, does she?"

I fought the urge to respond rudely.

"There was something about Elizabeth's inquest which doesn't seem quite right to me," I continued.

Cullen sighed, shook his head and resumed his writing.

I gave James my news report on the inquest. He read through it quickly.

"What doesn't seem right about it?"

"It's what the neighbour says. She says Mr Wiggins' drunkenness was out of character. Don't you think that's rather strange?"

"I don't suppose there's any harm in speaking to her about it," said James. "Given that two of Betsy's friends have died since then, there's a possibility that foul play may have been involved. I can't say L Division will like me interfering, though. They have already concluded their investigations."

"Do they need to know?"

"Probably not." He smiled, then retrieved his bowler hat and coat from the cloak stand.

"I won't be long, sir!" he said to Cullen.

The senior detective scowled in reply.

"Cullen really doesn't like me, does he?" I muttered to James as we left the building.

"Oh, I think he does really. He just doesn't like to show it."

I laughed. "You talk nonsense sometimes, James."

We hailed a cab on Whitehall, which took us alongside the

river and over Vauxhall Bridge. The warehouses and smoking chimney stacks of south London loomed ever closer.

"Well, look at that," said James. "Blundell's vinegar factory."

The enormous red-brick building had tall chimneys and a high wall around it. In giant letters supported by iron brackets on the roof were the words 'Blundell & Co'.

"And I suppose Ralph Lombard's place is also around here," I said.

"Just there," said James, pointing to a dirty cream building with lettering that read 'Lombard's Dry Gin' along the side.

The traffic on Wandsworth Road was slow-moving, and our cabman began hollering at the driver of a horse tram.

"So are you enjoying your freedom again, Penny?" asked James.

"I certainly am. The next time Conway and Sherman consider asking me to work as a maid, you'll stop them, won't you?"

"Of course." He smiled. "Although it was rather fortuitous that you were there when these unfortunate deaths occurred. It meant you were able to help me greatly."

"I wouldn't speak too soon," I replied. "The cases aren't solved yet."

"True."

I held his gaze and felt my face redden slightly. The small confines of a hansom cab placed us in close proximity to one another.

"I expect your Mr Edwards has been pleased to see you again," he said.

"*My* Mr Edwards?" I replied scornfully. "I have no possession of him whatsoever. He's merely a reading room clerk I happen to know."

"Of course." James smiled again. "Although I think if he

could hear how you have just described him he would be sorely disappointed."

"Well, I suppose it is inevitable that I shall disappoint him."

"Really?"

"I'm not looking for a husband, James. You know that. A husband would never tolerate my profession."

"I suppose it depends on the husband."

"No, it doesn't. Husbands don't expect their wives to work; in fact, many don't even *permit* their wives to work. That's the case for my sister, Eliza. She's given up trying to pursue a profession because George won't allow it."

"George sounds rather old-fashioned."

"Will you allow the future Mrs Blakely to have a profession?" I asked.

James opened and closed his mouth, as if unsure how to answer.

"She doesn't have a profession now," he replied. "She was a governess for a short while, but she cares for her mother now."

"What's the matter with her mother?"

"Between you and me, there's nothing the matter with her mother. But according to Charlotte, her mother suffers with nerves."

"Perhaps caused by the prospect of you marrying her daughter." I laughed.

"That's quite enough, Miss Green," chuckled James. "I think we had better get back to the matter in hand, which is a possible connection between the three deaths. Does this mean that you don't believe Maisie's death was a suicide?"

"No. I feel sure that someone else was responsible," I said. "I think that when I saw Maisie's door close for the first time someone else was in the room with her. That's why he or she didn't open the door when I knocked. And after I heard that horrible thud, I heard footsteps. That can only mean that someone else was around."

"The footsteps came from where?"

"The staircase, I think."

"Ascending or descending?"

"I can't be sure. It was only for a brief moment."

"I'm inclined to agree with you. Maisie didn't seem right when we interviewed her, did she? I said at the time that the girl was frightened of someone."

"That bottle of laudanum which was on her dressing table," I said. "The only other person I've seen with laudanum is Lady Wyndham. And it probably has nothing to do with anything, but I saw Lady Wyndham give something to Maisie at the dinner on the night of Miss Sophia's death. Maisie put it in her apron pocket, but I didn't see what it was."

"I need to speak to the Wyndhams again," said James. "We didn't get much from Lady Wyndham, did we? She very conveniently became too distressed to continue our interview."

We arrived at Gonsalva Road, where the trains rumbled behind rows of cramped brick houses. A pall of black smoke drifted across the rooftops.

The cab left us outside number sixteen, where Elizabeth and her husband had lived. A group of dirty-faced children paused from their game to stare at us.

"We need to find Mrs O'Donnell," I said to James. "She was the neighbour who spoke to the coroner at Elizabeth's inquest."

"We need to be careful, though," said James. "Bear in mind that L Division have already investigated this murder and are convinced that they have their man. We don't want to upset them."

"But what if they haven't investigated properly?" I asked. "If they've missed something important they should be grateful for our help, not upset by it!"

"In theory, it should work that way, but in practice it doesn't," said James with a grimace.

After calling at a few doors, we found Mrs O'Donnell talking with a friend further down the street. I recognised her from the inquest. She was a tiny lady with a firm jaw and piercing green eyes.

"Mrs O'Donnell?"

"Who's askin'?" She placed her hands on her hips.

"My name's Penny Green. I'm a news reporter for the *Morning Express*. And this is Inspector James Blakely of Scotland Yard."

Mrs O'Donnell groaned. "Not more of yer! I thought we was rid of 'em! It's Elizabeth you wants to talk about, ain't it?"

"Betsy. I knew her as Betsy. She worked as a maid for the Glenville family, didn't she?"

Mrs O'Donnell raised an eyebrow, intrigued by my knowledge. "Yeah, what of it?"

She removed her hands from her hips, but firmly folded her arms.

"I know the Glenvilles extremely well and their daughter Miss Sophia was terribly saddened by Elizabeth's death."

"I've 'eard she's dead an' all."

"Sadly, she is. And another maid, Maisie, has since died."

"Another one?"

"We're trying to understand why each of them died. I reported on the coroner's inquest into Elizabeth's death. And you gave a deposition, didn't you?"

"I spoke at it, yeah."

"I may have interpreted this wrongly, Mrs O'Donnell, so

do please correct me. But the implications from your deposition —"

"Yer what? You uses a lotta long words."

"What I mean to say is that you told the inquest Mr Wiggins didn't usually come home drunk and harm his wife?"

"Never 'eard 'im do it afore that time."

"So you had never heard him lose his temper before?"

"'E may 'ave done, but I ain't never 'eard it."

"And you mentioned at the inquest that he wasn't much of a drinker."

"I ain't never seen 'im drunk afore then, neither."

"So he had a sudden change of mood and drank heavily, then came home and murdered his wife?" asked James.

"Yeah, it was sudden, like. I dunno what 'appened that day in the fact'ry, but 'e'd drank a skinful and took it out on 'er. P'raps 'e couldn't take 'is drink. Some men can't when they ain't used ter drinkin' a lot. Then they drinks and they loses their mind. S'pose 'e regrets it now. What I don't understand is why they never asked that other bloke."

"What other bloke?"

"The bloke what come back wiv 'im from the pub."

"He brought someone back with him that evening?" I asked.

"He did, yeah."

James and I exchanged an astonished glance.

"How do you know that?" James asked.

"My Stan saw the pair of 'em walkin' down the street."

"Stan is your husband?" I asked.

"Yeah."

"Did Stan tell the police what he saw?"

"No one never asked 'im."

"Did he not wish to volunteer the information?"

"'E don't like talkin' to the police if 'e can 'elp it. They always go on and ask 'im abaht summink 'e ain't done."

"If I understand you correctly, Mrs O'Donnell, you're saying that on the night Elizabeth was murdered, your husband saw Mr Wiggins and another man return to the house Elizabeth shared with her husband," said James.

"Yeah."

"Did he recognise the man?"

"No, never seen him afore. Proberly someone from the fact'ry."

"Did your husband see the man leave?"

"Nah, my Stan went dahn the pub. All the 'ollerin' were over by the time he got back. 'E'd already killed 'er by then."

"Who? Mr Wiggins or the stranger?" I asked.

"Wiggins! That's what 'e got 'imself harrested for!"

"And what became of the stranger?"

"'Ow should I know?"

"Could the stranger have killed Elizabeth?"

"Why would 'e do that?"

"I have no idea," I said. "But is it possible that, amid all the shouting and banging you heard, the stranger could have murdered Elizabeth?"

"There were a lotta shoutin' an' bangin', so I s'pose 'e could of. But 'e weren't there when the police turned up."

"No, I don't suppose he would have been, would he? If he did murder poor Elizabeth, he presumably would have run away as quickly as possible afterwards," said James.

"Yeah, I reckon 'e would of."

"And allowed the drunk and insensible Mr Wiggins to take the blame," I suggested.

"That could of 'appened, yeah."

"So the stranger might be the murderer?"

"Yeah. But 'e ain't, though. Wiggins done it. 'E's the one what got harrested."

"Which factory did Mr Wiggins work at, Mrs O'Donnell?" asked James.

"Lombard's."

"Interesting," said James. "So before his wife was killed he presumably had a drink or two at a tavern near to the factory."

"Proberly. I can't say I know."

"I'd like to speak to your husband about this man, if you please, Mrs O'Donnell," said James politely.

"'E ain't 'ere," she replied gruffly. "And he don't like the police."

"Please reassure him that I have no interest in what he may or may not have done himself. All I wish to do is find out more about the man Mr Wiggins was with that night. When will your husband return home, Mrs O'Donnell?"

"This evenin'."

"I shall return then."

"And thank you, Mrs O'Donnell." I said. "You've been extremely helpful."

CHAPTER 42

"L Division completely ignored a witness!" fumed James as we walked up Wandsworth Road toward Lombard's gin distillery.

"I don't think they even knew about him. I suppose difficulties arise when potential witnesses don't wish to talk to the police."

"Of course it's difficult, but it's still their job to find these people! It doesn't sound as though Elizabeth's death was properly investigated at all. L Division arrested the most obvious assailant and considered their job done."

We jumped onto a horse tram and climbed its narrow, curving staircase to the roof.

"I'll return to Gonsalva Road this evening," said James as we sat down on the wooden bench. "And in the meantime, we need to find out which public house Wiggins was drinking in on the night that his wife was murdered. It's likely that he was accompanied by the man with whom Mr O'Donnell saw him."

"Do you think this other man might have deliberately encouraged him to become inebriated?" I asked. "It does not sound as though Mr Wiggins was a regular drinker, but this man may have coerced him."

"He may have indeed. I will speak to L Division and request a meeting with Wiggins. It may take a little while to persuade them, though. For the time being, we could go to the public houses near Lombard's and ask if anyone there saw Wiggins that night."

We got off the tram at Vauxhall Cross and found a number of public houses close to Blundell's and Lombard's. From what the landlords had told us, we ascertained that they were popular with the men from the factories as well as the men who worked in the nearby riverside wharves and gas works. And although they had all heard of Mr Wiggins' arrest for his wife's murder, we could find no one who could specifically remember seeing him that night.

"We'll have to keep searching," said James. "Let's try the other side of the railway lines."

We walked through the dark tunnel beneath the railway and were greeted on the other side by a large public house with a curved facade.

"The Royal Vauxhall Tavern," said James. "Let's try this place."

It was gloomy inside, with just a few gaslights burning. A smell of stale beer and tobacco smoke lingered in the air. A man polishing tankards behind the bar gave us a suspicious look.

"Yer the police, ain't yer?" he said to James. "I can always tell a police hofficer. But who are you?" he asked, addressing me directly.

He put down his tankard and cloth, and planted his two enormous hands on the bar.

"I'm Penny Green," I said. "A friend of Elizabeth Wiggins; the woman who was murdered in Battersea about five weeks ago. Do you know her husband? He works at Lombard's."

"Why d'yer wanna know?"

"I'm Inspector Blakely of Scotland Yard," said James. "Miss Green and I are trying to understand a bit more about what happened on the evening of Elizabeth's death. We're trying to find out if Mr Wiggins was drinking with an acquaintance that evening. Are you the landlord of this place?"

"Yeah, Smith's me name. I seen Wiggins come in 'ere. 'E weren't a regular."

"You knew him?"

"I knew *of* 'im. Heveryone knows of 'im since 'e murdered 'is wife."

"Did he drink in here on the night of the murder?" asked James.

"Yeah. I only realised it afterwards. Thought nothin' of it at the time," replied Smith.

I finally began to feel hopeful.

"Did you speak to him that night?" I asked.

"Don't recall as I did."

"We believe he was drinking with someone else that night," said James. "Did you notice him with anyone?"

"Man? Woman?"

"A man. Do you know of anyone who spoke to Wiggins and this friend that night?"

"Someone must of."

"You can't remember if he had an acquaintance?"

"Nope."

I began to feel frustrated again. "Would any of your regular patrons recall with whom Mr Wiggins might have been drinking?" I asked.

"That's a posh word to call 'em! Patrons, ha! Yeah, I can ask 'em."

"Would any of them be popping in today, do you think?"

"The regulars is always in."

"Fortunately, we've timed it right," said James, looking at his pocket watch. "They'll just be clocking off now at the factories."

As if on cue, the door swung open and the workers began to noisily fill the bar, their boots clattering on the floor.

"Whom should we speak to?" James called to the landlord.

"I'll find—" His voice was drowned out by the noise, and the tavern owner occupied himself with filling tankards of porter and beer.

We patiently waited, and I tried my best to ignore the leers from some of the factory workers. A man with wide-set eyes and a smattering of brown teeth sidled up next to me.

"I ain't see you in 'ere afore."

"I'm a news reporter."

He cackled. "What, writin' for the papers? No yer ain't."

"Do you know Mr Wiggins?" I asked.

"The wife killer? Yeah, I knows of 'im."

"Did you see him in here on the night of his wife's murder?"

"I 'eard 'e was in 'ere, but I didn't see 'im. Why yer askin'?"

"I'm a news reporter. I ask a lot of questions."

"Will yer put me in the papers if I tell yer I seen 'im?"

James noticed the man talking to me and joined us.

"I can put you in the papers," I said to the man, "if you're able to tell us something which will help the police investigation."

The man eyed James warily. "The police?" he sneered. "I ain't talkin' to no police."

He drifted away into the crowd. The room was noisy, and I began to feel hot in my woollen dress and jacket.

The landlord caught our attention with a loud shout. "Whippet's seen 'im!" he called out, pointing a large forefinger at a wiry man with sallow skin and yellowing whiskers.

"Whippet?" I said.

The wiry man pushed his way over to us. I hoped he had some useful information.

"Mr Whippet?" asked James.

He cackled in reply. "Mr Whippet! I likes that, I does."

He looked me up and down, then gave an appreciative nod. "We don't often see your sort in 'ere."

I felt an unpleasant taste in my mouth.

"Did you see Mr Wiggins on the night his wife was murdered?" asked James.

I held little hope that Mr Whippet could be of help to us.

"Yeah. I seen 'im. What of it? Who are yer?"

"Inspector Blakely from Scotland Yard, and this is Miss Green, a news reporter with the *Morning Express*.

Whippet's face split into a grin as he looked at me. "You ain't married, then?"

"Did you see who Wiggins was with?" asked James, ignoring the question and stepping between myself and Mr Whippet, as if to protect me from him.

"Yeah, some josser."

"Did you recognise the man he was with?"

"Can't say as I did."

Whippet's eyes rested on me again. He took a large gulp of beer, which trickled down his chin and into his whiskers.

"Can you remember what the man looked like?" asked James.

I was ready to suggest that James give up on the conversation. *How could we even trust that this man was telling the truth?*

Whippet paused for a moment and stared up into a distant corner of the room.

"'E were large; larger than Wiggins. I didn't know 'is face, and I didn't like 'is face, truth be told. 'E 'ad a look."

"What sort of look?" asked James.

"'E looked around a lot, like 'e were sizin' us all up. And 'e 'ad these funny eyes, what didn't look nice. I reckon 'e could of been trouble."

"Can you remember how he was dressed? Do you think he was one of the factory workers, or was he dressed differently?"

"'E 'ad a coat on. A long coat, yer know?"

"A frock coat?"

"Just a longer coat, and there was no 'oles in it or nothin'. It were nice. Proberly cost 'im a bit, I'd say. 'E 'ad money 'cause 'e were buyin' a lotta people a lotta drinks. That's 'ow comes I noticed 'im! He bought a lotta drinks."

"Was he older or younger than Wiggins?"

"Older." He shrugged, then peered over at me again.

"Did he seem friendly with Wiggins?" James probed.

"I s'pose so. They talked a lot."

"Did you think it was unusual to see him in here?"

"Not really."

"Did you hear any of their conversation?"

"No, I were too far away."

"Did you speak to Mr Wiggins that evening?"

"Can't say as I did. I'm bored o' them questions now. I can't remember nothin' else."

He stepped past James and lunged at me. "'Ow d'yer fancy a walk out in the fresh air, Miss Green?"

"No thank you, Whippet," I replied.

"Ah, come on."

I could smell beer on his breath.

"That's enough, Whippet," warned James, giving him a sharp shove with his elbow.

"Ow!" complained the man with a whine.

"Let's get out of here," said James, taking my arm and guiding me through the crowd.

CHAPTER 43

"I shall need to speak to Mr Wiggins next so we can find out the identity of the man he was with that night," said James as the cab took us back over Vauxhall Bridge. "I'm not sure if we've uncovered something useful here, or whether we're being taken on a wild goose chase."

"We must have. It seems that L Division didn't carry out a thorough investigation into Elizabeth's death."

"But how does it help us regarding Sophia Glenville? And Maisie?"

"Mr Wiggins worked for Mr Lombard," I said. "That has to be more than a coincidence, doesn't it?"

"I don't know. Lombard employs so many in Vauxhall and Battersea, and Wiggins' wife worked for Glenville, so perhaps he heard about an employment there from her?"

"I thought we were on to something, but my mind feels as though it's spinning in circles. Hopefully Mr Wiggins will be able to give us some clarity."

"Possibly, but it seems he was so insensibly drunk that night that he cannot remember what happened. I hope L

Division will allow me to speak to him. His trial has just begun and they won't welcome this new development."

"Perhaps they should have done their job properly the first time. It seemed very easy for them to decide that Elizabeth's death was a domestic incident."

"And perhaps it was. Perhaps the chap Wiggins supposedly had a drink with is a red herring."

"I hope not. If the work we've done today comes to nothing, what can we do next? We will likely have to rely on Cullen."

"No, there's more we can do yet. I want to return to the Glenville house somehow to look at the portrait of those ghost twins again."

"Why?"

"That bit of paper you found has to mean something."

"And how do you intend to get back into the Glenville house? Mr Glenville won't allow you inside."

"I'll find a way to win him over," James replied with a grin.

"Good luck. I don't think I could ever face Mr and Mrs Glenville again. I feel as though I betrayed them terribly."

"What do you mean? You never had any loyalty toward them, Penny. You went there for your undercover assignment."

"I lied to them about who I was."

"And you don't think Glenville lies to people?"

"To whom exactly does he lie to? Whenever he spoke to me, he sounded frank and honest."

James laughed. "I think you were charmed by him, Penny!"

"I was not!"

"There's no shame in admitting it. There's no doubt that he is a charming man. People like him are masters of manipulation. How else has a one-armed boy from an impoverished family risen to his position?"

"Through hard work and endeavour," I replied.

"You really believe that, do you?"

James laughed even louder this time, and I felt my jaw clench with anger. I flung open the hatch in the roof and ordered the cabbie to stop.

"Oh, don't take it to heart, Penny. There's no need to get out," said James.

I ignored him and opened the door in front of us. I twisted my ankle as I jumped down from the cab.

"We're right by Millbank Prison, Penny! It's not a nice place for a lady to be walking on her own!"

I continued to ignore him and hobbled on with my head bent low and tears stinging my eyes.

I didn't realise James had run after me until I heard his voice close to my shoulder.

"Penny!"

I stopped, but was too ashamed of my tears to look at him.

"I have no wish to argue with you," he continued. "Especially not about Glenville. I apologise for laughing as I did."

There was an uncomfortable pause, and I stared down at a crack in the pavement.

"Do you accept my apology?" he asked.

"Yes," I replied, turning my gaze to the bleak wall of the prison.

"I'm not sure that you do," he said softly. "What's the matter, Penny?"

I dug the tip of my tongue into my teeth, feeling too upset to speak.

"Penny?"

"Nothing's the matter."

"Funnily enough, I don't believe you."

"I'm just tired. A lot has happened. I suppose I'm upset about Maisie and Sophia."

I finally found the courage to meet James' gaze. His blue eyes were filled with concern, and I thought back to the moment we had shared inside Glenville's library in the flickering candlelight. Every encounter we had was heavy with unspoken words.

"Are you sure that you're making the right decision?" I asked.

"About what? Glenville?"

"No! Forget about him. Your marriage. Is it what you want?"

He raised his eyebrows, surprised by the directness of my question.

"It has been planned for a long time, Penny."

"Does that mean you know what you want?"

His brow crumpled. "I suppose so. I can't see that there's any question of it not happening. It's all been arranged. If I changed my mind now I could be tried for breach of promise."

"Would the future Mrs Blakely insist upon that?"

"I don't know. I have never considered it. Why are you asking the question, Penny?"

I felt angry all of a sudden. "Forget that I ever mentioned it, James."

I turned to continue on my way, but he caught my arm.

"No, I can't forget it now," he said. "You mentioned it for a reason, and I will be honest with you. I find myself in a complicated situation. I cannot deny that I have feelings for you. I have tried to deny it, but it's no good. I tell myself that perhaps once I'm married I will be devoted to my wife."

"And you wish to be devoted to her, do you?"

"I wish to be devoted to someone. Whether it is her or you I don't know."

"You *don't know?*"

"I'm sorry. I do know, but I can't see how it could ever

happen. You've made it quite clear that you have no wish to be married, and I'm engaged to be married to someone else. Although I find the situation frustrating, perhaps this is the way it is supposed to be. I enjoy working with you, Penny, and I always look forward to seeing you. I adore being in your company. Sometimes I feel that, should there ever be an attachment between us, it would ruin what we have."

"Perhaps it would."

I realised with sadness that James was keen to justify the choice he was making.

"I don't suppose there is much else to be said on the topic," I added tersely. "I'm tired, and everything seems worse when I'm tired."

James leaned forward and gave me a gentle kiss on my left cheek. I felt the skin tingle as he moved away and regarded me.

"I've never met anyone like you before, Penny."

I smiled. "Is that supposed to be a compliment?"

"Yes, it is."

CHAPTER 44

"Are you all right, Penelope?" asked Eliza as we stood on the doorstep of Mr Fox-Stirling's home.

"I'm fine, thank you, Ellie!"

I forced a smile and tried to push any thought of James from my mind. He had made it clear that his wedding was to go ahead as planned. My hopes that he would change his mind had been dashed. I reached up to feel for the ring which still hung on its chain beneath my blouse.

"Are you sure you're all right?" my sister probed.

"Yes. Now let's see what Mr Fox-Stirling has to say," I replied, pulling the bell pull rather harder than was necessary.

The housekeeper escorted us into a large room, where tropical plants basked in the light flowing through the three tall sash windows. There were bookshelves and lithographs of African hunting scenes on the wall. Eliza and I were instructed to sit in two comfortable chairs by the fireplace.

Mr Fox-Stirling joined us a few moments later. He was a stocky, fair-haired man of around fifty with suntanned, freckled skin. He wore a pale linen suit, and a small clay pipe was stuck to his lower lip.

"Mrs Billington-Grieg!" he said, spreading his arms wide in welcome. "And Miss Green! Remind me which one is the news reporter."

"That's me," I said.

"Marvellous! Your father would be so very proud," he said as he sat in one of the chairs opposite us and crossed one leg over the other.

"And I'm chairwoman of the West London Women's Society," said Eliza.

"Good, good. I understand you have some questions about your father's travels."

"Yes. I'm writing a book about them," I said.

"Writing a book! That really is marvellous. I've written several books about my travels, and I'm currently compiling a directory of Nepenthes. Carnivorous plants! You must visit the Nepenthes House at Wilde Nurseries. I'll get you in there. Many of the species are from samples I collected in the Straits Settlements."

I retrieved some papers from my carpet bag, then said: "It was while I was working on the book that I realised I couldn't complete it until I fully understood the last few months leading up to Father's disappearance."

"That's a very nicely drawn map," said Mr Fox-Stirling. "Let me see it."

I handed him the map.

"It's rather useful," I said. "An acquaintance of mine who works at the British Library sketched it for me."

"Your acquaintance is quite a draughtsman," he said, giving the map back to me. "The British Library you say? I wonder if your acquaintance has come across my own books in there."

"He may well have done. He has been helping me with my research."

"I think you would also enjoy reading them, Miss Green. In fact, there are some rather fine bookshops in the vicinity of the British Museum where you will find copies of my books. I hope it's not rude of me to ask whether you have purchased any of them?"

"Not rude at all. Mr Smith. I haven't yet, I'm afraid, but I shall seek them out."

"Please do, please do. I'm sure my books will answer any questions I don't have time to cover today. You'll find the account of my first journey to the Himalayas rather entertaining. The number of useful plant specimens I found within the first three months? Two. The number of tigers shot? Twenty-six! It should have been an animal hunting expedition rather than a plant-hunting trip. The darned animals are easier to find than the plants!" He slapped his knee with laughter and I began to doubt whether this meeting would live up to my expectations.

A maid brought in a heavy-looking tea tray.

"This is Darjeeling, which I brought back from India myself!" boasted Mr Fox-Stirling as he poured it out. After listening to a number of his travel anecdotes – during which he advised us that the full version of his tales could be found in his books – I eventually persuaded him to focus on his mission to find Father.

"Ah yes, it was a hellish crossing, that one, and I remember that we were held up somewhat. We finally disembarked in Savanilla, and spent some weeks in a steam boat travelling up the Magdalena. You can only get as far as Honda in a steamboat, so from that place hence it was a journey of more than two hundred miles by mule to Bogota. It was rather arduous, really.

"We were guests of a Dutch dignitary in Bogota, and what

a place! Wonderful fountains in the most beautiful marble courtyards. We drank the most marvellous guarapo. Have you ever tried it? I don't suppose you would have. It's the juice of boiled sugar cane, and if you allow it to ferment a little it's potent stuff, I can tell you!"

I noticed Eliza stifling a yawn.

"And when did you reach Tequendama?" I asked.

"Tequendama, you say?" He seemed to be put off by my interruption.

"Yes. Father's last known location was the Falls of Tequendama."

"That's right. Well, that's some miles southwest of Bogota. Before that we had to—"

"What did you find when you got there?"

"Bogota? Well, as I was saying, we stayed—"

"No, Tequendama. Did you find any trace of Father at Tequendama?"

"Not immediately by the waterfall, no. We found his hut at a nearby place. I forget what it's called now." He got up and walked over to his bookcase, pulled out one of his books and leafed through the pages.

"I recommend that both of you read this one. It's volume three of my collection *Travels, Trials and Adventure in the Andes* if you'd like to purchase copies. Ah yes, here's the place. El Charquito, a small village on the banks of the Funza. That's where I found where he'd been staying, because he'd left a notebook of sketches. Fine drawings they were too. Your father was an accomplished artist."

"And when you discovered the hut, what was it like?" asked Eliza.

"It was but a simple hut; of primitive construction, with everything in one room. There was a sleeping area, an open hearth and a rather ramshackle table, as I recall."

"Did it appear as though the hut been used recently?"

"I don't think so. Leaves and general detritus had blown in under the door. It was an ill-fitting door, I seem to remember."

"And his book of sketches was where? Had he left it on the table?" I asked.

"No, the old lady who lived next door was in possession of them. She thought I was the man himself, come back to retrieve them! She greeted me and swiftly handed over the book. I think she was worried that I would accuse her of stealing it. She had looked after it well, so she did us great service. And the book, as you know, is now in the possession of the British Museum's natural history department in South Kensington."

"Did the old lady tell you when she last saw Father?" Eliza queried.

"I'm sure she did. My Spanish has only ever been rudimentary, I'm afraid, and she seemed to speak with a strong dialect. From what I could understand, he hadn't been seen at the hut for a long time."

"But didn't the old lady think you were Father?"

"I think she probably did. If truth be told, I think we were as confused as one another!"

He chuckled, and I felt a ball of growing frustration in my chest.

"Did you not have someone with you who could translate properly between Spanish and English?" I asked.

"Not on that occasion. It's quite the feat to get yourself across the Atlantic and then travel for several weeks by steamboat and mule, you know, never mind finding a translator to come with you."

He seemed offended that I had suggested that the lack of a translator was a shortcoming on his part.

"Did you ask anyone else in the village if they knew what had become of him?" Eliza enquired.

"I did my best. The Spanish dialect was a hindrance, as I've mentioned. But if anyone had known something useful, I feel sure they could have communicated it to me one way or another. They could have led me to a gravesite, for example. I apologise for mentioning that, as I know you most probably harbour hopes that he is still alive somewhere. But searching for a gravesite was something I had to do."

"We realise that. Thank you, Mr Fox-Stirling," said Eliza. "I think if Father were still alive he would have contacted us by now."

"He may have done. He may not have done."

"What do you think could have happened to him?" I asked.

He puffed out a cloud of smoke from his clay pipe. "There are a number of possibilities. He might have been taken ill like poor Henry Chesterton, who died last year at Puerto Berrio. There are many tropical diseases to which our men have no resilience, you see. I suppose he might have been killed by red men. Explorers aren't popular with the red men in that part of the world."

I thought of the account of the massacre in Father's diaries, but kept quiet about it for the time being.

"If he'd died of an illness, I would have expected to find a gravesite," Mr Fox-Stirling continued. "Similarly if he'd died at the hands of the red men. Unless..."

"Unless what?"

"I can't recall now whether or not they practise cannibalism in those parts."

I shuddered, and he brushed the thought away with a wave of his hand.

"Or perhaps he met with an accident," he continued. "You say that his last known location was the Falls of Tequendama. Have you any idea what the place is like?"

"A little."

275

"The River Funza plunges from five hundred feet or so there. The effect is quite dizzying. Perhaps he missed his footing and fell down into the churning waters. I do apologise, ladies, for suggesting it. But you strike me as calm-headed women who understand that such possibilities must be considered."

"If the river had washed him away," said Eliza sadly, "where might he have ended up?"

"Well, from memory I think the Funza joins up with the Magdalena."

He stood to retrieve another book from his shelf. "Volume four of *Travels, Trials and Adventure in the Andes* is of great help on this subject."

We waited for him to flick through the pages again. "Ah yes, I've written here that the two rivers join at Girardot, and from thence the Magdalena flows northward. It meanders through for many hundreds of miles until it eventually reaches Barranquilla on the northern coast. I cannot imagine anything being carried so far in the river, however. I'm sure it would have been deposited somewhere along the way."

He closed the book and pursed his lips while he considered this possibility.

"So if he fell into the waterfall, his body may have been washed up anywhere along hundreds of miles of riverbank?" asked Eliza.

I looked down at my fidgeting hands, struggling to believe that we were even considering such a possibility.

"We understand now," I said. "There's no need to think on it too much, Ellie. It is too distressing."

"Of course it is. I'm simply considering all the possibilities, as Mr Fox-Stirling suggests."

"I think I've considered them enough for now," I said. "I can't imagine Father would have fallen into the waterfall, so I don't wish to pursue that avenue any further."

"Of course," said Mr Fox-Stirling, replacing his book onto its shelf and returning to his seat. "I must commend you both on being very strong-minded ladies. Few members of your sex would allow their minds to stretch to these unpalatable thoughts. Your father was a brave man, and he has two courageous daughters. I have run out of time on this occasion, but perhaps we can meet for dinner so I can share my memories of your father. You must bring your husbands, of course, and Mrs Fox-Stirling would be only too delighted to meet you both. You might find it useful to read my books before we meet again, just so I shan't be boring you with information you can find out another way!"

He chuckled.

Much as I wished to hear Mr Fox-Stirling's memories of Father, I struggled to endure the man's company.

"I don't have a husband," I replied tersely.

"Oh, I do apologise."

I felt a strange pleasure in seeing his face redden.

"It's *Miss* Green, isn't it? My mistake. I do hope you accept my most sincere apology."

"Perhaps you could bring Mr Edwards to dinner with the Fox-Stirlings," suggested Eliza as we walked along Chelsea Embankment. Large white clouds scurried over the Thames, and a steam boat puffed out a plume of smoke. "After all, he has been most helpful with your research."

"If I invite him, he will make assumptions about our current position," I replied. "I don't wish there to be any misunderstanding."

"What is there to misunderstand? You have already enjoyed a walk with him in Hyde Park!"

"There's a rather large leap between a walk in the park and marriage, Ellie."

"There is when you're a *young* woman," my sister replied. "But you're almost thirty-five. At your age, the leap must be taken as quickly as possible."

"I think it rather short-sighted of Fox-Stirling not to take a translator with him," I said, purposefully changing the topic of conversation. "How else could he have expected to speak to the local people about Father's disappearance?"

"He strikes me as the type of man who assumes he is adept at a certain skill until he has to try it out in a real situation."

"He didn't tell us much that we didn't know already, did he?"

"Not a great deal. I think it would be useful to meet him again," said Eliza. "I know you're not keen on the man, but we should take him up on his dinner invitation. There must be some new information for you to include in the book you're writing, Penelope."

"I suppose so. And as soon as it's published, I can pester Mr Fox-Stirling to buy it!"

We both laughed.

CHAPTER 45

"Your sister rides a bicycle, does she not, Miss Green?" asked Edgar Fish. "Is she aware that if she lived in Warwickshire she would be compelled to carry lights between sunrise and sunset? But if she lived in Birmingham, she would be permitted to drive *without* lights for an hour before sunset and an hour after sunrise?"

I paused from my typewriting. "I don't think she's aware of those rules."

"But only between the first of March and the thirty-first of October," added Edgar.

"But she lives in London," I said. "What about the bylaws in London?"

"I don't know. I haven't found those out yet," replied Edgar. "But I do know that if your sister rode a *tricycle* in Warwickshire, as opposed to a bicycle, she wouldn't have to carry any lights at all! Bylaws in Warwickshire don't cover tricycles."

"What a contradictory state of affairs," said Frederick Potter. "I think one would be better off riding neither."

"Sherman asked me to write a piece on the lack of uniformity concerning bicycle and tricycle laws," said Edgar. "And it seems the entire system is a Gordian knot."

"I still don't understand what it means for bicycles and tricycles in London," I said.

"That simply illustrates my point, Miss Green! A Gordian knot, as I say!"

I returned to my work, but soon became distracted by a jammed ink ribbon on the typewriter.

"It's the schoolboy inspector!" announced Edgar Fish.

I turned to see James in the newsroom, his bowler hat stowed in his hand.

"Must you still call me that, Mr Fish?" he asked.

"I suppose it's a habit now, Inspector Blakely," replied Edgar. "On account of your relative youth."

"Which is still significantly greater than the age of your average schoolboy," replied James.

He walked over to my desk. "Hello, Penny. How are you?"

I felt an uncomfortable twinge as I remembered that the last time I had seen him was on the occasion when I had walked away from the cab.

"I'm well, thank you, James."

We exchanged a smile. He appeared to have forgiven me for my bad temper.

"Have you managed to speak to Mr Wiggins yet?" I asked.

"Yes, that's why I'm here. L Division finally relented after a good deal of persuasion on my part. Mr Wiggins is not a well man. The arrest and trial have taken their toll on his health, unfortunately."

"That's terribly sad if he's an innocent man."

"It is indeed. And he remembers little about the evening on which his wife died. He doesn't even recall leaving the Royal Vauxhall Tavern. Until now, he had assumed that the man who had bought his drinks had made his own way home. Mr Wiggins seemed surprised when I told him that a neighbour had seen him with the man in his own street. The problem is that, because Mr Wiggins has no memory of the latter part of the evening, he actually believed that he had murdered his poor wife. He is filled with remorse and fear, and has made several attempts to take his own life.

"He has been unable to reconcile himself with what happened that night. When I suggested that the stranger who bought him drinks that evening might have been behind his wife's death, there was no relief in Mr Wiggins' eyes. Instead, I saw immense sadness. The events have broken him. I now fear that, even if this stranger is caught and it's proven that he was responsible for Elizabeth's death, Wiggins will never recover."

"The poor man. Did he tell you who the stranger was?"

"A man who called himself Mr Evans. Apparently, he approached Mr Wiggins a week before Elizabeth's murder and asked if Wiggins would like to work for him. He assured him the work would be better paid than his employment at Lombard's factory. Wiggins agreed to meeting him at the public house.

"Apparently, the man was initially reluctant to meet in the Royal Vauxhall Tavern, but Wiggins insisted on it because he wanted to be in a place where there would be other people he knew. He felt wary of Evans; he didn't feel sure he could trust him. He said the man was very generous in buying drinks. Wiggins admitted to me that he wasn't a regular drinker, and on the odd occasion when he did partake, he didn't drink much. But he said that after two drinks he began to feel rather odd."

"Just two drinks," I mused. "Do you think the man might have put something in them?"

"I suspect that he might have. He may well have administered a small dose of something which was enough to incapacitate Mr Wiggins but not cause him lasting harm. He says that his memory failed him for the remainder of that evening, and that he woke the next morning to find poor Elizabeth dead. At no point did he imagine that the stranger had anything to do with it. He blamed himself entirely."

"I suppose we cannot be completely sure that Mr Evans committed the crime."

"Not until we have managed to find the man himself. But it's a fair assumption to make for the time being."

"If Mr Evans approached Mr Wiggins a week before Elizabeth's murder, the attack was clearly planned well in advance. But if Mr Evans did kill Elizabeth, I cannot understand his motive."

"Me neither. I need to ask Elizabeth's brother, John Morrison, if he has ever come across the man before. There is another option, of course."

"Which is what?"

"That someone paid Mr Evans to carry out Elizabeth's murder."

"Why should they have done so?"

"Your guess is as good as mine. But it may mean that our Mr Evans has done this sort of thing before. Evans may not even be his real name. I've sent a telegram out to all divisions asking if they are aware of any men for hire operating in their area. It may be that he's known to the police. I have obtained a reasonable description of him from Mr O'Donnell. He describes him as a broad man wearing a long coat, so thankfully the description is similar to that given by the Whippet fellow."

"So who could have paid Mr Evans to carry out the attack? Viscount Wyndham? Mr Lombard? Dudley Lombard?"

"Or Mr Glenville, perhaps."

"But why?"

"I think *why* is the crucial question here, Penny. I need to find this Evans chap first. He may yet be an innocent man, after all. I wondered if the *Morning Express* might publish an appeal for information on the man. If he's of the criminal fraternity, there may be someone he has fallen out with who would like to inform the police of his whereabouts."

"Certainly. I should be happy to, James."

I glanced at my colleagues. They had lost interest in our conversation and were busy talking about cricket. I took the opportunity to whisper an apology to James for jumping out of the cab and walking away.

"There is no need to apologise, Penny," he replied quietly. "I shouldn't have laughed at you in that manner."

"It's because you don't like Glenville," I said. "But I don't mind that. You're allowed to dislike him."

"And you like him," said James.

"I don't suppose we can agree on everything, can we?"

He smiled. "No. Not until we can be certain of the truth. I'll keep you informed, Penny."

A messenger boy delivered a telegram to me the following week. It was from James. His message instructed me to meet him, Inspector Cullen and Inspector Trotter at the Glenville house the following day. They were ready to make an arrest.

CHAPTER 46

I approached the house in Hyde Park Gate with trepidation. Twelve days had passed since I had left and I'd hoped I should never have to return. *Who did James intend to arrest?* I had barely slept the previous night for thinking about it.

It was a warm spring afternoon and I wore my blue linen jacket with a lace collar and a matching linen skirt. As I drew closer to the house, I saw the short form of Viscount Wyndham and his petite wife walking up the steps to the door. I paused to watch them.

Were they James' suspects? Was he to arrest both or just one of them? If so, which?

I took a deep breath and continued walking. Mrs Craughton had already shown the Wyndhams into the house by the time I reached the door. She held it open for me as I climbed the steps, looking me up and down as I approached. I realised she was unaccustomed to seeing me in everyday clothes.

"How are you, Mrs Craughton?"

"You'll find them in the library," she replied sullenly.

The curtains in the house were still closed, but the gas lamps lit the way. When I reached the library, I was surprised by the number of people present. I could see the Glenville family and the Lombards. Viscount and Lady Wyndham were just taking their seats. Extra chairs had been brought into the room from the drawing room.

I caught Mr Glenville's eye. He glanced at me briefly before looking away. I cautiously approached him.

"I apologise if you think my behaviour deceitful," I said.

He rested his dark eyes on me and pursed his lips together.

"You may have noticed that nothing untoward has been written in the *Morning Express*," I continued. "I have been respectful of your privacy and the tragic events which occurred while I was working here."

"Do you wish me to congratulate you?" he asked bitterly.

"No. I only wish to explain myself."

I found a space to stand by the wall, not far from Mr Perrin and a newly appointed maid. Mrs Glenville was seated by the fire with Jane, her face veiled. Maurice sat on a chair by the window and the Lombard family sat silently on a row of three chairs. There was no sign of Tipsy the dog. Nor was there any sign of James. My stomach turned uncomfortably.

What was James planning?

He arrived a few moments later, accompanied by the barrel-shaped Inspector Trotter and Chief Inspector Cullen, whose thick grey moustache masked his mouth. James looked handsome in his sombre dark suit, and he raised an eyebrow in acknowledgement when he caught my eye. I smiled.

Chief Inspector Cullen began the proceedings.

"Thank you all for gathering here at such short notice, and thank you Mr and Mrs Glenville for allowing my colleagues into your home again. I realise how difficult the past few weeks have been for you and your family. Hopefully, we won't detain you for long. My colleagues Inspector Blakely and Inspector Trotter have almost completed their work on this investigation, and it has been far wider reaching than any of us could have envisaged. I will hand over to my colleague at Scotland Yard, Inspector James Blakely, who has some further information for you."

"Thank you, sir," said James, stepping forward. "I echo Chief Inspector Cullen's thanks to you all for gathering here today. It is a little over two weeks since Miss Sophia tragically lost her life. And as we remember her, I would also like to acknowledge a girl and another woman who have also passed away in recent weeks. The first is Maisie Brown, and the second is Elizabeth Wiggins, known to many of you as Betsy. Both worked as maids in this household."

He paused to allow for a respectful silence, then continued.

"Everyone who was present at Miss Sophia's birthday celebration is here today, with the sad exception of Miss Sophia and Maisie. Viscount Wyndham, was it a surprise to you and your wife to receive an invitation to Miss Sophia's birthday dinner? I understand your relationship with Mr Glenville had soured prior to the event."

"That's rather overstating it, Inspector," stated Mr Glenville. "But I will admit that Wyndham and I hadn't seen eye to eye, and I felt it was time to make amends."

"Is that your understanding of the situation, Viscount Wyndham?" asked James.

"Well, I suppose so. There's no need to make a fuss over the matter, though. What does it have to do with anything?"

"Let us consider now the cyanide with which Miss Sophia was poisoned," continued James. "An empty packet of the poison was found tucked behind the cushion of one of the chairs in the drawing room. It was ascertained that both

Viscount Wyndham and Mrs Lombard sat upon that chair on the evening of Miss Sophia's death."

As I watched James, I thought back to the moment we had first met on the steps of the British Library and how young and awkward he had seemed then. He seemed older and more assured now. I felt proud of him.

"I know what you're going to say next, Inspector!" Viscount Wyndham interjected. "Because I'm a photographer, I use potassium of cyanide on a regular basis. Therefore, I must have taken some of the supply from my dark room and brought it into this house in order to poison Miss Sophia. I cannot deny that there is some logic behind the suggestion, Inspector, but you're lacking a motive. Why should I poison the poor girl?"

"In revenge for the way Maurice has been overlooked," suggested James.

Lady Wyndham shrieked and covered her delicate features with her gloved hands.

"I beg your pardon, Inspector?" Wyndham cried out, jumping up from his chair. "Have you *lost your mind?*"

"Maurice, the only male heir in the Glenville family, was overlooked in favour of his sister," said James. "Despite the common perception that the boy is an idiot or a lunatic of some sort, both you and I know, Wyndham, that he is more than capable of inheriting his father's fortune."

"Yes, he is!" said Wyndham. "He is very capable of doing so, and over the years my wife and I have spent a great deal of time with the boy. He was lucky to escape an institution, but that doesn't mean that those in the Glenville household have had any time for him. The boy is continually ignored by them!"

"He is not!" objected Mrs Glenville, her face still hidden behind her mourning veil.

"Yes he is, Camilla! And as a childless man, I relished the

opportunity to play a fatherly role. Alexander and Camilla didn't like me doing so, Inspector, because I apparently undermine their role as parents. That's the argument that led to our estrangement. But you still managed to visit us a few times, didn't you, Maurice?"

The boy nodded in reply.

"But if you think that means I killed Miss Sophia, I'm extremely worried about the state of law and order in this country!" said Wyndham.

"Viscount Wyndham, I have more to say yet," said James calmly. "Please take your seat."

"But you have accused my husband of murder!" Lady Wyndham cried out.

"I have accused him of nothing, my lady, I merely stated that he had a motive for Miss Sophia's murder."

Viscount Wyndham stared at James for a while longer, then slowly sat down.

CHAPTER 47

"Miss Sophia Glenville was engaged to be married to Master Dudley Lombard," said James. "However, it is no secret to anyone now that she harboured feelings for another man."

I glanced over at Dudley, whose droopy features were turned down toward the floor. His mother's face was so stern that it might have been hewn from granite.

"Miss Sophia was in love with a gentleman called Mr John Morrison," said James. "The brother of Elizabeth Wiggins, known as Betsy during her time here."

"*What?*" Lady Wyndham called out. "In love with the *maid's brother?*"

Mr Glenville shook his head.

"Wasn't Betsy a *negro?*" asked Lady Wyndham. "Which can only mean that her brother is also a negro!" Her mouth hung open in a mixture of shock and amusement.

Dudley Lombard and his parents looked thoroughly downcast.

"Miss Sophia and Mr Morrison had been meeting in secret for approximately six months," continued James.

"Their last meeting before Miss Sophia's death was on Wednesday the twenty-sixth of March, three days before Miss Sophia died. Although the two met clandestinely, their relationship was no secret. Mr and Mrs Glenville were aware of the relationship, as was the housekeeper Mrs Craughton, and Mr and Mrs Lombard."

A number of glances were exchanged, but no one spoke.

"Mr and Mrs Lombard found out about the assignations because Mrs Craughton wrote them a letter informing them of it. Can you explain why you did so, Mrs Craughton?" asked James.

"They needed to know," replied the housekeeper with a scowl. "I don't like to speak ill of the dead, but the girl was being deceitful. I was trying to help the Lombard family."

"You had not been asked by the Lombard family to spy on Miss Sophia and report back?"

"No!"

"That is most interesting, because someone was tasked with spying on Miss Sophia. I shall get to that shortly. Mr and Mrs Lombard, the letter from Mrs Craughton must have caused some anger in your household?"

"Yes!" said Dudley, standing up. There were blotches of red on his cheeks. "I was the one who was angry! She was supposed to be my wife!"

His outburst surprised me. I wasn't aware that Dudley had known about the letter.

His lower lip began to quiver. "She didn't even apologise to me! She just stood and stared, as if I meant nothing to her!"

"You confronted Miss Sophia regarding the letter?" asked James.

"Yes! I expected an explanation and an apology! But there was nothing. She had a cold, cold heart."

"Why didn't you mention this in our interviews, Master Lombard?"

"It wasn't relevant." He sat down in his seat again.

"You should have been honest with the detectives!" Ralph Lombard hissed at his son. "You should have spoken up sooner and saved your embarrassment now. You've made a fool of yourself."

James addressed Ralph Lombard. "So concerned were you, Mr Lombard, about Miss Sophia's infidelity that you suggested a marriage with Miss Sophia's sister, Miss Jane, did you not?"

Jane Glenville stared at Ralph Lombard, but he averted his eyes from hers and cleared his throat. "Alexander and I had a brief discussion about it, but it came to nothing. It was never a serious conversation, you must understand."

"He propositioned me!" Jane piped up.

"Who did, Miss Jane?" James questioned.

"Master Dudley. He asked me if I would be his wife!"

The blotches spread further across Dudley's face, and Mr Glenville glared at him.

"You propositioned my fifteen-year-old daughter?" he asked angrily.

"Now hold on, Glenville," said Ralph Lombard, standing to his feet. "It was merely a thought Dudley had after the conversation we had. His intention wasn't serious at any point. You must remember that he was extremely hurt by Miss Sophia's betrayal."

"You should have kept her under control," Mary Lombard added coldly.

"How dare you!" cried Mrs Glenville, rising unsteadily to her feet.

"Perhaps a plan was being hatched between the two families," Viscount Wyndham chipped in. "Miss Sophia had behaved dishonourably, so maybe they decided it would be preferable to have the alliance founded on a more conventional marriage between Dudley and Jane."

Mr Lombard and Mr Glenville turned on him simultaneously.

"Watch yourself, Wyndham!" warned Mr Glenville.

"Apologise for your remarks!" added Mr Lombard.

Inspector Cullen stepped forward. "Now, now, gentlemen. You must calm yourselves. Tempers are running high."

"How dare he say such a thing?" said Ralph Lombard. "Wyndham knows he's the chief suspect, as he was the one caught with the cyanide. We have to watch him. He'll say and do anything to have the finger pointed at someone else!"

"Let us change the topic of conversation to Maisie," James suggested. "She joined this household a year ago, and was a chatty, carefree girl. However, she was devastated by Miss Sophia's death, not only because she had got on well with her mistress, but also because she feared she hadn't done her job properly."

He paused and looked around the room, as if gauging everyone's reaction to this statement. "Maisie was not only paid for her work as a maid. She was also paid to follow Miss Sophia's every move."

Mrs Glenville laughed. "How ridiculous, Inspector!"

"It explains why Miss Green heard Maisie's door close not long after Miss Green had encountered Miss Sophia on the servants' staircase on the night of the twenty-sixth of March. Maisie had been tasked with following Miss Sophia that evening."

Everyone turned to look at me.

"Did you actually *see* her?" Mr Glenville asked me.

"No, but I heard her door close," I replied. "It must have been her. I can't think who else it could have been."

"I'll admit that we paid the maid to follow Sophia," said Mr Glenville. "Camilla and I were worried about our daughter. We wanted to know where she was going, and with whom she was meeting. Sophia had unconventional notions about the world, and we were concerned that she was keeping company with the wrong sorts of people. Mrs Lombard helpfully told us a few moments back that we needed to keep Sophia under control. I can assure everyone here that we endeavoured to do so."

James nodded. "Thank you, Mr Glenville, for the clarification. An inquest has been opened into Maisie's death, and is currently awaiting further evidence about what happened to her on the night she died. It seems the girl wrote a short note, then threw herself down from the top of the servants' stairwell. Her death appears to have been a suicide; however, there are several factors which make me doubt this.

"Firstly, Maisie was illiterate and would have been incapable of writing a note. Secondly, Miss Green heard footsteps shortly after Maisie fell, which suggests that someone left the scene of her death. If that person witnessed her fall, why have they not come forward to explain what they saw? I can only guess that the reason they have remained silent is that the person in question murdered her. Maisie had scratches on her arms, which may have occurred during a struggle with the person who pushed her.

"An empty bottle of laudanum was discovered next to the supposed suicide note. I hope she won't mind me saying it, but I'm aware of only one person in this room who regularly takes laudanum, and that is Lady Wyndham."

I glanced at Lady Wyndham and saw her heart-shaped face crumple.

"What are you suggesting, Inspector?" Viscount Wyndham rose to his feet again. "That my wife gave the maid some of her own laudanum?"

Ralph Lombard snickered. "The Wyndhams and their poisons."

"This is not a laughing matter, Mr Lombard," scolded Inspector Cullen.

"Next we must discuss Elizabeth Wiggins," continued James, "who was known as Betsy while she worked in this household."

"But what about Maisie?" asked Mr Glenville. "I thought you said someone murdered her? If so, who was it?"

"I shall return to Maisie in due course," replied James. "During the time she worked here, Betsy formed a close friendship with Miss Sophia."

Mrs Glenville nodded. "Sophia didn't make friends easily."

"Betsy also got on well with Maisie," continued James. "And Betsy's brother tells me his sister discovered that Maisie was being paid to watch Miss Sophia. So close was Betsy's friendship with Miss Sophia that she informed her of this fact. Therefore, Miss Sophia knew the maid was following her during her secret excursions with Mr Morrison. Miss Sophia did not feel content with this situation, and often talked with Betsy and Mr Morrison about running away. Her greatest desire was to elope with Mr Morrison. However, the man had other commitments; namely his wife and child. He couldn't quite bring himself to leave his family.

"On the eighteenth of February, Miss Sophia left home and went to find Mr Morrison at Pattison's law firm, where he worked as a clerk. The young man told her that he would be unable to run away with her until he had organised some form of provision for his wife and child. He told her to bide her time, which she did. Miss Sophia returned to Hyde Park, where Mr Perrin found her wandering shortly before nightfall that day. Betsy was dismissed from service here on the twenty-second of February. Am I right?"

James looked at Mr Glenville.

"I can't be sure of the exact date, but February sounds about right," he replied.

"And it was shortly after Miss Sophia attempted to run away from home?"

"Yes."

"What was the reason for Betsy's dismissal?"

"Listening at doors," Mrs Glenville piped up. "The girl was terribly nosy."

"Were you concerned that she had overheard something she shouldn't have?"

"No, but overly inquisitive behaviour is not a good trait in a maid," replied Mrs Glenville.

"I concur that she was nosy," said Mrs Craughton. "I had noticed the same habit."

"And how did Miss Sophia react to Betsy's dismissal, Mrs Glenville?" asked James.

"She was extremely upset," she replied. "Far more distraught than was necessary."

"She was angry with you and your husband for dismissing Betsy?"

"She was. But then Sophia was angry about all manner of things. It didn't take much to upset her."

James consulted his notebook. "We are all aware that Betsy was sadly murdered on the fourth of March, and that her husband is currently on trial for her murder. Her husband, Mr Wiggins, worked at your factory, isn't that right, Mr Lombard?"

"Did he? I don't recall the chap, but I happen to employ in excess of seven hundred people."

"On the night of Betsy's murder, Mr Wiggins was out drinking with a stranger in the Royal Vauxhall Tavern," said James. "Do you know the place, Mr Lombard?"

He nodded in reply.

"The stranger called himself Mr Evans and had arranged to meet Mr Wiggins under the guise of offering him some employment. Not accustomed to heavy drinking, Mr Wiggins soon became incapacitated and was accompanied home by Mr Evans. We cannot rule out the possibility that Mr Evans had a hand in Betsy's murder."

"Why should he do that?" asked Mr Lombard.

"I have a theory," replied James, "which I will return to shortly."

CHAPTER 48

"Mrs Craughton!" James exclaimed.

"Yes?" the housekeeper replied nervously.

She glanced around the room and then smiled weakly at him.

James pointed toward the picture of the ghost twins. "May I ask your permission to remove this fine portrait from the wall?"

Mrs Craughton looked over at Mr Glenville, who nodded.

"Of course, Inspector," she said.

Mr Perrin helped Inspector Trotter take the portrait down. They carefully leaned it up against a cabinet. James examined the darker square of wallpaper where the portrait had previously hung. Then he lifted a finger and peered closely at something on the wall before turning to address Mrs Glenville.

"I believe the two boys in this picture are your ancestors," said James.

"Boys?" muttered Lady Wyndham.

"Yes, they were uncles of mine," replied Mrs Glenville. "Broderick and Snowdon Noel-Johnstone."

"Did you know them by any other names?"

"No."

"So the names Cubby and Bunty mean nothing to you?"

"Cubby?" jeered Viscount Wyndham. "Bunty?"

"Oh, those names," said Mrs Glenville. "Those were the nicknames I had for them as a child."

"Mrs Craughton," said James. "Are you in possession of a slip of paper which has the names Cubby and Bunty written on it?"

"No."

"Have you ever come across a piece of paper such as that?"

"No, I don't think I ever have."

"That's odd," said James. "Because when Miss Green was working here, she said she found a piece of paper bearing those two names hidden between two books in this very room."

Mrs Craughton gave me an icy stare.

"Miss Green says that you found her with the piece of paper and took it from her."

"Miss Green is a thief," she sneered. "She stole a key from my office, opened the drawers of Mr Glenville's desk and removed one of his books. Do you trust the words of a thief?"

"Miss Green was working here as an undercover reporter," said Mr Glenville. "She did not pilfer the book. She thought she could use it to find out more information about me. Although why she couldn't have asked me her questions directly, I will never know." He gave me a smile. "I'm sure Miss Green had every intention of returning the book, didn't you, Miss Green?"

I nodded, both surprised by, and grateful for, Mr Glenville's explanation.

"So you deny all knowledge of this piece of paper, Mrs Craughton?" asked James.

"I can't remember it."

"I believe the piece of paper Miss Green found was an instruction," James revealed. "It was left to describe the location of the hidden packet of cyanide to someone else."

"That makes no sense!" declared Ralph Lombard.

"If anyone wishes to examine the wallpaper behind the portrait of Mrs Glenville's ancestors, I invite them to do so," said James. "There is a small piece of wax on the wall to which the packet of cyanide was once attached."

James leafed through his notebook and found the empty packet of cyanide. He held it up.

"This is the packet of poison which was found on the chair in the drawing room. It bears testament to the fact that it was attached to something with wax."

"Why should someone wish to do that?" asked Mr Glenville.

"Perhaps they thought it was a safe place to hide their poison," said James. "After all, nobody would go looking for it there, would they?"

"This is ridiculous," said Mary Lombard. "How much longer do you plan to detain us, Inspector?"

"He's planning to bore us all until someone confesses," said Viscount Wyndham. "Whoever it was, own up now and put an end to this purgatory."

Wary glances were exchanged between those dotted around the room.

"Let me mention Mr Evans again," said James. "He was the man who accompanied Mr Wiggins home. The poor man experienced such an adverse reaction to his drink this evening that we speculate a poison of some sort may have been administered, mixed in with his beer. This would be impossible to verify unless we could speak to Mr Evans himself. Fortunately, I have managed to find him."

"You have?" I said excitedly.

"Yes I have, Penny. I'm most grateful to my colleague, Miss Green, in this matter. A few days ago, the *Morning Express* published a description of the mysterious Mr Evans, along with an appeal for information. The Yard was contacted by a gentleman who has now retired from a lifetime of criminal activity, but had certain scores to settle. He was able to inform us of Mr Evans' true identity and tell us that he is well known in criminal circles as a man who will 'dispatch' people in return for payment. We visited him at his home this morning and made the arrest."

"So you now have one criminal's word against another? That's not evidence! It's meaningless!" scoffed Ralph Lombard.

"Fortunately for us, Mr Evans was rather meticulous in his record-keeping," said James. "A search of his home and papers revealed a list of people for whom he has worked. Mrs Craughton, are you sure you no longer have the piece of paper you confiscated from Miss Green? It would be extremely convenient if I was able show it to everyone at this moment."

"I'll have a look in my office," she replied frostily, instantly leaving the room.

"When I first arrived at this house, I had a good look around," said James. "Without a doubt, one of the pleasantest rooms here is the conservatory. I imagine it requires a good deal of maintenance."

"It's my wife's pride and joy," said Mr Glenville.

"A tropical hothouse presumably attracts a few pests," commented James. "They attack the plants, do they?"

"We don't have too much of a problem with them," replied Mrs Glenville.

The housekeeper returned to the room.

"Mrs Craughton, when was the conservatory last fumigated?" asked James.

"About a month ago, I think, Inspector."

"Thank you. Did you manage to find the piece of paper?"

"I did, Inspector."

She held it out for him to take.

"You keep it for the time being, Mrs Craughton, and tell me in whose handwriting the names Cubby and Bunty are written."

Mrs Craughton glanced around the room and moved her lips, but no sound came out.

The room was so silent that I hardly dared to breathe.

"Mrs Craughton?"

"I... What will it mean when I say the name? Will this person be in trouble?"

"Let's worry about that later. Whose handwriting do you see on that piece of paper?"

"It's... er... the handwriting belongs to Mrs Lombard."

CHAPTER 49

"**N**o! I didn't write it!" Mary Lombard cried out, her violet eyes wide in her pale face. "You're mistaken, Mrs Craughton. Why should I have written it?"

"Let me take a look at it!" demanded Ralph Lombard.

He strode angrily across the room toward Mrs Craughton. He snatched the piece of paper from her hand and glared at it.

"That is not my wife's hand, Inspector!" he appealed to James. "If you need a sample of her handwriting we can provide it, can't we, Mary? This is a setup!"

"What are the implications for the person who wrote on that bit of paper?" asked Viscount Wyndham. "Does it mean the writer is a murderer or not?"

"Let me see," said Mr Glenville, peering over Ralph Lombard's shoulder at the paper. "I don't even recognise the writing," he said. "Inspector Blakely, this is preposterous! What are you trying to do to us here? Rile us up until we all claw each other's eyes out?"

"Not at all," said James. "I've almost finished. If everyone can quieten down, I will conclude my explanation. Please hand me that piece of paper, Mr Lombard."

Ralph Lombard thrust it at him and returned to the seat next to his wife. Most of the faces in the room were turned toward Mrs Lombard. She seemed to be suffering terribly in response to the suggestion that she had written the brief note.

She produced a fan and wafted it beneath her chin. Her husband clasped a protective arm around her shoulders. I watched carefully and tried to imagine them causing Sophia any harm. I decided that they were capable of it. After all, Sophia had been unfaithful to their son. Her murder might have been an act of revenge, and they had no doubt hoped that Dudley could be married to Jane instead.

"Mrs Craughton," James continued. "When a hothouse or conservatory is fumigated, potassium of cyanide is usually used, is it not?"

The housekeeper remained silent, but glanced around the room, as if the answer lay somewhere within it.

"Answer the question, Craughton," barked Chief Inspector Cullen. "Did you use potassium of cyanide to fumigate the conservatory?"

"Yes."

"So it's reasonable to assume that there is a supply of cyanide somewhere in the house or inside the storage shed out in the yard?" asked James.

"It's possible."

"I find you quite evasive, Mrs Craughton," said James. "You know more than you're letting on, and I surmise that you're either protecting yourself or someone else. I suspect it's a bit of both."

The housekeeper stared at him.

"It's not true," she said coldly.

"It's not Mrs Lombard's handwriting on this piece of paper, is it?" said James. "It is, in fact, yours."

There were gasps from the attentive onlookers.

"You have no proof," the housekeeper retorted.

"Actually, I do," said James, leafing through his notebook again. "I kept the sketches of the drawing room everyone drew for me and Inspector Trotter. The writing on your sketch matches the handwriting on this piece of paper."

"I didn't draw that sketch," she said. Her grey eyes were cold and reptilian.

"You can deny it all you like, Mrs Craughton," said James, "but there's no escaping the truth. It will be far easier for you if you're honest with us now. It may have been you who secreted the packet of poison behind the portrait, but you didn't carry out the poisoning of Miss Sophia on your own. You simply did what you had been asked to do. You carried out orders. Am I right, Mrs Craughton?"

The housekeeper said nothing.

"You're extremely loyal to your employer, are you not? It was Mrs Glenville who instructed you to put the packet of poison in a place where she could secretly access it that evening."

"That's not true!" said Mrs Glenville defensively, rising to her feet. "I had nothing to do with it!"

I stared at her veiled face, struggling to believe the woman could have poisoned her own daughter.

"I think the jury will deliberate over the extent of your involvement, Mrs Glenville," said James.

"No!" she shrieked. "No, they won't! I had nothing to do with it! It was all *him!*"

She pointed at her husband.

Mr Glenville laughed. "You'll try anything to escape your guilt, won't you, Camilla? You would even accuse your own husband!"

"But it *was* you!" she cried. "*You* poisoned our daughter!"

"Why should I do that?" Mr Glenville asked with a smirk. "You're suffering from delusions again."

"She was in the way of your plans. She didn't do what you wanted her to!"

"I do apologise, Inspector Blakely," said Mr Glenville. "My hysterical wife is preventing you from finishing your most eloquent speech."

Mrs Glenville charged towards her husband.

"Tell them the truth!" she screeched.

She lunged wildly at him, and I gasped as he grabbed her wrist.

"Camilla, please calm yourself," he said softly.

"Tell them what you really wanted to do! How you planned for Dudley to marry Jane instead!"

"No!" Jane entreated. "Please no! Mother! Tell them it's not true!"

Mrs Glenville tried to wrestle her wrist free from her husband's grasp, but he gripped it firmly.

"You knew Jane would do anything you told her to," she cried. "Once that gin distillery was yours, Ralph Lombard would have had no chance. You wanted to push him and his son out the way, just as you did with Archdale. It has only ever been about you!"

I felt my heart pounding heavily as I listened to Mrs Glenville's words. *Was there an element of truth to them? Or was she desperately trying to deflect from her own guilt?*

"That's enough, Camilla," said Mr Glenville. "Why don't you lift your veil and show them your face? The face of a murderess who pushed her own maid down the stairs."

He let go of his wife's wrist and pulled up her veil to reveal deep scratches across one cheek.

Mrs Craughton let out a cry. "My lady!"

"No!" Jane screamed.

Mrs Glenville's face remained impassive. She pulled back the veil and made a move to leave the room. Inspector Trotter quickly caught up with her and took her arm.

"You're right, Inspector Blakely," said Mr Glenville. "Maisie had scratches on her arms because she put up a fight. It seems she injured the face of her killer."

"Come with me, please, Mrs Glenville. The air is rather warm in here," lisped Inspector Trotter.

Mrs Glenville said nothing as he led her out of the room.

CHAPTER 50

"Well done, Inspector," said Viscount Wyndham cheerily. "I can scarce believe it, though. Could Camilla really have done such a thing? Whatever possessed her?"

"Maisie must have known who was behind Miss Sophia's death," replied James. "As each day went by, Mrs Glenville grew increasingly terrified that Maisie would talk. Unfortunately for Mrs Glenville, hers was a rather clumsy attempt at pretending that Maisie had taken her own life."

Ralph Lombard stood to his feet. "Glenville," he barked. "Is there any truth in what your wife says?"

"Nothing but the ramblings of a hysterical woman," replied Mr Glenville.

"Am I in the clear now, Inspector?" asked Viscount Wyndham. "Are you satisfied that the potassium of cyanide on the chair I selected had nothing to do with me?"

"We're not quite finished yet, Wyndham," said James. "Bear with me for a moment longer. Remember our Mr Evans; the man we think murdered Elizabeth Wiggins? A cursory search of Mr Evans' papers this morning revealed that he had been in contact with someone within this room." He paused to look around. "And that person is Mr Glenville."

I gasped.

"You're wasting your time now, Inspector. You already have your culprit," argued Mr Glenville.

"Have you ever met with a professional criminal who calls himself Mr Evans?"

"No."

"Mr Evans' papers reveal that you paid him the sum of one hundred pounds at the end of February. Is that correct?"

"I don't recall giving money of any amount to a man called Evans," replied Mr Glenville. His dark eyes never wavered from James' face. "Perhaps he used a different name, but I certainly wouldn't have paid money to aid someone in carrying out a nefarious deed."

"Mr Evans is a nefarious man, Mr Glenville," said James. "You paid him to murder Elizabeth Wiggins. It seems the nosy maid had heard too much."

Mr Glenville laughed. "Wherever have you got this idea from, Inspector?"

"Elizabeth Wiggins, who you knew as Betsy, overheard you and your wife discussing how to rid yourselves of your troublesome daughter."

"What nonsense, Inspector. You have no evidence to back up your preposterous claims!"

"As Miss Sophia grew into a young woman, she demonstrated an independence of mind and a strength of character incongruous with your plans for her," said James. "She was a modern woman who identified strongly with social reform, such as women's suffrage and fair conditions for factory workers.

"Having betrothed her to Dudley Lombard while she was a young girl, you and your wife increasingly despaired as she became less consistent with your plans with each year that passed. As the wedding drew near and you learnt of her indiscretions, you felt that the girl had become more trouble than she was worth. Perhaps you had both hoped she would elope with her lover, and that would be the end of it. Only her lover wasn't ready to leave. He had a family to support."

Mr Glenville assumed a bored expression. "You're an excellent storyteller, Inspector," he said.

"In addition to your worries regarding how this rebellious young girl could ever manage the family business, you were also concerned about the shame she would inevitably bring to your family," continued James. "Her attempt to run away was an embarrassment too far. What if the establishment discovered the trouble you were having with her?

"She was engaged to be married to the son of your friend, but then you have another daughter, don't you? You considered whether Jane would be a more suitable wife for Dudley, and Mr Lombard had already proposed such a match. As your wife suggested, once the Lombard gin distillery was owned by your daughter Jane, it wouldn't have been too much trouble to push the Lombards out."

Mr Glenville chuckled and shook his head.

"Together, you and your wife hatched a plan to be rid of your daughter and fix the blame on Viscount Wyndham, a man you had many disagreements with over your son, Maurice. One of you deliberately planted the empty packet of cyanide on the chair upon which he had been sitting to shift the suspicion onto him."

"Sheer foolishness, Glenville!" laughed Viscount Wyndham. "Looks like you'll be needing a lawyer now, eh?"

"You're a fool if you believe a single word of this, Wyndham!" snarled Mr Glenville.

He turned back to James. "If this is what happened, Inspector, how would my wife or I have emptied a packet of poison into Sophia's glass without anyone noticing? It would have been impossible!"

"But not completely impossible," said James. "The best theory I could come up with is as follows. You emptied the packet of cyanide into your own glass, Mr Glenville. Then somehow you created a diversion which allowed you to exchange your glass with your daughter's while everyone's attention was elsewhere."

I thought about the moment just before Sophia had died, when we were all distracted by Tipsy, the trick-performing dog.

Mr Glenville laughed. "If only I were that clever, Inspector!"

"You are, Mr Glenville. And I suspect that your loyal butler, Mr Perrin, and equally loyal housekeeper, Mrs Craughton, were willing to turn a blind eye or even assist where required. Miss Sophia was also a great nuisance to them.

"And as your daughter lay dying, you placed the empty packet of poison on Viscount Wyndham's chair. You probably hoped he would return to the same one so everyone would connect him with the cyanide. However, Mary Lombard sat down on the chair, which perhaps diluted the intended effect."

"This fairy tale involves an awful lot of conjecture, Inspector," said Glenville. "This is little more than a story you have concocted to suit your own means. You have no proof of anything. You entered my home because you were already carrying out an investigation on the behalf of a man who bears me nothing but animosity. You thought I didn't know about Mr Conway and his intentions to ruin me? And then you encouraged *this woman*," I jumped as Mr Glenville turned his eyes toward me, "to use lies and subterfuge to gain access to my home."

I met his dark gaze and my knees suddenly felt weak.

"Is it any coincidence that my daughter died within a few days of Miss Green beginning her work here, under the pretence of being a maid? And notice how she conveniently uncovered the so-called evidence. It was Miss Green who discovered the note in the library. It was Miss Green who encountered my daughter on her return from an alleged encounter with her suitor. Miss Green who heard Maisie after she had followed Sophia one evening. And Miss Green who discovered Maisie after she fell! There is too much coincidence in that, Inspector."

"Miss Green is a respected news reporter," said James.

"This is all part of a plan masterminded by Scotland Yard and the *Morning Express*," said Mr Glenville.

"With all due respect, Mr Glenville, you are quite mistaken," Chief Inspector Cullen interjected.

"Miss Green was sent here to charm me, and once she had done that she set about framing me for the death of my own daughter."

"It's not true, Mr Glenville," I said. "Mr Conway asked me to work undercover in your household, and during my time here I mistakenly believed that you were an honest man. I defended you when others criticised you, and up to the very last moment I could never have believed that you would cause your daughter any harm. I still struggle to accept that you and your wife have done such terrible things to these innocent young women. As a reporter, I pride myself on being a good judge of character, but on this occasion I have been wildly mistaken."

I felt a lump in my throat, and Mr Glenville smiled at me.

"We got on well, didn't we, Miss Green? I can't tell you how disappointed I was when I discovered the truth about you. There was something that didn't seem quite right about you from the start, but in a pleasant way. You were different from everyone who had worked here before. That's why I kept searching your room. I wanted to discover the real you. And I did. It turns out you are even more fascinating than I first thought. The daughter of a famous plant-hunter, nonetheless! It's a terrible shame you allowed yourself to be talked into this scam by Scotland Yard. Why do you wish to make it look as though I murdered my own daughter?"

"Because you did." I felt tears in my eyes.

Mr Glenville shook his head.

"No. I see now that you're a part of the conspiracy against me," he said. "I can't tell you how disappointed that makes me feel."

"Come along, please, Mr Glenville," said Chief Inspector Cullen. "We need to take you down to Church Court station."

He took Mr Glenville's arm, but my former employer shrugged him off. Within a couple of strides, Mr Glenville had reached my side. He held his hand up around my throat in a vice-like grip.

My head knocked against the wall, and I couldn't breathe. My wide eyes stared into his.

"And to think I once had faith in you," he snarled. "You're nothing more than a temptress!"

I tried to pull his hand away, but it felt like a steel clamp, gripping harder and harder.

I tried to mouth the words, "*Let go!*" but already my vision was becoming cloudy. I could hear distant cries and shrieks. Glenville was speaking to me, but his words were too muffled for me to understand. My sight and hearing were closing down. My body fought for air, but Glenville was too strong.

I had once trusted this man, and now I was to die at his hands. In front of everyone else. In front of James. Why wasn't someone stopping him?

CHAPTER 51

Wen I came to, I discovered that I was lying on the floor of the library. My head throbbed with pain.

The portrait of the ghost twins swam into view as it sat close by, propped up against the cabinet.

"Penny," I heard James say softly.

My throat hurt too much to reply. James' face was directly in front of me, but I flinched, frightened that Glenville was somewhere nearby.

"It's all right, Penny," James said soothingly. "He's gone now. Cullen's taken him away."

Another face joined James'.

It belonged to Lady Wyndham.

"Would some laudanum help?" she asked gently.

I managed to shake my head.

"No thank you," I mouthed. "I just want to leave this accursed place."

CHAPTER 52

"Well done, Penelope!" Eliza said encouragingly as she rode alongside me on her bicycle. "You've managed to walk half the length of North Ride! She's recuperating well, isn't she, Mr Edwards?"

"Wonderfully well," said Mr Edwards with a grin.

"You're both speaking about me as if I were a small child," I replied sullenly.

The trees in Hyde Park were in full leaf. Nearby, some children were throwing bread to a flock of pigeons. The sun felt warm on my face, but my legs were feeble.

"You survived strangulation, Penelope!" said Eliza. "We've been so worried about you, haven't we, Mr Edwards?"

"Terribly worried," he added.

"I'm fine," I said, lifting my hands to my neck, which still felt tender.

"You've only been resting for two days," continued Eliza. "It's not enough. You should have spent at least a week in bed!"

"I don't want to be in bed, Ellie. I need to be out and about."

"Stubborn," whispered my sister to Mr Edwards. "She's always been terribly stubborn."

"I can hear what you're saying about me," I said. "I'll come out for a walk on my own next time."

"You'll do no such thing. You'll be attacked or murdered. You're a magnet for trouble," scolded my sister.

"I don't do it on purpose."

"Of course you don't. No one *intends* to attract trouble, do they?"

I rolled my eyes and continued walking. Up ahead, I could see a man and two women walking towards us.

"I remember the last time we were here, Mr Edwards. You regaled us with a most fascinating history of Hyde Park," said Eliza. "Remind me when it was first opened to the public again?"

"During the seventeenth century," he replied. "King Charles the First admitted the public at that time. Before that, it was a hunting park originally created for King Henry the Eighth."

"I do love your head for facts, Mr Edwards," said Eliza.

He blushed at the comment.

"King Henry may have charged after a deer on his horse along this very stretch!" she continued.

"It's unlikely that this path was here at the time."

"But he might have ridden in this location."

"He might indeed."

I watched the approaching threesome and thought that the man looked familiar.

"The park also used to be a popular duelling spot," added Mr Edwards.

"Did it really?" said Eliza. "Call me a silly romantic, but I always fancied the idea of two men fighting a duel over me!"

The man approaching us wore a bowler hat.

It was James.

"I say! Isn't that your inspector?" asked Eliza.

"The chap who came into the library a few weeks ago?" asked Mr Edwards.

"Is it?" I said. "Oh yes, I suppose it is."

I noticed James' step falter slightly as he realised who I was. Then he grinned and strode on ahead of his companions.

"Penny!" he called out. "What a pleasant surprise!"

"Hello, James!"

My eye was drawn to the women behind him. One looked older than the other, and was leaning on a walking stick for support.

"Good afternoon, Mrs Billington-Grieg and Mr Edwards." James stopped and doffed his hat.

Mr Edwards did the same.

"How lovely to see you all. What a lovely Sunday afternoon!" said James.

He spoke through a fixed grin, and I felt as uncomfortable as he looked.

The two women joined us, and I knew who they were before James introduced them. The younger woman had a wide, apple-cheeked face, with fair curls peeking out from beneath a flowery bonnet. The older woman had the same face, but with rather more lines. Both had smiling blue eyes.

"This is Charlotte and her mother, Mrs Jenkins," said James.

He told them our names and my face began to ache from the false grin I had adopted.

"It's lovely to meet you at last," I said to Charlotte, keen to demonstrate that I was entirely comfortable with her status as James' fiancée. "I've heard so much about you."

"Likewise!" she giggled. "James has told me all about you. You must be a very clever woman to be a news reporter!"

"Has he?" I replied with surprise. "You don't have to be

particularly clever to be a news reporter. In fact, I often think you need to be rather foolish."

Everyone laughed politely.

"Much like being a detective, in that case!" giggled Charlotte.

The others laughed politely again.

"The police force," tutted Mrs Jenkins. "I always told Charlotte: 'Whatever you do, don't go marrying someone in the police force.' And what does she do?"

I noticed that James' face was rather red. I had never seen him so flustered before.

"What a lovely bicycle you have there, Mrs Billington-Grieg," said Charlotte. "Are you permitted to ride it in the park?"

"I should hope so. No one has arrested me yet," replied Eliza.

"How are you faring, Penny? Are you fully recovered?" asked James.

"Oh yes. I'm fine, thank you," I lied.

"She's not really," interrupted Eliza. "She's still rather weak. I told her she should be in bed."

"Absolutely," added Mr Edwards. "Miss Green is trying to do too much too soon."

"Well that's Penny for you." James smiled. "I'll let you know as soon as I have the start date for the Glenvilles' trial, Penny. We're about to charge Craughton and Perrin for aiding and abetting."

"That's impressive work, James," I said.

"With assistance from Cullen and Trotter, I should add. Actually, I'm not sure how much assistance Trotter has given us, but he likes to remind us that it was his case to begin with."

"Naturally," I said with a laugh.

"That's enough shop talk, darling," said Charlotte. "I'm

sure Miss Green doesn't want to be bothered about work on a lovely Sunday afternoon."

"It's what police officers do," said Charlotte's mother. "They're married to the force first. That's what I have to constantly remind you of, Charlotte. Police force first. Wife second."

"Penelope also has an obsession for her work," Eliza chipped in. "She regularly works on Sundays."

"It's the same with James!" laughed Charlotte. "Goodness, you can see why they get along so well, can't you?"

I exchanged a glance with James. We both wished we hadn't had to meet under these circumstances.

I reached for the chain around my neck and pulled it up from beneath my collar.

"I almost forgot. I need to return this to you, James," I said as I detached his grandfather's ring from the old locket chain.

"Oh that? There's no need."

"But you gave it to me for luck while I was working undercover. Although I'm not sure how much luck it brought me in the end."

"Isn't that your grandfather's ring?" asked Charlotte, eying it curiously.

"I think it is, yes," James replied uncomfortably.

'But isn't it precious?" asked Charlotte.

"Not really. Only sentimentally. A little bit."

James coughed, and I could see that whatever he chose to say would offend either me or his wife-to-be.

"Hang on to it for now, Penny," he added.

"If you're sure. I thought you might want it safely returned."

"Well, we must continue with our stroll. How lovely to meet you all!" said James with forced cordiality as he doffed his hat again.

"And lovely to see you," I said politely.

James gave me a good-humoured grimace when no one else was looking. We all bid each other goodbye and walked on.

I overheard Charlotte asking James about his grandfather's ring again. I smiled, wondering, whether it would cause trouble between them.

"Well that was rather neat and tidy, wasn't it?" said Eliza once they were out of earshot. "You both met each other with each other's partners!"

"*Partners?*" I replied. "Mr Edwards is an acquaintance, Ellie. The word partner suggests a much stronger attachment."

"Perhaps an interested and hopeful acquaintance would be a better description," proposed Mr Edwards.

"Possibly, but it's rather a mouthful," said Eliza. "Charlotte seems a pleasant lady, but a little plain. You may be much older than her, Penelope, but you have a prettier nose."

"There is no need to compare me with the future Mrs Blakely, Ellie."

"She has fair hair like you," said Eliza. "Men often fall for a certain type."

"Type?" asked Mr Edwards. "I hope you're not suggesting that Miss Green is Inspector Blakely's type?"

"Absolutely not," said Eliza mischievously as she pedalled on ahead of us. "That would be highly inappropriate, wouldn't it?" she called back over her shoulder.

"It absolutely would," said Mr Edwards.

He stopped and gave me a suspicious look.

I glanced back at James' retreating form and noticed that Charlotte was holding on to his arm. I tucked my hand into the crook of Mr Edwards' elbow and his face broke into a smile.

"It's time to find somewhere for our afternoon tea," I said.

"Absolutely!" he replied. "Let's catch up with our chaperone. Although, on second thoughts, would it be so utterly terrible if we lost her?"

"Yes it would, Mr Edwards. Let's run and catch up with her."

THE END

THANK YOU

Thank you for reading *The Maid's Secret*, I really hope you enjoyed it!

Would you like to know when I release new books? Here are some ways to stay updated:

- Join my mailing list and receive a free short mystery: *Westminster Bridge* emilyorgan.co.uk/short-mystery
- Like my Facebook page: facebook.com/emilyorganwriter
- View my other books here: emilyorgan.co.uk/books

And if you have a moment, I would be very grateful if you would leave a quick review of *The Maid's Secret* online. Honest reviews of my books help other readers discover them too!

HISTORICAL NOTE

Hyde Park Gate is the name for two streets in Kensington which are situated close to the Royal Albert Hall and opposite Hyde Park. The area has long been associated with the wealthy and that's still the case today. The young Virginia Woolf lived at number twenty-two and Winston Churchill spent some of his later years at number twenty-eight, he passed away there at the age of ninety.

By contrast Gonsalva Road was a row of terraced homes which housed workers for south London's industry and railways. My interest in the street arose from the discovery that my great grandmother and her family lived there for many years. The area suffered bomb damage during World War II and was cleared for redevelopment in the 1950s and 60s. It's now home to the Westbury Estate and would be unrecognisable to my ancestors, although the railway lines are still there.

In Victorian England cyanide, and other lethal poisons, were easily obtainable. Prussic acid – hydrogen cyanide – was even found in skin lotions! Potassium cyanide and sodium cyanide were used as insecticides and potassium cyanide was also used in photography and gilding. A search of the British Newspaper Archive reveals a number of suicides by cyanide including a bereaved photographer, Alfred Matcham, who in 1884 drank a 'large quantity of cyanide of potassium'. A large dose is fast-acting and the effects are unpleasant as the poison deprives the body of oxygen. Antidotes can work if they're delivered swiftly enough.

My Gonsalva Road great-grandmother was working as a housemaid by the time she was 14 in 1891. Millions of women and girls did the same as her in the nineteenth and early twentieth century. In England in 1900 domestic service was the largest female occupation with a third of women aged between 15 and 20 working as servants. Servants weren't just the preserve of the wealthy, many self-respecting middle-class households had at least one servant.

My idea for Penny to work undercover as a maid is not a unique one: in the 1864 novel *Revelations of a Lady Detective* by William Stephens Hayward, the female detective works undercover as a maid in the home of the Countess of Vervaine in the story *The Mysterious Countess*.

Blundell's vinegar factory and Lombard's gin distillery are fictional. Legislation to protect factory workers from exploitation and accidents struggled to keep pace with rapid industrialisation during the nineteenth century. Despite countless factory acts being passed, workers still had to endure long days, low pay and dangerous working conditions. The London matchgirls strike of 1888 was prompted by poor working conditions in the Bryant & May match factory and the debilitating condition 'phossy jaw' which some of the workers suffered from. The women were supported by the

social activist Annie Besant and were eventually able to nego-
tiate better working conditions. Sadly, almost 130 years later,
worker exploitation still makes the headlines.

The Royal Vauxhall Tavern was built in the 1860s and is now
a famous gay venue. Many of the buildings which neigh-
boured the pub have since gone but the Tavern is set to
remain there for a long time yet having been made a Grade II
listed building in 2015 in recognition of its importance to the
LGBT community and history.

If *The Maid's Secret* is the first Penny Green book you've read,
then you may find the following historical background interesting. It's compiled from the historical notes published in
Limelight and *The Rookery*:

Women journalists in the nineteenth century were not as
scarce as people may think. In fact they were numerous
enough by 1898 for Arnold Bennett to write *Journalism for
Women: A Practical Guide* in which he was keen to raise the
standard of women's journalism:-

*"The women-journalists as a body have faults... They seem to me
to be traceable either to an imperfect development of the sense of order,
or to a certain lack of self-control."*

Eliza Linton became the first salaried female journalist in
Britain when she began writing for *the Morning Chronicle* in
1851. She was a prolific writer and contributor to periodicals
for many years including Charles Dickens' magazine *Household Words*. George Eliot – her real name was Mary Anne
Evans – is most famous for novels such as *Middlemarch*,
however she also became assistant editor of *The Westminster
Review* in 1852.

In the United States Margaret Fuller became the *New York
Tribune*'s first female editor in 1846. Intrepid journalist Nellie

Bly worked in Mexico as a foreign correspondent for the *Pittsburgh Despatch* in the 1880s before writing for *New York World* and feigning insanity to go undercover and investigate reports of brutality at a New York asylum. Later, in 1889-90, she became a household name by setting a world record for travelling around the globe in seventy two days.

The iconic circular Reading Room at the British Museum was in use from 1857 until 1997. During that time it was also used a filming location and has been referenced in many works of fiction. The Reading Room has been closed since 2014 but it's recently been announced that it will reopen and display some of the museum's permanent collections. It could be a while yet until we're able to step inside it but I'm looking forward to it!

The Museum Tavern, where Penny and James enjoy a drink, is a well-preserved Victorian pub opposite the British Museum. Although a pub was first built here in the eighteenth century much of the current pub (including its name) dates back to 1855. Celebrity drinkers here are said to have included Arthur Conan Doyle and Karl Marx.

Publishing began in Fleet Street in the 1500s and by the twentieth century the street was the hub of the British press. However newspapers began moving away in the 1980s to bigger premises. Nowadays just a few publishers remain in Fleet Street but the many pubs and bars once frequented by journalists – including the pub Ye Olde Cheshire Cheese - are still popular with city workers.

Penny Green lives in Milton Street in Cripplegate which was one of the areas worst hit by bombing during the Blitz in the Second World War and few original streets remain. Milton

Street was known as Grub Street in the eighteenth century and was famous as a home to impoverished writers at the time. The street had a long association with writers and was home to Anthony Trollope among many others. A small stretch of Milton Street remains but the 1960s Barbican development has been built over the bombed remains.

Plant hunting became an increasingly commercial enterprise as the nineteenth century progressed. Victorians were fascinated by exotic plants and, if they were wealthy enough, they had their own glasshouses built to show them off. Plant hunters were employed by Kew Gardens, companies such as Veitch Nurseries or wealthy individuals to seek out exotic specimens in places such as South America and the Himalayas. These plant hunters took great personal risks to collect their plants and some perished on their travels.

The *Travels and Adventures of an Orchid Hunter* by Albert Millican is worth a read. Written in 1891 it documents his journeys in Colombia and demonstrates how plant hunting became little short of pillaging. Some areas he travelled to had already lost their orchids to plant hunters and Millican himself spent several months felling 4,000 trees to collect 10,000 plants. Even after all this plundering many of the orchids didn't survive the trip across the Atlantic to Britain. Plant hunters were not always welcome: Millican had arrows fired at him as he navigated rivers, had his camp attacked one night and was eventually killed during a fight in a Colombian tavern.

My research for The Penny Green series has come from sources too numerous to list in detail, but the following books have been very useful: *A Brief History of Life in Victorian Britain* by Michael Patterson, *London in the Nineteenth Century* by Jerry White, *London in 1880* by Herbert Fry, *London a Travel*

Guide through Time by Dr Matthew Green, *Women of the Press in Nineteenth-Century Britain* by Barbara Onslow, *A Very British Murder* by Lucy Worsley, *The Suspicions of Mr Whicher* by Kate Summerscale, *Journalism for Women: A Practical Guide* by Arnold Bennett, *Seventy Years a Showman* by Lord George Sanger, *Dottings of a Dosser* by Howard Goldsmid, *Travels and Adventures of an Orchid Hunter* by Albert Millican, *The Bitter Cry of Outcast London* by Andrew Mearns, *The Complete History of Jack the Ripper* by Philip Sugden, *The Necropolis Railway* by Andrew Martin, *The Diaries of Hannah Cullwick, Victorian Maidservant* edited by Liz Stanley, *Mrs Woolf & the Servants* by Alison Light, *Revelations of a Lady Detective* by William Stephens Hayward and *A is for Arsenic* by Kathryn Harkup.

The *British Newspaper Archive* is also an invaluable resource.

THE INVENTOR

A Penny Green Mystery Book 4

❦

Electricity pioneer Simon Borthwick lights up Victorian London with a stunning illuminations display – then shoots himself in the back of a hansom cab.

Plucky Fleet Street reporter Penny Green witnesses the inventor's death and suspects the clue to his suicide lies in a mysterious letter he left behind. But can she persuade Inspector James Blakely of Scotland Yard that a crime has been committed?

Borthwick isn't the only person who died that day and Penny soon encounters a shadowy world which the police can't get close to. When the intimidation begins, Penny starts to fear for her own safety. James does what he can to protect her, but is it enough?

Find out more at: emilyorgan.co.uk/the-inventor

GET A FREE SHORT MYSTERY

❧

Want more of Penny Green? Sign up to my mailing list and I'll send you my short mystery *Westminster Bridge* - a free thirty minute read!

News reporter Penny Green is committed to her job. But should she impose on a grieving widow?

The brutal murder of a doctor has shocked 1880s London and Fleet Street is clamouring for news. Penny has orders from her editor to get the story all the papers want.

She must decide what comes first. Compassion or duty?

The murder case is not as simple as it seems. And whichever decision Penny makes, it's unlikely to be the right one.

Visit my website for more details:

emilyorgan.co.uk/short-mystery

THE RUNAWAY GIRL SERIES

෴

Also by Emily Organ. A series of three historical thrillers set in Medieval London.

Book 1: Runaway Girl

A missing girl. The treacherous streets of Medieval London. Only one woman is brave enough to try and bring her home.

Book 2: Forgotten Child

Her husband took a fatal secret to the grave. Two friends are murdered. She has only one chance to stop the killing.

Book 3: Sins of the Father

An enemy returns. And this time he has her fooled. If he gets his own way then a little girl will never be seen again.

Available as separate books or a three book box set. Find out more at emilyorgan.co.uk/books